Hot as a Firecracker

Margarite St. John

Published & distributed by:

BAUER
communications

Bauer Communications
Fort Wayne, IN
www.reviveworldmedia.com

ISBN 1479122726
Second Edition

Cover design by Angie Underwood, BookCoverPro.com, and Sara Norwood,
www.norwoodarts.com.

Coding and page layout by Sara Norwood, www.norwoodarts.com

Library of Congress Control Number: 2012952919

Printed in the United States of America.

Books by Margarite St. John

The Florida Murder Mysteries
Face Off
Monuments to Murder

The Fort Wayne Murder Mysteries
Murder for Old Times' Sake
The Girl with a Curl
Hot as a Firecracker
Agenda for Murder

The Christmas Novel
Postcards from a Tuscan Christmas

Non-Fiction
Finding Mrs. Hyde: Writing Your First Popular Novel

Our Loyal Readers Say About:

Face Off

"I really enjoyed *Face Off*. It is far better than James Patterson, Patricia Cornwell & Stuart Woods I also read over the past few months. I have recommended it to friends!"

- Jamie

"Easy and enjoyable reading. . . . The pace compelled me to read just one more chapter. . . . explosive beginning and end."

- A fan, Marco Island

"Well-written and fast-paced. . . .characters are thoroughly fleshed out. . . surprising and very exciting."

- Anne-Marie

"Interesting characters. . . compelling story line. . . easy comfortable writing style keeps you involved and draws you on. . . I'm left wishing for more!"

- pageturner

"Couldn't put the book down! Extremely well-written . . . suspenseful plot . . . interesting characters. Each chapter ended with a hook, so I couldn't wait to start the next one!"

- Heather

Monuments to Murder

"It took me only two days to read this book. It was funny, disturbing, educational, enlightening, and ended with a good twist. I'm hooked on this author."

- Anne-Marie

"This is the second book from this author that I have read and I absolutely loved it!! Suspenseful, interesting characters with whom it was easy to identify, and a plot that was both intriguing and yet easy to follow. I literally could not put down my Kindle for 2 days until I finished it! I would say that this author has exactly what it takes to please the suspense novel fan and keep them coming back for more! Can't wait to read her next novel."

- Heather

Murder for Old Times' Sake

"The characters are very interesting, the story compelling, and the who-done-it suspense kept me reading to the funny and fitting end. The author fleshes out the good guys, bad guys, and the somewhere in-betweens, as people the reader can sympathize with and understand their motivations and mindsets. I am looking forward to the fourth book."
- Anne-Marie

"Third book from this author that I have read and just a wonderful suspense novel all the way around! Very interesting characters combine with an exiting plot to keep the reader coming back for more. Details are woven in carefully giving the reader the sense that they "are there" as things are happening. Just loved it!"
- Heather

The Girl with a Curl

"A favorite author of mine. This latest novel of hers won't disappoint."
- Heather

"I enjoyed the perspectives of each character. . . . The ending was a complete surprise."
- Anne-Marie

"A fantastic fifth murder mystery by this author. I could not put this down and I had no idea who the murderer was until the very end. I found the business with the tarot cards fascinating . . . A lot of great research. . . . There were laugh out loud parts. . . . I highly recommend this book."

-Anne-Marie

Hot as a Firecracker

"A fantastic fifth murder mystery by this author. I could not put this down and I had no idea who the murderer was until the very end. I found the business with the tarot cards fascinating . . . A lot of great research. . . . There were laugh out loud parts. . . . I highly recommend this book."
-Anne-Marie

Postcards from a Tuscan Christmas

"I loved this Christmas story, its romance, intrigue, and beautiful Tuscan setting. Tales of redemption . . . illustrate the meaning of Christmas."
- Anne-Marie

Table of Contents

Part One

Part Two

Part Three

Author's Note

Part One

He who walks with the wise grows wise,
but a companion of fools suffers harm.

Proverbs 13:20

"Reading is a disease. I blame writers."

Atticus Solon

1

Prologue
Atticus Solon
Wednesday, February 29, 2012

Alastair Rutherford Digby III sat unmoving in a wingback chair, staring out at the peaceful boulevard. Though an enthusiastic gardener, he seemed oblivious to the hyacinths that had made an early appearance in front of his Tudor Revival house. He did not return the wave of a neighbor walking her dog. He did not pick up the ivory receiver of the vintage phone ringing near his elbow. A rare leather-bound book of drawings lay at his feet on the Sumak carpet, splayed open, pages hopelessly creased. The grandfather clock in the dining room chimed the notes for twelve noon without rousing him to action.

Alastair would have sat there forever if Desmond Digby hadn't used his own key to enter the house. He was there to pick up his eldest brother for a meeting with their late aunt's estate lawyer. Alastair had a car but was an indifferent driver and, though meticulous in most things, was always so late for appointments that the only way to ensure his timely presence was to pick him up.

When Alastair didn't answer his insistent ring, Desmond entered and shouted his brother's name. No answer. He wrinkled his nose at the familiar aroma of Murphy's oil soap, old books, pipe smoke, and dried lavender.

After banging the door shut and dutifully removing his shoes, he made his way straight down the long, dark hallway to his brother's study at the back of the house. He expected to find Alastair at his desk, finishing another one of his scathing book reviews. Writing for a well-known political rag was the only source of income Alastair now had other than an ever-decreasing trust fund. Little did his admirers know that their favorite reviewer, using the *nom de plume* Atticus Solon, was neither a philosopher nor a law-giver but merely a failed writer living out his years in an obscure Midwestern city.

Alastair's elegant Louis XVI desk chair, black lacquer with gilt trim, had been pushed back from the Empire desk and left at an angle instead of being returned to the kneehole and positioned just so. Papers and books were stacked in neat piles on the credenza. Scholarly journals and "serious" magazines were fanned out on a coffee table. But the laptop centered on the desk was open and powered up. Perhaps Alastair was in the middle of writing a review, but when Desmond bent down to read the screen, he was puzzled.

Fool --

You'll never hurt anyone again

Desmond straightened up. Who was Alastair calling a fool? Who had hurt him? Was this just a passing angry thought or was it a message he planned to send to the "Fool?"

Then he noticed a large, brightly printed card, somewhat larger than an ordinary playing card, positioned upside down next to the laptop. He picked it up and turned it right side up. On it was pictured a young man in tights and a colorful tunic, holding a wand, a dog nipping at his heels. He was standing on the edge of a precipice, gazing over his shoulder at the sun instead of down at the void below. The legend under his feet read "The Fool."

Desmond screwed up his face in thought. What the hell was this? He tossed the card back on the desk and looked around.

Without knowing why, Desmond suddenly felt the pinpricks of dread. He spun on his heel and shouted his brother's name. No answer. Frozen, he strained to detect any sound at all. Nothing. Sometimes stillness meant all was well, but sometimes, Desmond knew from a lifetime of living in Indiana, it meant one was standing in the eye of a tornado.

Desmond left the study and hurried through the back hall to the service stairs, taking two steps at a time to the second floor. Perhaps Alastair had had another dizzy spell. Because of high blood pressure, he had been forbidden by his doctor to take hot baths, but listening to directions was never Alastair's strong suit. He always knew best. Desmond tried not to picture his brother passed out in a tub of bubble bath.

The bed had been made up and the tub was dry. A quick tour of the second floor yielded nothing. Relieved but still puzzled, Desmond returned to the first floor and began striding through one room after another, starting with the kitchen. No Limoges teapot on the marble counter. No precious plate of cream puffs and turkey bacon.

Finally, he reached the living room. Quiet as a tomb. He halted and turned his eyes to the street as if he might find his brother standing out there, waiting for him. When the ivory phone suddenly rang, he jumped in response. As he walked toward it, wondering if he should pick it up, he found himself looking straight at his brother's slightly distorted reflection in the leaded glass windows overlooking the boulevard.

Desmond, furious, let out an explosive breath. *What kind of game is this?* "Alastair!" he said, glaring at the man's reflected eyes. "What in hell do you think you're doing, not answering me, making me run all over the damn house? Get up. I don't have time for this." He checked his watch. "We're late already."

Alastair just stared back. Shaking his head, Desmond walked over to the chair and gave his brother an angry little shove on his shoulder.

As Alastair slowly fell forward and rolled off the chair in an undignified heap, Desmond yelped and leapt back a step. He reflexively examined his hand, as if it had of its own demonic volition caused his brother's collapse.

He walked around the chair and bent down, ready to help his brother up. Only then did he see the hole in the back of Alastair's neck, a trickle of dried blood disappearing below the silk collar of the smoking jacket.

Desmond, dumbfounded, stood up and slowly took a few steps backward, considering what to do next. The scene was humiliating. Alastair's body now lay awkwardly across an open book of Edwardian homoerotica, his hips half concealing a line drawing of two men doing unnatural things to each other, as if Alastair were attempting a virtual *ménage-à-trois*. His cravat and smoking jacket were askew. A cut glass tumbler smelling like scotch rested on a silver coaster near the now-silent telephone. A Meerschaum pipe lay upside down in a crystal ashtray in a heap of tobacco ash.

Knowing how private Alastair was about his peculiar life, how proud he was of his house and its contents, Desmond desperately wanted to retrieve the book and dispose of it before it was found by a policeman too unsophisticated to appreciate the art. He wanted to clean the chair to Alastair's standards, then return his brother to his original position. Then he would straighten his cravat, retie the belt on his smoking jacket, replace a brocade slipper, maybe even put the pipe in his hand, so he looked like the elegant intellectual he'd always been. He wanted to report to their youngest brother Carleton, a very dignified estate lawyer in Fort Wayne's most esteemed law firm, that Alastair had simply died in his sleep.

Yes, he wanted to stage the scene as if Alastair Rutherford Digby III had slipped away naturally and peacefully after thinking deep thoughts about Aristotle's *Poetics*.

Then the pinpricks of dread struck again. Whoever had done this to Alastair might still be in the house. Maybe the murderer, not Alastair, had left the message on the computer and the strange picture card beside the keyboard.

What a fool he was to have walked through the way he had, yelling his brother's name, touching everything, paying no attention to places a murderer might be hiding.

He ran outside to the sidewalk, still in his stocking feet. Keeping an eye on the front door, he called 911 from his cell phone.

1

Keep This on the Cutie
Wednesday, February 29, 2012

In Gretna Green, Plato Jones strode around the magnificent home gymnasium, admiring his handiwork. He had designed the entire setup by himself. Well, not entirely by himself. His girlfriend, Petra Kuzmin, had edited his designs so they were actually buildable. In Russia, she had studied architecture. In America, she hawked men's toiletries at Macy's.

One day he was walking through the store, just to be among people, when a tiny, curvaceous brunette ambushed him with a bottle of Calvin Klein *Man* cologne. He raised his hands in surrender, graciously allowing her to open fire. In a foreign accent, she informed him that the top notes were spicy but the bass notes were woody -- very, very woody. Her heavily fringed eyes were black and flirty; her lips were luscious. What did he think of that? she asked with a little wiggle. Finding the power of suggestion working all too well, he bought a gift set from her, then asked her out. That was two years ago. Now they were a power couple with dreams of becoming internationally famous fitness gurus.

Plato and Petra's dreams were made manifest in this home gymnasium. Mirrored walls and concealed lighting made the room sparkle. A specially laid bamboo floor was just bouncy enough to be easy on the joints and cushion a fall. Ballet bars were mounted on one mirrored wall. Wall-mounted speakers allowed his favorite

7

synthesizer music to envelope the room in surround sound. Four ceiling-mounted televisions meant users could view the latest exercise videos without straining.

And, of course, the room was studded with the most expensive home gym equipment he could find. He had spent a month personally testing leg presses, cycling bikes, electronic steppers, treadmills, and cardio machines. If things worked out the way he hoped, in a year or so he'd suggest to the owners that the equipment was hopelessly outdated and needed to be replaced. He'd take it off their hands and, with a little financial help, refurbish and expand his 24-hour fitness center on Dupont.

Cellphone in hand, he began snapping pictures from every angle. The stone archway on the south end led to a coffee bar, lounge chairs, showers, and a blue-tiled lap pool, with a view of the manicured grounds through floor-to-ceiling windows. He hadn't designed the lap pool area, but it was beautiful just the same. He took more pictures.

Then he returned to the workout room, mounted a cycling bike, tipped his head so it didn't shine, and snapped himself reflected in a mirror. Yes, sir, he was a very fine specimen of his own art. A little short, perhaps, and a head that was just a tad small for the size of his body, but nothing he could do about that. Despite his artificial tan, his skin was oddly yellow. Perhaps he needed more supplements. He stroked his chinstrap beard, which rakishly balanced his shaved scalp. He was well-defined, not muscle-bound at all. He looked good in regular clothes.

When Steven and Alexandra Wright first approached him about designing a home gym, he had floated the idea of doing everything in secret and then surprising them with a fabulous reveal, the way HGTV designers did it. A video crew would be present, of course. But Mrs. Wright was having none of that. Though she was heavily pregnant when she hired him, she wasn't the pushover he thought she'd be. She insisted on overseeing absolutely everything. He'd hoped to fudge a little on the expenses, but that hadn't been possible either. He and Petra, who thought of themselves as wily foxes, quickly learned what it felt like to be the quarry in an English

8

fox hunt.

Still, he had fallen hard for Mrs. Wright the way a courtier falls for a queen. He didn't want to get into her bed. Like the landless knights of old, he wanted to get into something else entirely -- her treasury. If he could convince her to finance the business he had in mind, he'd never have another worry in his life and Petra would finally have to admit he was worthy of her.

But it wouldn't be easy, as he'd already discovered. Though Mrs. Wright was kind in ways that Petra was not, she did not let her good nature blind her to weakness or risk. Her dark brown eyes saw through his nascent schemes before he could put them into words.

His pride in his work and his desire to share in Mrs. Wright's fortune were so intense that he wanted this room and the lap pool area to be featured in a luxury magazine like *Unique Homes* or *Architectural Digest*. True, he'd get the credit and his career would finally take off, but he insisted to himself and Petra that *his* fame wasn't the main point. *Mrs. Wright's* was. When Petra pointed out that Mrs. Wright -- whom she privately referred to as the Duchess -- was already famous and didn't need his help, he pretended not to hear her.

He put away his camera and removed a tub of disinfectant wipes from the storage closet behind a mirrored door. He was wiping down an already gleaming machine when Mrs. Wright appeared around the corner in gray yoga pants and a purple razorback top. Even with her blond hair in a ponytail, not an ounce of makeup visible, and ten pounds too many around her middle, she was beautiful.

"Mrs. Wright! You're looking fit today."

Lexie made a face. "I look like crap and you know it." She patted her muffin top and still bulging tummy. "It's been two months since Lacey was born and I just can't get rid of this."

He eyed her middle professionally. "We're gonna work on that today. I'll get out your exercise mat and we'll start with the Sahrmann exercises again."

"Oh, that's so boring." Lexie made a sweeping gesture. "All

these machines I paid for and mostly I just lie on the floor and push my legs around or stretch myself over an inflatable ball. I could have bought what I needed for twenty dollars."

"We'll get to the machines, I guarantee that, but *postpartnumb* stuff, that's what we've got to work on."

"Post what?"

"Part*numb*," he said, emphasizing the last syllable. "You've heard of it, I'm sure."

"Not quite that way, but I like the 'numb' part. I was definitely numb for awhile." She checked a clock over the archway. "Let's get going. I have an appointment at four."

"Anyway, the exercises we've been doing are the best thing for you. No crunches or pushups or anything to put a strain on your back or those delicate woman parts."

"If you ever gave birth, Plato, you'd take back that word 'delicate.' There's nothing delicate about what Lacey did to me."

He surprised himself at what came out of his mouth next. It was unsettling the way his secrets slipped out in the Duchess' presence. "I'd do it, you know, if I could."

"You're kidding. A tough guy like you?"

"I want a son the worst way but Petra's not interested. She says if I want a kid so bad, I should go ahead and have it."

"Not an easy thing to do."

"Don't I know it! Now let's start with the basic breath." He placed his hand on the abdominal muscle she was supposed to contract. "I told her, on that score, I just can't pass the *mustard*."

In the middle of trying to contract the right muscle without arching her spine, Lexie laughed. "Or the ketchup. Plato, you crack me up."

"Don't know how that happens, ma'am. Petra says I'm boring, the most *sloporific* person she ever met. I don't think she means it in a nice way."

Lexie rolled to her side and laughed. He thought he heard her say, "I need to start taking notes."

When the exercises were done, after handing the Duchess a towel and a bottle of water, he once again broached the idea of having a luxury magazine do a photo spread on the beautiful room he had designed for her. "I don't want to *rehatch* the subject, but I think you should give it a little more consideration."

When Mrs. Wright smiled and started her reply with a heap of compliments, he knew she was going to refuse. "It's a wonderful room, Plato, and you should be very proud of it. It's a happy enough gym I look forward to working out . . . most of the time."

"It has great energy. That's what Petra says, anyway. Kind of a spiritual place, don't you think, specially when the lights are dimmed and the music's playing?"

"I never know what people mean by good energy and spirituality, Plato. Very overused words, I think, a little too New Age for my taste. And all these mirrors," she said, gesturing at them, "root me in the material world, not the spiritual." Catching his stricken look, she softened her tone. "But I understand why you want to let the world know about it. It's very clean and efficient, and it works amazingly well."

"So . . . ."

"So I'll think about it, but don't get your hopes up. My husband is adamantly opposed to that kind of publicity -- too much of a security risk these days. A photo spread would just fire up every scammer and burglar in the country. Steve's so concerned about security, he replaces his Expedition every year in the same color with the same wheel covers so nobody knows the truck is new." She patted Plato's shoulder. "I don't even want my neighbors to know I have a home workout space this grand, so let's keep this on the QT."

"*Cutie*? What's 'keep this on the *cutie*' mean?"

He heard her laughing all the way to the end of the hallway.

2

Another Note
Wednesday, February 29, 2012

Todd caught up with Miss Royce, still in her workout clothes, as she was hurrying toward the stairs to the second floor. "Ma'am, wait up." He brandished a piece of paper. "I found another note."

Lexie stopped dead. "Where?"

"On your car."

"It's still in the garage, isn't it?"

"I just washed it -- outside of course -- but then I pulled it inside and half an hour later when I walked by I spotted this note on the passenger window."

"You didn't see who put it there?"

He shook his head.

"Did you read it?"

Todd closed his eyes. "I have to confess I read it right away, yes, I did, couldn't stop myself. It worries me, can't tell you how much, somebody leaving notes everywhere soon as my back is turned. I never even spot a shadow on the wall or hear a footstep on the floor. It's like the notes just fly around, landing here and there, the way us kids let loose paper airplanes in school, launched by an unseen hand."

"Very poetic." With a resigned shrug, Lexie unfolded the note and read the lines aloud.

12

The rose is red, the violet blue
Who wouldn't fall in love with you?

"What child wrote this?" Lexie asked.

"You think a child wrote it?"

"Not really, Todd. The rhyme is just so simple-minded, the printing style so primitive. If some adult is leaving these notes, why doesn't he sign them?"

"But very adoring, wouldn't you say? The admirer leaving them thinks a lot of you, that's for sure. Anyway, how many notes does that make now, ma'am?"

"I haven't kept count, but there's a growing pile in my cubby." She handed the note back. "Phyllis knows where the others are, so give it to her for safekeeping."

"You think you should go to the cops?"

"It's creepy, I grant you that, but the notes never threaten me, so what am I going to say?"

"I don't like it, even if the writer of these notes is in love with you. Which, by the way, I think they are. It's not right, though. If you love somebody, just say so. No sneaking around. If Lieutenant Powers saw these, I bet he'd take them seriously. I'm no cop, of course, I'm just sayin'."

"I'll think about it, Todd -- when I have time. If I don't get upstairs this minute, I'm going to be late for my meeting."

3

Talisman

Wednesday, February 29, 2012

Drago Bott was the happiest he'd been in months. Just that day he'd learned that at the age of 65, his boss, Nate Grabbendorf, was finally retiring. The old fart had been the assistant manager and then, when Isaac Royce died, the big kahuna operations manager of Summit City Metals and Scrapyard for almost forty years. When Nate told him about retiring, Drago had tried not to look overjoyed.

"What do you plan on doing with all the free time coming your way, Nate?"

"I'm going to fish every goddamn day remaining to me. I've got a little boat up on Lake James. The wife's family has had a cabin there for years. Nothing to look at, mind you, and in need of a lot of work. Beulah's probably going to try to get me in the habit of sprucing up the place." He shifted the toothpick to the other side of his mouth and with a penknife began trimming his nails. "But I plan to die with a fishing pole either in my hands or up somebody's butt."

Now there was room at the top for a young, ambitious guy with lots of new ideas and strong ties to the Royce family.

Drago was not a man for writing lists on paper, but he could make them in his head. Mentally, he drew a vertical line down the middle of a piece of paper and began his list of pros and cons

-- why Mizz Royce should or should not make him the new manager.

He decided to run through the cons first. He was sure it was the shorter list.

He was young, just twenty-seven.

He'd been in the scrap business only three years.

He hadn't gone to college.

He didn't have a trade or special skill that any other boss would value.

He had a record -- a couple of bar fights, car windows tinted too dark, possession of an unregistered gun, speeding tickets, that kind of thing -- but nothing serious or recent.

His work history wasn't something he could put on paper. Before Mizz Royce gave him a job at the Scrapyard, he was in the drug business with her brother, Rolie. For over five years after graduating from high school, he was Rolie's chauffeur and enforcer. He'd killed a rival drug dealer who was about to get the draw on him. He'd also helped his mother conceal the murder of his father.

Well, that was it for the downside. He stared at the wall of his cubicle, surprised not to see a longer list there, glowing like phosphorescence.

Now for the upside. Mentally, he moved to the right column.

He was tough, loyal, and ambitious, in excellent health.

He was married with two kids and two dogs.

He'd graduated from high school, on time, with a respectable C+ average.

With the help of both Nate and Trude Weide, the Scrapyard bookkeeper and office manager, he'd learned every trick there was for spotting drivers who stole scrap, tried to cheat the scales, and pretended they'd left their driver's license at home. He knew how a worker could cheat on his time card. And thanks to his own experience on the wrong side of the law, he could spot every shady character who passed through the gates before they had a chance to try out their dark arts.

He'd gotten an at-a-boy last year from Lieutenant Dave Powers for stopping a cemetery thief in his tracks.

He not only knew what went on in the Yard but, thanks to Trude, understood a fair amount about government permits, accounts receivable and payable, taxes, and the basic rules for hiring and firing.

He'd made sure all the clunkers in Fort Wayne ended up in the Scrapyard when the government was foolishly paying cash for them, for which accomplishment he received a small bonus.

As part of management, he was paid for forty hour weeks but typically worked at least fifty without complaint, and he hadn't had a raise in almost a year.

He never missed a day of work and was never late.

The men in the Yard respected him.

True, he'd been in the drug business, but weed only, nothing stronger.

He was tight with the Royces. His mother, Phyllis Whitlow had worked for them as cook and housekeeper since shortly after he was born, and a couple years earlier he'd saved the lives of Mizz Royce and her husband, Steve.

And he wanted the job. He really, really wanted the job and the extra money. He'd heard that really wanting something could make it happen.

Lost in thought, Drago absently extracted a coin from his pocket and bounced it in his hand. It was a very special coin he'd found in a parking lot: an 1885 Morgan silver dollar. One side showed Lady Liberty in profile with 13 stars; the other depicted an eagle with its wings spread. This coin spoke to him because he was born exactly a hundred years after it was struck. After he'd checked with a coin dealer and discovered it was authentic, not rare but fairly valuable, Lucy, his wife, told him it was a talisman, a good luck charm he should hang on to.

"I don't believe in luck and charms," he'd told her.

"You should. If your dad hadn't practically beaten you to death . . . if your mother hadn't protected you the way she did . . . if Rolie hadn't gotten himself in too deep in the drug business . . . if Mizz Royce hadn't taken you under her wing as a consequence

. . . if not for all those ifs, where would you be? There was a long string of luck there, Drago. Some bad, I grant you, but it ended up good."

Now he took a long look at the talisman. He flipped it onto his desk to see if it would tell him which way Mizz Royce's decision would go. Lady Liberty, no way; eagle, yes, he'd be the big kahuna. And then the strangest thing happened. The coin, perfectly balanced, spun on its edge but didn't fall in either direction. He couldn't believe it. He'd performed a magic trick without knowing how.

He glanced at the wall again, hoping to see an explanation glowing there. He hoped the weird event had nothing to do with a warning he'd received the week before. He hadn't known how to respond. Like the coin, he was balanced on a knife edge, his response suspended.

When he heard Trude close the door on her little office and walk toward his cubicle, he hastily pocketed the coin and stood up so she could see him. "Is the queen leaving early?" he asked, thrusting his wristwatch in her direction.

She laughed. "The queen leaves no later than six and has many other duties, so, yes, she's leaving. You can escort her to her carriage if you want."

On the way out, after turning out the lights and locking up, he told her he needed her advice about something. Could he take her to dinner?

"I've gotta get home first, Pup, feed Lord and Lady MacDuff, then, if I'm going to eat dinner out, shower and change clothes. How about seven-thirty somewhere?"

"It's a deal."

"You've never taken me to dinner before. I take it something's up."

"You got it."

"Give me a hint about what you need to talk about so I can be prepared."

"Not here, okay?"

"Nate's retirement?"

17

"No. Something that happened last week. It's been on my mind awhile."

They agreed to meet at a little diner in Leo.

⚜

4

Important Woman
Wednesday, February 29, 2012

When Lexie got home from her meeting a little after five, she found Astrid Wikfelder, the new *au pair*, sitting in the kitchen, chatting with Phyllis, the cook, and Todd, the man-of-all trades. When they spotted Lexie, all three put their fingers to their lips and nodded in the direction of the pumpkin seat, where Lacey was sleeping, her fists bracketing her rosebud mouth. Her cheeks were wet.

"She cried for an hour," Astrid whispered, standing up, "and she's finally quiet."

"But I want to pick her up," Lexie whispered back with a frown. The frown wasn't just about having her maternal instincts thwarted but about Astrid's appearance -- too damned attractive. She wondered if it had been a mistake to hire a tall Swedish blonde, just twenty-one, with a figure both sexy and athletic. Was her whole closet nothing but spandex? And how was it the girl could look so good without makeup? Lexie wouldn't feel quite so threatened if the girl was unlikeable -- but, wouldn't you know, everybody loved her.

Phyllis tiptoed toward the family room, signaling Miss Royce to join her. "Trent's waiting for you upstairs. Lacey will be ready for some action when you get done up there, so you won't miss out on a thing and you'll get Trent out of the way. Dinner's going to be ready at seven."

"What are we having? It smells good."

"*Coq au vin*, Steve's favorite."

"Mine too. Well, everything you make is my favorite. Is there enough if I invite Trent to join us?"

Phyllis frowned. "Of course. I'll make a bigger salad and bake a few more popovers before I leave. You'll find six chocolate mousse cups in the fridge in the butler's pantry. All you have to do is spoon on the whipped cream."

Lexie rubbed her waistline. "Thanks, Phyllis, for helping me diet."

"You don't have to eat dessert, you know."

"I know," she said in a resigned voice. "Back in an hour -- I hope."

Trent Senser was waiting at the top of the stairs. He was dressed in a perfectly tailored black suit, as if he were her butler. "Ah, Alexandra, I have so much to show you."

"Have you been waiting long?"

"No. The perfect amount of time to get everything ready for you."

"The suits are back already, altered to your specifications?"

"That's what we're going to find out -- whether they fit the way we want." He showed her the Spanx he'd bought her. "Let's put this on, then the suits."

"I've heard of Spanx."

"Every woman's best friend."

When she emerged from her dressing room, wearing a silk kimono over the Spanx, she told him she couldn't breathe.

"Good. That means it's doing its job. Now, go put the black suit on."

When she reemerged, he looked stunned in the happiest way possible. He wasn't acting. He loved, loved, loved being Alexandra Royce Wright's stylist, and as a result of her recommendations to a few other rich women, he'd been able to leave his old career as a paralegal. But Mrs. Wright would always be his favorite client: beautiful, inscrutable in the nicest way, accommodating, rich.

"Perfect. Notice how the peplum -- which is very fashionable -- hides that little tummy without making your butt look big, which you were sure would happen."

"I'm noticing. You were right, I was wrong. And it fits perfectly."

"I knew it would. I have a couple new things for you to consider. One is this Panthère de Cartier necklace. I just have a picture, of course, from *WSJ Magazine*, so we'll have to go to New York if you're really interested in seeing it for yourself. Animal pendants are all the rage, and you'll notice how the emeralds set off the white and black diamonds. It would be perfect with the camisole you're going to wear under the jacket . . . and it's a good investment. Gold and diamonds -- I hear they're appreciating like mad. Of course, no one would know that better than you. I've taken the liberty of looking through your jewelry collection and you don't have a thing like it."

"For a bloody good reason, Trent. It probably costs the earth."

"But it's worth it. An important woman must wear important jewelry. Now hold out your wrist, I want you to try this Christian Lacroix perfume. The seashell bottle is just stunning, don't you think? It's not even that expensive but it smells like heaven: top notes of mandarin and coriander, middle notes of orange blossom, base notes of cedar and vanilla."

"How do you know all this?" Lexie asked sniffing her wrist. "I do like it."

"I research everything. Anyway, notice how beautiful the bottle will look on your dressing table. Which, by the way, could use a little upgrading. I know just the silver lamp and crystal vases that would raise it to a new level."

"I'm sure you do."

Focus, he thought. Best to ignore the hint of sarcasm. "We need to have Armstrong Flowers bring in fresh white bouquets at least once a week to give your *boudoir* that French look I love. I can arrange that, if you like. Maybe we need an imposing arrangement downstairs in the entryway too."

"We?"

Should I smile or not? No. "A grand house like this deserves fresh flowers."

Suddenly, Lexie laughed. "You're so serious about the most frivolous things, Trent. I love it."

Adjusting the bright yellow silk handkerchief peaking out of his breast pocket, he adopted his most philosophical look. "Beauty is not frivolous. If we can't have a little beauty, what's life really worth?"

"I think we'd find out in a nanosecond if there was no food. Speaking of which, do you want to stay for dinner?"

He willed his face not to look too eager. "Let me call Cricket, but I know she'll understand. What's Mrs. Whitlow making anyway? If I were anybody else, I'd be drooling, it smells so divine."

5

Find the Snake
Wednesday, February 29, 2012

Tucked into a corner booth at the diner, Drago and Trude both ordered fried chicken dinners with mashed potatoes and gravy. When they were sipping iced tea and waiting for their salads and dinner rolls, Drago began recounting the unscheduled meeting he'd had the week before.

"Picture this. I'm in Dick's Sporting Goods, looking at work boots, when this lady comes over to me, lays her hand on my arm, says she knows me. I take my time turning my head to look at her without saying a word, acting like she's interrupting something important, pretending I don't know who she is. But I recognize her. She's one of those street hustlers trying to shut down the Scrapyard. Somewhere around forty, I'd say."

"Tall, thin, deep creases in her forehead? Her nose pinched like she smells something dead -- you, maybe? A staccato way of speaking?"

He laughed. "To a tee. How'd you know?"

"It's gotta be Doreen. She's a Soren, but I hear she's married now. Don't know her new last name."

"The strangest thing is, what's going through my mind isn't what she's saying. It's her color. Lucy's pale pink, Mom's really, really pale, you're sort of a soft red in my mind, like you just won a fight."

"Soft red? Just won a fight? Are you referring to my rosacea?"

"It's a compliment, Trude. Goes with your spiky white hair. You're a scrapper, like me."

"And you're mocha. That's a compliment too, by the way. Mocha's my favorite drink."

He ducked his head in acceptance. "You know what color Doreen is?"

"Kind of beige with purple undertones. Hair, skin, eyes -- all the same color."

"I don't know about the purple undertones, but a kind of grayish beige is right. Looks like she lives under a rock, eats dirt, comes out only at night. Anyway, what do you know about her?"

"Miss Royce has no time for her, even though they're sort of related. She's the niece of Miss Royce's step-mother, Matilda. The woman's an activist, all about saving the earth."

"A do-gooder?"

"In her mind, she's a woman with a cause. Hates industry, oil drilling, cars, banks, shopping malls, that kind of stuff. Loves unions, windmills, and free medical clinics. So what's she want with you?"

"I'm trying on boots, she takes the chair next to me. She asks me how many hours I work a week -- she hears it's a lot more than forty. She wants to know whether I'm paid overtime and treated fairly."

"And you say what?"

"I ask her how she knows how many hours I work. She says she has her sources."

"What sources?"

"Don't know. Then she asks as a black man how I like working for rich white people."

Trude reached out her hand to take the salt shaker from him, which he was twirling around.

He held on to the shaker but put it back on the table with a thump. "Sorry about that. Anyway, I tell her rich people are the only ones who've ever paid me a salary and I don't give a flying fuck what color they are."

"You didn't say that. The bad word, I mean."

"I did. Then she says it's easier to organize a union these days, thanks to a man in the White House who looks a lot like me."

"White mothers, black fathers. You two look alike, you should think alike. Is that it?"

"I don't like people telling me how I should think, know that."

"I do know that."

After their salads were in place, Drago resumed his story. "She wants me to talk to the guys in the Yard about why they should vote for a union. Says I'll be more persuasive than anybody else."

"And what do you say to that?"

Drago pushed his salad away. "You know, I've never liked salad. Lucy thinks a meal isn't complete unless she shoves a pile of raw greens at me." He grabbed the salt shaker again. "I hate when anybody tells me to do something that's good for me."

Trude laughed. "You're repeating yourself. And you're avoiding my question, Drago."

"I said I'd get back to her."

"And that's it? She let it go at that?"

Drago paused when he saw the waitress approaching with their dinners. "That was fast," he said, a little irritated. For once, food was less important than talking. After taking a few bites of chicken, he resumed. "No. The woman says she has a lot of muscle behind her, friends in high places, stuff will happen. A demonstration, bad publicity, maybe even a court order to shut down the joint. She asks if I know about the Wall Street occupiers."

"And what do you say?"

"I say I'd have to live under a rock not to. She tells me unless I get back to her with the right answer, all hell will break loose, just like on Wall Street. This chicken, by the way, is pretty good, don't you think?"

"Agreed." Trude put down her drumstick, wiped her hands, and sipped her tea. "Did she give you a date for when the protestors are going to show up at the Yard?"

"No. She doesn't even say it will be at the Yard. She mumbles something about going to the houses of the one percent."

"So she's threatening you, maybe even Miss Royce at home."

"It's obvious, isn't it?"

"I know what I think about it, but first let me hear what you think, Drago."

Drago closed his eyes in thought. "I don't want people pooping in the Yard, throwing garbage around, yelling and screaming, breaking things for the hell of it, so let's start there."

"Good place to start."

"And I want to run the place, I won't lie. The way I see it, a union's only going to make it tougher, don't you think? More hassle every which way."

"Of course."

"But if I let the place go union, that avoids a big, expensive fuss, a battle I might lose just when I'm trying to make a good impression on Mizz Royce. Maybe a union's inevitable anyway."

"So you're caught between a rock and a hard place: resist or surrender."

"Not the first time."

"So what's the answer?"

He grinned at her. "That's why I'm paying for this expensive chicken dinner, your ladyship. You tell me."

"Bear with me if I go round the barn before answering."

"Take your time. There's a lot of chicken here."

"I've worked at the Yard ever since graduating from high school. I've never had any other job, and I need to work another fifteen years before I retire. I'm not married, so nobody's got my back. I still have a mortgage to pay, I like to trade in my truck every three years, and I go on a two-week cruise every autumn. This year I've signed up for the same river cruise Matilda and Grace were bragging about at Miss Royce's baby shower, and it isn't cheap, believe me. I breed Shelties, as you know, but they don't pay their own way."

"Life is expensive."

"I don't have a lavish lifestyle, but I admit it's way beyond what a Walmart greeter can afford, so if I lose this job, I'm in deep trouble." She paused as the waitress refreshed their iced tea. "Now, let's take you. You need the job too, and even if the economy was good, finding work paying this well would be hard. No offense."

"None taken."

"So if anybody asks, I'm going to recommend that you take Nate's place. There are lots of reasons why you might not get the job, chiefly your age, so it's a bit of a long shot, but Miss Royce may have her own reasons for elevating you. If anything you do ends up unionizing the place, however, you'll find yourself out on the street, no matter how much Miss Royce cares for you. Business is business."

"I thought you never liked her, but you seem to be taking her point of view."

"Some things are neither black nor white, Drago, and personal feelings change as circumstances do. I don't hate her; I never did... . Put it this way. I got used to the way Isaac, her dad, did things, so I never liked the kids poking into the business. But he's been gone for a long time and I've come to respect her. In any case, she's got the power and the money, so go with it."

"Your advice, then, is to resist Doreen the street hustler."

"Community organizer. Activist. I think that's what she calls herself. . . . We can use whatever words we want in private, but in public let's not disrespect her, okay?"

He frowned. "Okay."

"What I'm saying is, I need the job and so do you. Things are damn good just the way they are. You want to change that?"

"No. So now what?"

"You're going to have to do quite a few things all at once. Find the snake who's crawling around the Yard, whispering our secrets to Doreen. Tell Miss Royce what you told me. Then you'll know what to say to the men and the answer to give to Doreen. But you're going to have to act fast."

Lost in thought, he pushed his plate to the side and tore open a wet-wipe package so he could wash his hands. "You know, Trude, life is funny as hell. First time I saw you, I was scared to death -- a woman, for Pete's sake, scaring the crap out of me! It was something about your eyes, the way you looked through me, not so much with hatred as with laughter. Nobody ever laughed at me when I was working for Rolie, know that. It was a new experience. I wasn't scared of the Bosnian gang or Rolie when he was drunk or anything else, but being laughed at made me shake in my boots."

"I have that effect on men and dogs," she murmured ruefully. "And now?"

"I'm glad you have my back, that's all."

"Meaning you want me to be with you when you talk to Miss Royce."

"That's what I mean."

6

Ostara
Wednesday, February 29, 2012

Mama Bee is unable to sleep, despite having drunk a pot of chamomile tea. She has too much on her mind.

For a hundred dollars apiece, twelve women have been accepted for her Ostara Celebration of the vernal equinox, to be held in less than three weeks. Her acolytes were reminded that the equinox means spring, and spring means rebirth. Her invitations -- to almost fifty women -- warned that since attendance was limited to twelve goddess-celebrants (she would make the thirteenth) they should reply as quickly as possible. She had to turn down half a dozen women eager to pay the fee, but of course they are fodder for the next celebration.

She prefers outdoor parties. Her summer solstice celebration in late June is always celebrated in a white gazebo behind her house. The gazebo is perched in the middle of a large manmade lake, connected to land by arched bridges, and ringed with statues of Greek and Roman goddesses. Given its setting, the gazebo can be made ethereal with white scrim hung between the pillars, strings of fairy lights reflecting off the water, and pots of incense scenting the air. She always serves up soothing music and fruity spiked punch to open her guests' chakras to the mysteries of the universe and their minds to the need of another reading.

But March 20 might not lend itself to the gazebo. Though

Fort Wayne's winter has been unusually mild, the weather might be windy and cold that day.

She sighs, not with despair, but with pleasure. She has choices. Over a decade ago, she helped an addled old widow lift a life-long curse with weekly séances. She did not charge a fee. Instead, she simply pointed out that the more generous the donations to the spirits, the faster the curse would be lifted. Unfortunately, the widow died before the curse was fully lifted, but the cumulative donations to the spirits were enough to let her build a rather grand house on two acres just inside the city limits.

On the east side of the house, she designed a hexagonal room -- the Crystal Cave. Floor-to-ceiling windows allow her clients to project their third eye toward the spiritual center of Mother Earth -- Jerusalem, Mecca, Varanasi, Alexandria, Delphi, depending on their preference. The room is large enough to hold a round table seating thirteen.

Aside from the table and chairs, the room is sparsely furnished. A huge custom-made Persian rug mutes sound. On either side of the doorway stand glass étagères. One, crowned with a bust of Buddha, displays crystals, pyramids, obelisks, and stone eggs. The other, crowned with a celestial globe, holds the tools of her trade: crystal balls, decks of cards, incense sticks, bells to summon the spirits, an onyx wand, and a gold crown for very special occasions.

Dark blue draperies, embroidered with gold and silver signs of the zodiac, can be closed if the mood suits her. Often it does suit her, for she has discovered that when no one else is in view, when the only sounds in the room are sitars and tablas, when incense dulls the senses -- that is, when wisdom is confined to the quiet mystery of the Crystal Cave -- a querent's mind opens to Mama Bee's words of comfort and, with that, her wallet.

Mama Bee has already done a lot of planning for Ostara. The women have been told to wear all white with green jewelry in honor of spring, preferably real emeralds, Tsavorite, peridot, or jade. Imitation jewels offend the spirits. Real jewels gladden the heart of a hungry fortune teller.

Each celebrant will be given a sparkling green bindi to paste

30

on her forehead where the third eye is located.

Then each guest will be given a sprig of green herb, revealing something about her soul that needs to be brought to consciousness. The herb will be hidden in an egg marking each place setting, but a guest's given name will not be written on the egg. Instead, a word or phrase about the ancient meaning of each goddess' name will appear, so she has to exercise her intuition about who she really is. Each guest will get a short individual reading, but the one who finds a crystal in her egg will get something longer and more detailed.

Names, she knows, are important. Most mothers select them much too carelessly. But her family doesn't. For instance, Ama, her daughter's name, means "difficult birth" in both West African and Native American languages. Ama's birth was indeed difficult; in fact, her whole life has been, and though Mama Bee is third-generation American, she identifies herself as a citizen of the world for whom color, culture, and language are mere accidents of nature. Ama in turn named her only daughter Umbra, meaning "ghost" or "the darkest part of a shadow" -- which indeed the poor girl is. Mama Bee's own name -- Belinda -- sounds too common to be special, but in fact it means "beautiful serpent." Her mother was prescient.

What Mama Bee has not decided is what kind of reading to give. Each of the short ones can last no longer than five minutes, ten at the most, or the evening will be too long.

The list of readings she is comfortable with is short: palm reading, crystal ball gazing, numerology, and Tarot cards. She rarely reads astrological charts.

Palm reading is the easiest. She is confident of her powers, having studied for a week in India when she was young. She can give a reading in her sleep.

Crystal ball gazing isn't particularly difficult either. She can envision whatever comes to mind; her client, who has no hope of seeing what she does, can only marvel at her mystical powers.

Numerology is boring and astrological charts are alarming, requiring a tiresome amount of work. She has never really understood a thing about them. Just looking at a chart makes her dizzy.

Tarot cards are different. She is very attracted to them herself, though they make her uneasy. There are 78 cards in a deck -- a lot to memorize. In a reading she can't use a cheat sheet lest she look unprofessional. The strange pictures on the cards are inscrutable, replete with hidden meaning. The same card upright means one thing, in reverse another -- and still another thing depending on which cards are proximate and which spread she uses. Interpretation is supposed to be specific to the client's subconscious, but how is she to know that?

Because clients can see the same cards she is seeing, they often think they know as much as she does and are doubtful of her reading. In her experience, the client can sense when a reading is really intuitive rather than just a lot of mumbo-jumbo.

A knowledgeable client is a client who doesn't return.

Yes, she will read the palms of eleven guests but favor one with a Tarot reading, which will take much longer than five minutes. Now, who should be favored? She reviews the twelve responses she has accepted.

The younger goddesses include a trio of friends: Cricket Grinderman, Lucy Bott, and Sally Westfield. Trent Senser too -- not a woman but, as Cricket's shadow, he fits in. Three of the four friends attended Vicki Grinderman's palm-reading session three years earlier. The other three young women are new to her: Astrid Wikfelder and Ivana Starr, recommended by Trent; and Petra Kuzmin, recommended by Cricket.

The older goddesses include Grace Venable and her little cabal: Grace's friend Matilda Royce; Matilda's older sister Abigail Soren and Abigail's daughters, Doreen Soren-Kawzy and Shayla Soren. In this group, the only one she knows personally is Grace.

Palm reading for the Cricket group is popular, though now it might be just a little tarnished. She drastically misread Vicki Grinderman's palm, after all. Perhaps they remember that. And any reading for Grace is fraught with problems; her eyes danced with skeptical amusement when her palm was read last year. Still, both

Cricket and Grace are returning, so they must have some faith in her.

Yes, she will read eleven palms -- five minutes apiece should do it -- and then do a longer Tarot reading for the special goddess who finds a crystal in her egg. She can't leave the special goddess to chance, of course. It might be amusing to put a crystal in Trent's egg. His name means "traveler." Or in Astrid's egg. Her name means "beautiful goddess." Both lend themselves to positive predictions. She'll have to think about that.

Mama Bee leaves the Crystal Cave for her study. Once more she sits down at her computer and calls up a YouTube video she has watched many times before. It features Denzel Washington, Robin Williams, Oprah, and other fine actors who describe how they sometimes call upon the spirits in order to play a difficult part. When they feel their minds and bodies being taken over, when they have been transported into another dimension, then mystical powers allow them to give the performance of their lives -- a performance they can't explain rationally.

Mama Bee wants what they have. She is tired of being a fraud. She wants real power, real knowledge.

But she is unsure of something. Where do the dark spirits live that fine actors call upon? Is it in the air or in the underworld? She knows it isn't in trees or rocks or lakes because she has tried conjuring up spirits in the natural world and nothing ever happens.

She wants to give a Tarot reading that sets her client's hair on fire. To do that, she will have to try something new.

So, after a little hesitation and feeling rather silly, she gets down on her knees, spreads her arms like wings, empties her mind of thoughts about the Ostara party, and summons the spirits lurking in the great void.

"Oh, iridescent plumèd one, the feathered ruler of the air and the underworld, enter me. Great dragon, the speaker of proud words, transform my soul."

After a few seconds, she feels her head drooping. Her eloquence has departed as suddenly as it appeared; no other supplication comes to mind.

Besides, the material world, the world of the body, has rudely asserted itself. She is too old for kneeling. Her back aches and her knees hurt, and she is suddenly cold. So she struggles to her feet and goes to bed.

7

Entourage

Wednesday, February 29, 2012

It was almost midnight and Lexie and Steve were still sitting in the atrium, a glass of wine beside Lexie's chair, a tumbler of scotch beside Steve's. Though they had many rooms to choose from, the atrium was their favorite. No television, no distractions. If the stars were out, they could see them. Lightning storms were amazing, viewed from the comfort of a glass room. But tonight there were no stars, nor any lightning either. All was calm.

"How is it Astrid always sits next to you at the dinner table?" Lexie asked teasingly.

"Does she? I didn't notice."

Lexie made a scoffing sound.

"If she does, I suppose it's so Lacey will be at my elbow. I don't get to see her all day, you know."

"Who don't you get to see all day -- Astrid or Lacey?"

He laughed. "Silly woman. Where's Henry, by the way?" Henry was the German Shepherd Lexie adopted from a shelter a few months before their marriage.

"Sleeping outside Lacey's door. Sometimes he pushes it open and Astrid finds him under her crib in the morning. By the way, did you feel the tension between Astrid and Ivy?"

"Can't say that I did."

"Of course not. You're a man. Well, I felt it."

"What's that about?"

"Not sure. They're both great at what they do. I try to treat them the same."

"Do you really need Ivy?"

"Jean's already pregnant, as you know. Her doctor says she's pre-diabetic and her blood pressure's high, so she might have to take a long maternity leave. I have to have somebody ready to take her place at a moment's notice."

Jean Arnold was Lexie's office manager and executive assistant. They'd been friends since high school, and though once upon a time Jean seemed to have a thing for Steve, that was long forgotten. Two months earlier, Jean had married Dover Pitt, Steve's golf pro, at a New Year's Eve wedding in Indianapolis.

Coincidentally, Jean had met Ivana Starr at the Conrad Hotel, where Ivy, as she was known, had managed the hotel's end of the wedding arrangements. She was the most organized woman Jean had ever met other than herself. A month ago she'd urged Lexie to interview Ivy for the position of office assistant.

"Ivy's kind of a cool customer, don't you think? Very reserved, always dressed like she's a spokesman for the State Department." Lexie shot her husband another teasing look. "And Astrid's hot as a firecracker, all dazzling light, bouncing around in short shorts, joking and laughing, not only flirting with you but with Trent too. So I suppose in this case opposites don't attract; they repel."

"Like those little scottie-dog magnets we used to play with."

"Was it their butts or muzzles that repelled?"

"Butts I think."

Lexie laughed. "What a visual!"

Steve wasn't particularly intuitive but he was sensitive enough to pick up on something. "You mention Astrid a lot. Are you hinting at something?"

"Maybe."

"Well, put your mind at rest about that. And I might point out that all those little notes you've been getting -- some guy thinks he's your lover. Unrequited, I trust."

"You trust right. I have no idea who it is, so you can put your mind at rest too."

"How's your book doing, by the way?"

"You're referring, of course, to *I'm the Boss: A Field Guide for Women Who Mean Business.*"

"Have you written another book since I last noticed?"

She laughed. "I don't intend to write another in this lifetime. It was going gangbusters for a few weeks, but as you know that review in *The Nation* a month ago was the equivalent of a grenade exploding at a party."

"Very mean words, I thought. I recall several mentions of the word 'hubris' -- you're full of it, you know. And you're a free-market ideologue on the wrong side of economic history. Most serious of all, we're going to have to get your *Weltanschauung* fixed, whatever the hell that is."

"My world view. Atticus Solon accused me of having rigid principles instead of being a flexible pragmatist. I stand accused and plead guilty."

"You're also an heiress pretending to be a self-made woman."

"I resemble that remark. I admit it's partly true. If Dad hadn't lent me money, I couldn't have gotten started. And if I hadn't learned the scrap business from him at the dinner table, Without a Shred and Junk in the Trunk would never have occurred to me as viable businesses. On the other hand, Dad gave me more criticism than advice once I got started, and if I'd failed, he wouldn't have rescued me. I explained all that in the forward, but maybe Atticus skipped it."

"Did you ever find out who Atticus is?"

"No. It's obviously a pen name, but until he reviewed my book, I'd never heard of him -- maybe because I'm not an intellectual. It's probably somebody I offended when I was in business -- except I never dealt with anyone with a vocabulary like that."

"The pen name sounds like a man's."

"But the attack is so personal, so bitchy, maybe a woman."

"Bettina can't be happy."

Lexie pictured her literary agent, Bettina Lazare -- the eponymous owner of The Lazare Group -- sitting in her hard-edged New York office, draped in Donna Karan garments, screaming at somebody to find the reviewer and kill him. "She isn't. She's furious. I got a big advance, you know, so the book needs to stay on the best-seller list a lot longer for Bettina to make her money. Friday I'm going out to New York to meet with her."

"You could do that by Skype, couldn't you?"

"My book isn't the only excuse for the trip, if you must know. Trent's lined up a few showings with clothing designers and a private viewing at Cartier to look at some panther necklace he says I can't live without. That can't be done except in person."

"You've booked the private jet?"

"I have."

"And you're staying at the Hôtel Plaza Athénée again?"

"I've taken a two-bedroom suite so Trent will have his own room but have access to the same luxury I do. He's so excited, I couldn't do anything else."

"My God, Lexie, Trent will dine out on that trip for the next five years -- when he's not dining in with us." He stood up and stretched. "How does he manage that schedule, by the way -- always around when dinner's about to be served?"

"Ivy does the same thing. Practically every day around six-thirty, she arranges to have something for me to sign. She's so quiet, new to Fort Wayne, works so late -- I feel guilty not including her at dinner."

"Every night we eat with an entourage -- the nanny, the stylist, the maid, sometimes the cook and the handyman. It's like living at Downton Abbey except there's no downstairs."

Lexie smiled. "Speaking of Downton Abbey, who would you want to be?"

"Lord Grantham's dog, of course. How about you?"

Lexie collapsed in giggles. "The Dowager Countess. She had the best life of them all. And I like the way she thinks."

"I note she's a widow. Is that something I should keep in mind?"

Lexie rose and took his hand. "Are you crazy?"

"When are you getting back from New York?"

"Saturday afternoon."

"Then I'm going to make reservations for two at Joseph Decuis that evening. No entourage."

Lexie stretched to kiss his cheek. "I know a place where there's no entourage."

He gave her a real kiss in return and then led her upstairs.

8

Put a Sock in It
Friday, March 2, 2012

Friday in New York City was even colder and rainier than in Fort Wayne, but Trent barely noticed the weather. He'd never ridden in a private jet before; in fact, this was only his second airplane ride ever. The comfort of the glove leather seats, the attention of the steward, the legroom -- everything was phenomenal, and Ivy, it turned out, had arranged for them to be served Starbucks lattes and cheese danishes before takeoff. Then there was the sleek black limousine waiting at the Teterboro airport in New Jersey. Trent sat beside Mrs. Wright, sipping ice-cold water from the bottle he found in a miniature bar, feeling important but a little tense too, wondering if he should say something or wait for his boss to speak first. Mrs. Wright seemed to be lost in thought, so he allowed himself to concentrate on the panorama sliding by: the George Washington Bridge, the Hudson River, the skyscrapers and traffic jams of Lower Manhattan, the rivers of people flowing up and down the streets.

One question he couldn't help asking out loud. "Why is there so much garbage on the sidewalks?"

"The city doesn't have alleys, so that's where garbage gets picked up."

"Ick. I don't like that." He caught himself. "But everything else I love."

After they'd checked into the hotel, they took a seat in the lobby to review their schedule. Trent looked around. "Is it okay if I take a few pictures for Cricket?"

"Be discreet. We don't want to look too much like tourists."

"I don't suppose everybody in New York lives like this."

"Some do. Most live in shoeboxes." She checked her lipstick in a pocket mirror. "Do you want to come with me to The Lazare Group or spend some time alone, wandering up Fifth Avenue, checking out the shop windows? It's okay if you do. I don't know how long my meeting will last and I don't want you to be bored. I'll call you when I'm done so we can meet up."

Trent wrestled with competing desires. He couldn't wait to see the treasures offered in every shop. On the other hand, he was a little intimidated by the sheer size and bustle of the city and wanted to stay close to his patroness, like a lion cub with his mother. "I'll stay with you."

Bettina Lazare, as always, was very busy, dictating letters, shuffling manuscripts to various editors, asking one of her harried assistants where the hell her coffee and fruit cup were. But she didn't keep Alexandra Royce Wright waiting.

"Have a seat. How was the trip?"

"Uneventful -- the way I like a flight to be. This is my stylist, by the way. Trent Senser."

He held out his hand. "Glad to meet you. You're wearing Donna Karan, aren't you? Love it."

Mrs. Lazare, who had sat back down before she could grasp his hand, shot him a quick glance and then turned her attention back to Lexie. Confused, Trent shut his mouth and made a little half bow before taking the other guest chair.

He only half listened to the women's discussion of sales figures and royalties. He'd never been good with numbers. Then the subject changed to Mrs. Wright's book tour.

Lexie was examining a schedule. "I'll do the rest of this book tour -- though Detroit seems like a big waste of time. Just so you know, I'm not reading from my book any more. People are bored to death with that. It's not the kind of book that lends itself to a reading anyway, and even the little lecture I sometimes give instead on the history of women-owned businesses puts women to sleep."

"So then what do you propose, Alexandra?"

"Questions and answers. I do that at the end anyway and people like it. So I'll just do a half hour or so of Q and A and then sign books."

"What kind of questions do you get?"

"Mostly about my private life. How I manage husband and baby and business without going insane."

"Okay with me so long as you sell books."

Before Lexie could respond, Bettina leaned forward and changed the subject. "My investigator found Atticus Solon."

Trent perked up. He'd heard that name over the dinner table. At first, he'd assumed it was a heroic figure played by Brad Pitt in an action movie co-starring Angelina Jolie and loosely based on some historical event. He knew better now. The thing Atticus Solon wrote about Mrs. Wright's book was a hot topic of conversation one evening among the staff. He was prepared to hate Atticus Solon without ever having met him.

"Really? Who is it?"

Bettina reached to the side of her desk and picked up a black folder. She let the tension build as she opened the folder and silently read a page. "The answer will surprise you. First of all, he lives in Fort Wayne."

"You're kidding."

"On Forest Park Boulevard."

"I used to live there!"

Bettina found a sheet of paper and handed it to Lexie. "Here's a picture of his house and the address. A picture of him too."

"Oh, my God, I recognize that old Tudor -- and the man. I used to live a few doors down across the street."

"So you know who it is."

"Alastair Digby."

"To be precise," Bettina said, consulting another sheet of paper, "Alastair Rutherford Digby III. Born in 1942. Third-generation scion of a family that made its fortune in World War II in magnet

42

wire, whatever that is."

"Of course. The Digbys are still around, but they sold the company years ago."

"According to our research, he attended Andover Phillips Academy in Massachusetts, where he was a member of the German Club, wrote for *The Phillipian*, and did some acting. He went on to study at Columbia University's school of journalism and after graduating got a gig reviewing books for *The Nation*. He was briefly married. Then he lived with an artist friend in Manhattan, but when the friend died a few years ago, he quietly returned to the city of his birth." Bettina looked up from her folder. "I take it you didn't know Alastair wrote book reviews for an East Coast publication?"

Lexie shook her head. "No. I saw him on the street a couple of times, met him at a party once. He was wearing a double-breasted suit and talking through his nose about some subject I don't even remember. But I never heard how he made ends meet. I just assumed he was living off the family fortune because he never mentioned a job and he hardly ever left the house."

Bettina reached for the paper Lexie was holding and replaced it in her folder. "You know, of course, that he's dead."

Lexie nodded. "It was in the paper yesterday. He was found dead in mysterious circumstances, possibly a homicide, the paper said."

"Possibly?" Bettina laughed. "*Possibly* a homicide?" She paused for effect. "He was ice-picked in the back of the neck."

"Oh," Trent exclaimed, wincing and grabbing his neck.

Lexie put her hand on his arm to steady his nerves. "By whom?"

"Still to be discovered. Did the paper mention that he was Atticus Solon, the influential but pseudonymous author of *On the Shelf*, a book review column for *The Nation*?"

"No. I would have remembered that if it had."

"His brother Desmond was the person who found Mr. Digby dead in his house. He told my investigator that a Tarot card was found upside down near the computer keyboard. The Fool. That was the card. Know anything about Tarot?"

Trent raised his hand. "I do. I've had my cards read."

"Does the card mean anything?"

"All by itself? Just that one card?"

"That's my understanding."

"I don't remember exactly, but in my reading the Fool turned up. It meant I was embarking on a new adventure -- which I was without knowing it. Mrs. Wright here," he said, touching Lexie's arm, "hired me a few weeks later."

"Does it matter if the card is upside down?"

"I'm not sure. According to Mama Bee, Tarot is complicated."

"Mama Bee?"

"The reader I went to."

"Well, the Tarot card wasn't the only thing Desmond found. On his brother's computer screen, there was a message." Bettina picked another sheet of paper out of the black folder and read aloud: "'Fool -- You'll never hurt anyone again.'"

"Very mysterious," Lexie said. "Was Mr. Digby the author of the computer message, or was the ice-picker leaving a calling card?"

"My investigator is still looking into that."

"Who's your investigator?"

"Let's just say an opposition research firm that digs up dirt on political candidates owes me a favor."

"I'm a little puzzled, Mrs. Lazare. Why did you go to so much trouble to find Atticus Solon -- even if the investigator didn't cost you anything?"

"He's hurt more than one of my writers -- and me too. He's been on a tear lately, excoriating old-line agents like me, saying the only books we publish are by famous people who barely speak English and certainly can't write it. He claims we're too lazy to ferret out great new authors and promote them. If a writer doesn't already have a public platform, he whined, then good writers can't get in the door."

Well, that's true, isn't it? Lexie thought. *If I hadn't been featured in Forbes' 40 under 40, you'd never have known a thing about me or asked me to write a book.*

"You know what else my investigator learned?"

Lexie and Trent shook their heads in unison.

"Alastair Digby had two boxes full of an unfinished manuscript entitled . . . let's see," she said extracting another sheet of paper from her folder, ". . . *Musket Misfire: How the British Lost the American Colonies by Winning the French and Indian Wars.*" She looked over her glasses at her visitors. "Desmond said his brother had been working on it for thirty years, so if anybody asked, Alastair always said he was a writer and historian. Now I know he was just an embittered old man who couldn't finish his book and probably couldn't have found an agent if he had, so he had to spew his bile on successful agents like me and real writers like," cough, cough, cough, "you."

"Poor man," Lexie murmured. "Do you need some water?"

Bettina shook her head. "Poor man indeed! That stuff he wrote about your little celebrity book was just crazy. Do you even understand what he meant about your 'shadowy metaphysics of inherited wealth' or 'antediluvian dogma of individuality?'"

"No. My husband commented on that part about my being an heiress."

"Or your failure to understand the 'Nietzschean evolution of economic theory?'"

"No."

"Such big concepts to attack a little book. His review was like killing a mosquito with a shoulder-fired weapon."

"My little celebrity book is a mosquito?"

If Lexie's question registered with Bettina, she didn't acknowledge it. "Anyway, a few weeks ago, I'd just had it. I wanted to find out who the schmuck is. At that point, he wasn't dead yet, but by the time my investigator got on the job, he was."

"So you didn't have him killed."

Bettina smiled. "Can't nail me with that one."

"What were you going to do if you found him alive?"

Bettina fell back in her chair with a laugh that made Trent jump. "I was going to tell him to put a sock in it. And if he didn't,

I'd put it there myself."

Trent stared. Her oversized bosom was shaking so hard he knew she wasn't wearing Spanx. He wanted to give her a few hints about shapewear.

Still laughing, she pushed up her glasses and wiped her eyes. "Thank God, somebody beat me to it. Don't you love it when you get revenge without even trying?"

9

Lexie Is Flexy
Friday, March 2, 2012

When Jean Arnold entered the office off the courtyard of Steve and Lexie's estate, she found Ivy Starr already at her desk. Jean looked at her watch. It was eight in the morning. For days she'd been arriving five minutes earlier than the day before, but she never beat Ivy to work. It was starting to grate on her nerves.

"What are you doing here so early?"

Smiling, Ivy carefully inserted a bookmark and closed the book she'd been reading. Then she got to her feet. "Getting a start on the day. My, you look nice. The coffee is ready. I'll get you a cup."

"I'll get it myself -- but thanks for making it. What are you reading?"

"Miss Royce's book. I love it. Such a charming mixture of memoir, anecdote, and practical advice. Every time I read it I find something new -- something I didn't grasp the first time around."

"Is it really that complicated?"

"I wouldn't say complicated. But it's rich with ideas. I thought I learned a lot about business at the Conrad, but, really, I didn't know a thing."

"Have you completed Lexie's February expense report?"

"Right here, ready for your review. I also had a look at all the solicitations that came in last month. Each is stapled to my analysis and recommendation -- subject to your judgment, of course. I found out all I could from the Internet about each of the charities and individuals who've written to Miss Royce, as you'll see. If you want the backup research, I have a folder I can give you. Of course, I don't expect you just to take my word for anything."

"Of course not," Jean sighed. The woman's efficiency was beginning to set her teeth on edge. "Anything else?"

"I'm taking a course in accounting at IPFW, so if you want, I can help you with organizing Miss Royce's investment records. And I've been collecting information on pioneering industries she might want to take a look at. I know she likes to stay ten steps ahead of everybody else. I've got a couple of ideas for selling the wind farms, by the way. She told me if she'd known how many birds the windmills kill and how much they heat up the air around them, she'd never have invested in them. They take a lot of land away from food production too."

"I don't think those are the reasons she's selling them."

"You don't?"

"No. Whatever you heard, she gave the real scoop to me. At some point, she thinks, the government is going to stop granting tax credits for them and she wants to get out while she can. She's trying to make money, you know, not save the earth from fossil fuels."

"Oh. I have so much to learn."

Yes, you do. Like, stop trying to pretend you know Lexie better than I do.

"Before I forget, you might want to take a look at this," Ivy said, holding out a piece of lined notepaper. "It was scotch-taped to the office door this morning when I got here. It's a limerick."

Jean took a look. "I know what a limerick is." She read it aloud:

> There is a nice lady named Lexie
> Who is the epitamie of sexy
> She lites up a room
> She makes my heart boom
> She works out so much she's flexy

"I don't like this," Jean said, snapping the paper.

"I don't either. 'Epitome' and 'lights' are misspelled . . . and is 'flexy' even a word?"

Jean frowned at her assistant. "The misspellings and contrived rhymes are the least of my worries. Who the hell would write crap like this?"

"Gosh," Ivy mused. "Let me think." She snapped her fingers. "Maybe Plato. He misuses words, probably can't spell them either, and that part about working out -- isn't that what he would notice about Miss Royce?"

"Plato's harmless. He doesn't see Lexie as sexy. He sees her as rich. No, it's not him. And he has no reason to be here today anyway because Lexie's in New York."

"How do you know he didn't sneak in early?"

"How could he sneak in? The courtyard gate is locked until one of us arrives."

"It sounds like him though," Ivy said stubbornly. "Maybe he scaled the wall."

Jean scoffed. "It wasn't Plato."

"I don't understand how you can be so sure."

"Because I know people, that's how."

Ivy reached for the note. "I'll give it to Miss Royce."

Jean drew back her hand and threw the note on her own desk. "I'll give it to her myself. What a crappy way to start the day. I think I'll just go throw up now, get it over with."

10

The Fool Is Missing
Friday, March 2, 2012

Friday afternoon, when Mama Bee rolled into her driveway, she was startled to notice a black sedan pull in behind her. It was shiny and clean and sported big spotlights. When a black man, dressed in a tan shirt and jeans, got out and began walking toward her, her heart skipped a beat. Was he here to rob her?

The man held out his badge. "Lieutenant Dave Powers, Fort Wayne Police. Are you Belinda Cripps?"

She'd never really seen a police badge up close before, but it looked authentic enough. Taking a step backward, she nodded. "You're not in uniform."

"Plainclothes. I'm a detective. I wonder if I could talk to you a few minutes."

"About what?"

"I hear you're an expert on Tarot cards."

She put her hand on her heart, flattered but still wary. "Who says?"

"Are you an expert or not? I don't want to waste your time or mine."

"I read Tarot cards for people who want to know their future."

"Then you know more than I do. I'd like to show you a couple of photographs but out here is a little inconvenient."

She stared at Lieutenant Powers. He was medium height,

very fit, almost handsome, mid-thirties. Unusually well developed forearms, thick neck, wide shoulders. Intelligent eyes, a firm but unthreatening voice. His unmoving stance signified quiet authority.

She looked toward the road, as if searching for an escape route, then back at him. Her instinct whispered that he was who he said he was. She hoped her instinct was right.

"Okay."

Mama Bee led him to the Crystal Cave. The drapes were open, the room flooded with indirect light. After inviting him to take a chair, she asked, "So what do you have to show me, Lieutenant?"

Dave laid two color photographs on the table. "This is what we found at a recent murder scene."

"May I?" she asked, reaching for one of the photos.

"By all means."

Mama Bee slipped on a pair of glasses and picked up the photo. "This is a card from the Rider-Waite Tarot deck. That's a deck published in London more than a hundred years ago. Very popular, especially with beginners." She glanced at Lieutenant Powers. "Should I go on?"

He nodded.

"The card pictured here is the Fool. Notice that he's carrying a rose in one hand, a bundle of possessions on a long stick in the other. You see he's standing on the edge of a precipice, a dog at his heels. The sun is shining."

"He looks like he's paying no attention to where he's going."

"Very observant. The Fool is part of what's called the Major Arcana -- mostly representing virtues and vices. The Fool is given the number 0 in this deck, sometimes no number at all in others. He's also called the Jester, the Beggar, or the Madman."

"So what's it mean?"

"Was this the only card you found?"

"Yes."

"At a murder scene, you say."

"Right."

"Well, then, it doesn't mean much. In a Tarot reading, the reader lays out the cards in a certain pattern called a spread, and the meaning of a particular card changes depending on whether it's upside down or right side up. The meaning also depends on what cards are next to it."

"It was alone and upside down."

Mama Bee cocked her head. "Well, being upside down matters. What was it next to?" She pushed her cornrowed braids away from her face. "I know you said there were no other cards, but what about other objects?"

"It was lying next to a computer keyboard. There was a message on the screen. Here it is," he said, sliding the second photo toward her.

Mama Bee picked it up. "'Fool, You'll never hurt anyone again.'" She looked at Lieutenant Powers. "Who left this message?"

"We think it was the murderer."

"So the murder victim is the fool?"

"That's what we think."

"This message suggests the murdered person hurt somebody -- so badly he or she deserved death. Was the murdered person a man or a woman?"

"Don't want to say for now. What would you have to know to make sense of this scene?"

"Something about the victim -- the fool." When Lieutenant Powers didn't respond, she added, "A Tarot reading isn't a stab in the dark. The reader is supposed to talk to the querant -- ."

"The what?"

"The person who wants some spiritual insight. The person who comes here for a reading. The questioner."

"I see."

"Anyway, I need to know what kind of spiritual question is on the table. Most of my querants are women. Usually, they want to know about relationships or job prospects or travel opportunities or financial problems or somebody's health. Here," she said, tapping the photo of the computer screen, "the victim is accused of hurting people, so I suppose that's a spiritual clue."

"He did hurt people. He was secretly in the business of trashing other people's creations."

"What do you mean?"

"That's all I can say for now."

"Oh, dear, how terrible! Trashing people's creations -- well, that's just unforgivable. And the card was upside down, you say."

Dave nodded.

"When the card is upright, the Fool usually means new beginnings or adventures, sometimes good, sometimes rash. When the card is reversed, the Fool often means a faulty choice, a bad decision, a stupid action, something like that."

"So the victim made a faulty choice. He might have trashed the wrong person's creation."

"I can't say for sure, but that's not a bad interpretation." She checked the impulse to pat Lieutenant Powers' hand and teasingly suggest that he become a fortune teller.

"What is Tarot, by the way?" Dave asked. "This is all new to me."

"It's a way of telling the future, exploring spiritual dimensions, though some people just use it to play a card game."

"One of the women at the office said Tarot is evil."

Mama Bee looked away, an image of the feathered serpent coming to mind. "I've heard that too, but I don't believe it. The Major Arcana -- 22 cards known as trumps -- include cards about spiritual matters and big, important trends in the querant's life. As I said, the Fool is part of that group. So maybe the card left near the victim's computer is a comment on his or her spiritual life and what was going to happen if the victim -- the fool -- kept on doing what he or she was doing." She smiled for the first time. "The victim wasn't a nice person, at least in somebody's estimation. A card like that could be a warning."

"In this case, it was obviously more than a warning. Somebody stopped the victim dead in his tracks."

"*His* tracks.' So the victim is a man?"

Lieutenant Powers picked up the photos and got to his feet. "His or her tracks, I should have said. I'd appreciate it if you'd keep this visit confidential." He held out his hand. "You've been very helpful."

"Pardon me for being personal, Lieutenant, but are you married?"

"Yes, I am."

Mama Bee rose too and walked over to one of her étagères. "Then let me give you my card. Your wife might be interested in a private reading or even my solstice party in June. Unfortunately, my Ostara party a couple weeks from now is all booked up, but I'd be happy to put her on the mailing list for June."

He took the card without comment. He was pretty sure Sheila would no more be interested in landing on Mama Bee's mailing list than on Gloria Steinem's. He eyed a shelf holding crystal balls and decks of cards. "Do you happen to have a deck like the one in the photo?"

"The Rider-Waite deck. Of course, I do. Every reader starts with that deck." She found the right package of cards. "Here," she said, trying to give it to him.

Dave backed up a step, his hands in the air. "You hang on to it, but I wouldn't mind seeing the Fool card up close again."

Mama Bee took the package back to the table, sat down, and carefully removed the deck. "After I use a deck, I always re-sort the cards into groups, so the Fool should be on top."

Dave moved to stand over her shoulder. "That deck looks like you've had it awhile, used it a lot."

"That's true."

The first card to show up, however, wasn't the Fool but the Magician.

She couldn't believe it. She quickly riffled through the Major Arcana -- finding no Fool -- then set it aside for the moment. Maybe the Fool had gotten misplaced.

So she began laying out the rest of the cards, starting from the bottom of the deck. The Minor Arcana: Pentacles, Cups, Swords, and Wands, 14 cards each. Complete.

Now she fanned out the cards she had set aside, the Major Arcana. There should be 22 but in fact there were only 21. No Fool. She counted again, this time making sure no card was stuck to another.

She felt her stomach knot up. She looked around the room in disbelief. Where was the Fool? What kind of coincidence was this? "The Fool's not here," she murmured.

"You sure?"

"I'm sure."

"Could one of your cards have been stolen?"

"No."

"You sure?"

"Pretty sure," she said.

"What do you think happened?"

She stood up. "It got put into the wrong deck or it fell under a piece of furniture or something."

He handed Mama Bee his business card. "Perhaps you'd come down to the station with me, take a look at the card we found. It's in an evidence locker at the moment, so I couldn't bring it with me. Bring this deck along -- maybe we can figure out if it's the missing card."

Mama Bee again put her hand to her heart. The last thing she wanted was a visit to the police station. When the addled old widow's children complained about the looting of their mother's estate, Mama Bee had consulted a lawyer and discovered she'd broken no Indiana law. Still, her brief encounters with the police had been nerve-wracking.

She wished she'd never opened the Rider-Waite deck.

11

Stakeholders
Wednesday, March 7, 2012

Drago and Trude were ready for their meeting with Doreen Soren-Kawzy, the president of The Kekionga Center for Community Justice.

Miss Royce had given them strict instructions. Doreen would be allowed to enter the Yard with two supporters of her own choosing. They were to listen to Doreen without engaging in argument. They would respectfully accept any paper she wanted to give them. Ivy Starr would be present as Lexie's eyes and ears.

Private guards were posted at the gate and strategic locations around the Yard. The conference room, small and always sparsely furnished, had been emptied: no table, no chairs. No coffee was brewing and there was no heat. Because the room was cold and empty, the Doreen contingent probably wouldn't want to stay long anyway, but in any case the meeting was to last no longer than a half hour. A guard would be stationed at the door to the office. All visitors would be relieved of their electronics; they would have to show photo identification and sign a guest log. No exceptions.

By the time Doreen Soren-Kawzy reached the conference room, she was livid and almost incoherent. "What are you running here, a police state?"

"It's private property," Trude said quietly.

"Where is your great leader?"

"You mean Miss Royce? She's not here. This is Ivy Starr, her assistant. I'm Trude Weide and you've met Drago Bott."

"Why isn't Alexandra here?"

"She couldn't make it."

"That's not a reason." Doreen looked at Drago. "I told you, very clearly, that your boss had to be here."

"She got your message."

Doreen scanned the empty room. "Where are we meeting?"

"Right here. This is where we hold our meetings," Drago said.

"But it's cold in here."

"It's not that bad," Trude said. "Besides, the cold keeps our minds sharp."

"And we don't like to waste resources," Drago added, barely able to conceal a smile.

"Where are the blasted chairs? We need to sit down."

"We like to hold our meetings this way," Trude said. "Now, we've taken time out of our day to listen to you, and the minutes are ticking away, so let's get started, shall we? Why don't your companions introduce themselves first?"

A tall, skinny man wearing a hoody and enormous black-rimmed eyeglasses introduced himself as Maynard Philpot. A short plump woman in overalls and a windbreaker said, in a timid voice, that she was Lois Smith.

Maynard then spoke up. "We're here on behalf of the community. From everything we can see, this place is being run strictly for the one percent. That violates our principles."

"Which are?" Trude asked.

Maynard handed her a piece of paper. "Here's our mission statement."

"May I read it aloud for the sake of my colleagues?"

"It's kind of long. Why don't you read it later?"

"I think the three of us need to know all we can about you, so if you'll bear with me. 'The mission of The Kekionga ...'" She stopped and looked up. "Kekionga. You mean the old name for Fort Wayne?"

Maynard nodded.

"Well, you know your history. I congratulate you." Trude continued reading. "' . . . The Kekionga Center for Community Justice rests on six progressive pillars: world peace, community engagement, social justice, diversity, universal welfare, and environmental sustainability. It is our intention to serve the community by identifying every form of institutionalized discrimination, including but not limited to racism, sexism, classism . . . .'" Trailing off, Trude looked at Doreen. "Is classism really a word?"

"Yes," Doreen barked.

Trude nodded "Everyday I learn something." She returned to the mission statement. "'. . . ageism, flat-earthism, and homophobia wherever they're found.'" She looked up again. "Flat-earthism?"

"Global warming and evolution deniers. Fundamentalists. Right-wing zealots."

"I see. 'As the representative of community stakeholders, The Kekionga Center for Community Justice engages institutions in democratic dialogue and, if necessary, takes such action as may be necessary to transform pernicious discrimination into societal justice.'" Trude stopped and turned her attention to Drago and Ivy. "There's more here but you get the picture, I think."

"And a very interesting picture it is," Drago said. "So what is it you want with us?"

Doreen, who had been leaning against a wall, straightened up. "We want justice for you and everyone who works here."

"What kind of justice?"

"An equal place at the table with management."

"We are management," Drago and Trude said in chorus.

"Titles!" Doreen scoffed. "Your boss calls you management so she doesn't have to pay you overtime." She glared at Drago. "I know you work ungodly hours. Are you paid for them?"

"I'm paid well enough."

"Don't you know when you're being exploited? Don't you want equality with real management -- by which I mean Alexandra?"

"What have you got in mind?" Drago asked, knowing full well

what she had in mind.

"Unionize. We have a list of demands. We'd like to know the names of your workers, their ethnicity and gender, their age and disabilities, the wages they're paid, the hours they work, the benefits they get. We want to see your log of workplace injuries. And we want to put a monitor in here to ensure there is no discrimination or other unlawful practice."

"A monitor?"

"Someone to ensure the company is obeying the law. Either someone from our Center or one of your workers. He'll report to us."

"Do you have a worker in mind?"

"Buck Tiddly," Maynard blurted out before Doreen could stop him.

"Why Buck?" Drago asked.

"He's respected by the other guys," Maynard answered.

"And by you?" Drago asked.

"It doesn't have to be him," Doreen said, giving Maynard a harsh look. "All we're saying is it's our prerogative to select the person who will act as monitor so we can be sure he isn't in Alexandra's pocket."

"Do you have your demands in writing?" Trude asked. "It's a lot to remember, you know."

"We do," Doreen said. "We are also demanding permission to spend the next two weeks here getting signatures for a union petition without being hassled. That's in writing too."

Trude checked her watch. "We only have a couple minutes left. Tell me about that idea of stakeholder. I don't understand it."

"The community has just as much of a stake in this operation as your boss does. She may have the money, but it's the community's welfare at stake."

"Welfare?"

"Jobs, health, traffic, noise, safety, aesthetics."

"Tell me -- and pardon my ignorance -- what community are you talking about and how did you become its representative?"

"Oh, for Christ's sake. The community is everyone with an

interest in worker welfare. And the Center speaks for it because nobody else will. Stepping up to the plate like we have means that we're entitled to have this piece of shit operation answer to us. We have the workers' interests at heart even if nobody else does." Pause. "Though, frankly, it's no business of yours who we represent."

"When do you expect a response?"

"How about tomorrow?"

Trude waited a few seconds to respond. "It won't be that soon, you understand. There's a lot to be digested. We'll see that Miss Royce gets all these papers in the next day or two, but I'm not authorized to speak for her."

"Well, maybe that woman is," she said, pointing at Ivy Starr. "I notice she hasn't said a word. What is she, a spy?"

"A spy?" Ivy asked, confused.

Trude patted her arm. "Never mind." Trude directed herself to Doreen. "No one's authorized to speak for Miss Royce until she's had time to consider your demands."

"Then this meeting was a waste of time," Maynard said, leaning down to grab his messenger bag. "Negotiations don't work unless both sides are . . . ."

"We just had negotiations?" Drago asked.

Doreen gave him a withering look. "Not much of a democracy here, that's for sure, if you people can't speak for yourselves, let alone your boss!" Getting no response, she continued, "Tell *Alexandra* -- ," saying the name between her teeth, " -- that next time she better meet with us personally or . . . ."

"Or what?"

"She'll wish she had."

"Could you be more specific?" Trude asked.

"There'll be so many people camped outside your gates, you'll be shut down for the next month. Is that specific enough?"

"Is that in writing?"

"No," Doreen practically screamed. "But maybe somebody's pea brain can remember that much."

*   *   *   *   *

After the Kekionga contingent left the Yard and Ivy headed back to Miss Royce's office, Drago turned up the thermostat and followed Trude to her office, where she brewed a pot of coffee.

"That was more fun than I expected," Drago said.

"I'm hungry. Let's have some coffee cake." She pushed a wax-paper package in his direction and kept one for herself. "This is homemade, fresh last night."

"Thanks." He took a bite and sipped some coffee. "I like it. What is it?"

"Apple cinnamon, cream cheese center."

"Thought so. Anyway, Buck's the snake, isn't he?"

"We weren't supposed to know that," Trude said, laughing. "Did you see Doreen's face when Maynard blurted out Buck's name?"

"I did. I hope she didn't notice my face. I couldn't believe the guy was that stupid." He reached for a napkin. "I should have known Buck's the agitator, right? Sucking up to me, trying to find excuses to come into the office and hang out, always worrying about how hard I'm working."

"Have you been putting notes in Buck's personnel file every time he's late or doesn't follow orders or breaks something or otherwise messes up?"

Drago waggled his head. "Not every time. I guess I should step up the game."

"I'll look at his file. We may already have enough to get rid of him. Firing somebody right off the bat is probably a good way to get everybody else's attention. Then we'll call the other guys in, remind them of the favors Miss Royce has done them."

"So that's the strategy?"

Trude nodded. "The oldest strategy in the book. Love and fear. Works with dogs and kids every time."

"Who are you calling a dog?" he said, tossing the wax paper into a waste basket.

"Nobody. Just a joke. All I mean is, some people do the right thing out of love, but others only do it out of fear of what you'll do to them if they screw up."

"You're a wise old bird," Drago said.

Trude shook her head. "Not so wise. It's just that I've known a lot of screw-ups."

12

Matilda's Agenda
Saturday, March 17, 2012

Trent was fluttering around the nursery, folding blankets, straightening pictures, plumping cushions, turning on table lamps. He spent ten minutes rearranging a shelf of stuffed toys, first by color, then by size, finally settling on an artistic jumble.

Though he wouldn't be part of the portrait, he again checked himself in a full-length mirror. Yes, he was nice-looking, if not movie-star handsome. He was only medium-height and very slender, but in the crisply tailored suits he was partial to, he looked like somebody worth knowing. Women always commented on his full head of hair, fashionably spiked, and friendly brown eyes.

When he heard Mrs. Wright coming down the hall, he once again began fluttering, unsure whether to strike a casual pose or businesslike attitude. Businesslike, he decided. It was all he could do not to salute when she entered the room.

"Astrid's right behind me with Lacey. And Phyllis just let Jolene, the photographer, into the house, so she'll be up here in a few minutes too, setting up. She might need your help."

"Did you use the new BB cream I brought over?" Before Lexie could answer, he stepped closer to take a good look at her face. "I can see you did. The matte finish is perfect for photographs, don't you think? I like the cowl-neck on your sweater, by the way. Why don't you sit on this bench and let me style your hair."

"You already styled it."

"Just a little tweak here and there and it will be perfect. We want to be perfect, don't we?" He looked at his watch. "Where is your step-mother? Am I going to have time to fix her makeup or hair?"

"Speak of the devil," Lexie said, looking at her cell phone, which was playing *Nine to Five*. She put the phone to her ear. "Matilda. You're on your way?" Lexie nodded at Trent. "In ten minutes? Don't rush; nothing's worth a speeding ticket. It'll probably be close to a half hour before we're ready to start shooting anyway. What are you wearing?" Lexie winked at Trent. "A white silk suit. Sounds perfect. All three of us will be in white." Pause. "Okay, then. Ten minutes."

"Oh, I love it," Trent said. "All white is so virginal."

"Not the right word, I think, for a portrait of step-grandmother, mother, and baby. If I were a virgin, there'd be no baby, you know."

Trent blushed. "I know. But there's a word for it somewhere in my brain. White is just so . . . so clean and innocent. That's what I mean. Innocent. . . . I've never met your step-mother, you know."

"I've only seen her once myself since Lacey was born, so don't feel bad."

"I take it she's not the kind of grandmother to bake cookies and babysit."

"You take it right. She's much too busy with bridge and travel and golf. She shops a lot for entertainment and gets her hair and nails done once a week."

"A *Dynasty* kind of grandmother."

Lexie laughed. "I don't mean to sound so critical. She just has her own life -- which she's entitled to. And even if she's not willing to babysit, she's generous in other ways. Lacey already has a string of pearls, you know."

"I found them -- so tiny and lustrous. I laid the necklace out on the dresser. Pearls shouldn't be kept in a box, you know. They'll turn to dust. Remember that story about one of the grand ladies in New York City who traded her townhouse for a million-dollar string of perfect natural pearls? After she died, when the safe deposit box was opened, the pearls were nothing but dust."

"I hate to burst your bubble, Trent, but that's an urban legend. What really happened was in the intervening half century, cultured pearls were invented and instead of the natural pearls being worth a million dollars, they were only worth a tenth of that. And the townhouse Mrs. Plant foolishly traded is the Cartier building you and I were in a couple weeks ago."

"Is that true? We were in that very building?"

"We were."

"I wondered if it had been somebody's house, it was such a strange place. Not like a shop at all."

"Tell me your ideas for how the three of us should be posed."

"I've thought and thought about it. The two of you ladies could be bending over the crib, gazing at Lacey, but gravity does bad things to women's faces, so that won't work. Or your step-mother could sit in the rocker, Lacey in her arms, you kneeling beside them, gazing adoringly at the baby. But I don't like that either. You should be the center of attention. So maybe your step-mother should be standing behind your right shoulder. Then you'll be in the middle of the frame holding Lacey, whose head is to the left. The photographer can do something interesting with light and shadow."

"I suspect my step-mother wants to be in the center holding Lacey. And since this is all her idea and she's paying, she gets to call the shots."

"Don't mean to pry or anything, but why does she want a portrait now? I'm not saying you shouldn't take pictures any time you want, the more the better, but Lacey's not even three months old. There's no significant calendar date to celebrate, is there?"

Lexie moved to the rocker. "No, there isn't. I've wondered too. With Matilda, there's always an agenda. I have no doubt I'll know in a couple of hours."

And indeed Lexie did know a few hours later. She and Matilda had retired to the atrium with a bottle of chilled white wine and a plate of Phyllis' famous chicken salad sandwiches, cut in quarters, no crusts. Astrid had put Lacey down for a nap --

which she desperately needed, having fussed through the most of the session.

"Well, that went pretty well, I think," Matilda said.

Lexie laughed. "You don't mean it."

Matilda laughed too. "I'm trying to find the positive."

"Unfortunately, four in the afternoon is the arsenic hour for Lacey, so if there's even one good shot of her, it'll be a miracle. Anyway, you look lovely -- ."

"As do you."

Lexie made a face. "Thanks, but I'm still trying to lose ten more pounds."

They talked awhile about diets and exercise and then Matilda, after accepting another glass of wine, abruptly said, "Doreen came to see me. She's very upset with you, you know."

"With me?"

"Don't pretend you don't know what I'm talking about."

"What did she say?"

"She complained that it was very arrogant of you not to meet with her at the Scrapyard."

"Wasn't it arrogant of her to demand a meeting?"

Matilda looked faintly startled. "She just wants the best for our workers."

"So do I."

"Well, let's put that aside. She says the only responses she's gotten from your staff are so confusing she doesn't know what you're going to agree to -- if you're going to agree to anything."

"Why did Doreen come to you?"

"She's my niece. She knows I still have an interest in the Scrapyard."

"I mean, what does she expect you to do? Take her side of things?"

"Maybe."

"Did she ask you to talk to me?"

"No. . . . Not exactly."

"What motive would you have to do what she wants, Matilda? If our costs go up -- which they will if the place is unionized

-- your share of the profits goes down. Besides that, I don't think Doreen gives a bean about the workers. She's just looking out for herself."

"Oh, I don't agree. She's a very sincere woman. She wants to make the world better."

"Implying that I don't."

"I'm not implying anything."

"I think you are -- or at least Doreen is. Let's remind ourselves of something. We have a special fund set aside to take care of employee catastrophes -- and you fought me every step of the way when I established it."

"I didn't fight you -- ."

"You did. Now let's tick off a few items. Last year Dick Shogunner's baby was born with a heart defect. We covered all medical costs the insurer didn't and paid Dick for the time he had to take off. You weren't on board with that."

"I just thought you went a little too far."

"Exactly. Then there's Mick Kerry, returning from Iraq missing a leg; we rehired him anyway. We arranged for physical therapy he wouldn't have gotten otherwise and remodeled his house so it's easier for him to get around."

Matilda, her eyes averted, sipped her wine.

"Then there's Pedro Gonzales. When his wife died, for six months we paid for a baby-sitter to take care of the pre-school child and be there when the other children got home from school. Otherwise, Pedro couldn't have kept working."

Silence.

"All that largesse goes away if we have the expense of a union. Plus we have to decide what kind of health care benefits to offer our employees now that the price of insurance is going through the roof -- if we offer any. Our advisors tell us it'll be cheaper to dump them into public health exchanges, but that's downright cruel. I don't want to be cruel."

More silence.

"You started this conversation, Matilda, so talk to me."

"I didn't bring up Doreen's visit because I agree with her."

"Then why did you bring it up?"

"Doreen says there's no way to stop her group from occupying the place. There'll be violence -- ."

"She threatened violence?"

"She didn't *threaten* it. She just said there probably would be violence."

"That's a threat in my book."

"She pointed out that we'll look bad no matter what we do. And the operation will be shut down for a long time."

"Which means our profits go into the toilet."

"Agreed. So I want to sell the Scrapyard now. Get out while we can. Avoid the property damage, the shut-down, the bad publicity."

"You know I don't want to do that. The Yard's been in the family over a hundred years. Selling it is like wiping out our history."

"I knew you'd probably feel that way, but that's just sentiment talking. You're a businesswoman who uses her head, not her heart."

When Lexie started to protest, Matilda held up her hand. "So hear me out. I have another reason for selling now. While I'm still alive, I want to have the money to do something significant for the community."

"The community! You sound like Doreen."

"When you get to be my age, you'll understand. It's time I do something to benefit mankind. If I'm going to be remembered for something, I want it to be big. So I'm going to endow a chair to study climate change at my alma mater."

"The Isaac Royce Chair of Global Warming?" Lexie made a gagging gesture. "Dad's rolling over in his grave."

"No. The Matilda Pinserman Royce Chair for Climate Change Studies. Something like that."

"Not the Isaac and Matilda Royce Chair of Something or Other?"

"I've never had anything that was just my own. I deserve a little recognition too, if only because I married a workaholic ten years older than me who already had a child I was expected to take care of. He openly favored you over Rolland, you know. I blame Isaac for Rolland's death."

Dad was too old for you? You felt burdened taking care of me? "Matilda! Dad was already dead and he had nothing to do with Rolie's drug and gambling career."

"You'll never understand."

No I won't. "Of all subjects, how could you even consider the climate change kooks? Are you aware they want to wipe out industries like ours -- the one that has supported you in very high style for thirty years?"

"Maybe they're right about the way we're destroying the earth. Don't you ever feel a little guilty about living off the Scrapyard?"

"What's wrong with the Scrapyard?"

"All that energy we use. The noise and dust. It's not a pretty place."

"You can't crush a car and recycle the metal without some noise and dust. You can't reclaim precious metals without finding the energy to light a very hot fire."

"Well, it bothers me. We should be making money from something cleaner, more respectable. Like investing in green technology."

"Living off the Scrapyard doesn't bother me one bit. I'm proud of the Scrapyard. Matilda, and it's pretty green. Dad used to tell me about how hard his grandfather worked, how he started out as a rag-and-bone man. It took almost his whole lifetime to build the Yard and make it prosperous enough to support a family. Think of it, Matilda. Edward Royce came here from England, twelve years old, all alone, with a couple dollars in his pocket. And he left us this."

"As I said, you're getting sentimental. Maybe it's the birth of Lacey that's made you this way, but I say get rid of the damn thing while there might be some fool out there stupid enough to buy it."

Lexie had begun to shake, she was so angry. She stared at her step-mother. *You're using Dad's money to honor yourself? Worse, to fund a cause inimical to our business? You slight the achievements of four generations as if they meant nothing. And you're not leaving family money to Lacey, the only grandchild you have, the one you pretend to love so much?*

"I tell you what, Matilda. If you feel guilty about living off the Scrapyard, then I can stop writing checks to you."

Matilda was suddenly on her feet, her mouth a snarl. "You do that and you'll hear from my lawyers."

Fortunately, before the argument could escalate, Ivy popped in, Trent right behind her. "Oh, excuse me. I hope I'm not interrupting anything," Ivy said, giving Matilda an apologetic look, "but it's almost dinnertime, Miss Royce."

"We're having crown roast of pork with apple dumplings," Trent said. "And we have so much to talk about."

"I have a bunch of letters for you to look over and sign," Ivy said, clutching a leather portfolio to her chest.

"Is Lacey awake?" Lexie asked.

"She's in the kitchen, looking happy as can be."

"Of course, now that the photo session is over." She looked at Matilda. "In any other circumstances, I'd invite you to stay for dinner, but -- ."

"Thanks, but I have plans."

"Oh, well, another time."

Lexie's gratitude for the sudden end to her conversation with Matilda was tempered by a new worry: what had Ivy and Trent overheard? Family fights were not a matter for public consumption. And gossip about what might happen to the Scrapyard could only add fuel to Doreen's fire.

13

Heavy Metal
Monday, March 19, 2012

For once, Lexie beat Plato to her home gym. It was unusual for him not to be waiting for her, polishing a piece of equipment or unrolling her special mat. Once in awhile she caught him preening in a mirror or taking pictures.

She was shocked at the way he looked when he appeared a few minutes after two. "Good heavens, Plato, you're as yellow as a sunflower."

"I know. I just got back from having my blood drawn at the lab. My doctor thinks some of the supplements I've been taking are destroying my liver."

"How?"

"Some, he said, contain lead or mercury. He mentioned arsenic too and something else, sounding like cad- . . . *cadbury*."

She was amused. "I doubt that he meant chocolate. I think he had cadmium in mind."

"That sounds right. He said they're heavy metals. I told him the powders I put in my morning milk aren't heavy at all. There aren't any metal shavings I can see and they don't taste metallic. But he just smiled and said I should stop taking them until the lab results come back."

"Are you going to do what he says?"

"What do you think I should do?"

"Throw the powdered stuff away and eat right. Aren't you always telling me to munch on raw carrots when I get hungry?"

"And do you?"

She gave him a grim smile. "Usually not. So I know how hard it is to quit doing something you like and start doing something you know is right. Well, what are we doing today?"

"More Sahrmann exercises."

Lexie groaned. "I'm sure it's okay for me to cycle or use the treadmill by now."

"I almost forgot," Plato said, extracting a piece of folded paper from his duffel bag. "This was taped to the gate on your auto courtyard. Your name is printed on it."

She hastily took it from him. "I bet I know what it is."

"Read it to me."

"It's a poem." She read aloud:

> I see my real true love
> flutter like a little dove.
> as she flies off to the wood.
>
> She sits up in a laurel tree
> The freest of the free
> While I just stand and brood.

She put her head in her hands. "I am so sick of this stupid doggerel I could scream. Somebody must have followed me home."

"Dog what?"

"Doggerel. Bad poetry."

"Who's it from?" Plato asked.

"That's the whole problem, Plato. I don't know. In fact, I don't have a clue." She gave him a thoughtful look. "You found it. You didn't put it there, did you?"

He put his hand on his heart. "No, I swear. I don't know nothin' 'bout poetry."

That's probably true, she thought.

"Well, why don't we get started, Mrs. Wright, get your mind

off the dog stuff."

For once, Plato didn't chatter for the next fifty minutes. But that was only because he was saving himself for a speech before he left.

"I don't want to *suppose* on you, Mrs. Wright," he said, handing her a bottle of water, "but Petra and I really need to upgrade our gym. We want to expand Plato's Studio so we can have a guy give sports massages and put in a juice bar. We can make a ton of money selling supplements but right now we don't have the room."

"Like the supplements that are killing you?"

He took a step backward. "Well, not the ones I'm taking. We'll find the good ones. Anyway, we need a partner. I hear you have a hand in a lot of businesses in town."

"Oh, for goodness' sake. Where do rumors like that get started? The only business I own here is the Scrapyard."

"Don't you own this subdivision?"

"My husband does -- the golf club and unsold lots. In my own name, I don't own anything except this house."

"Well, then our gym would be a first for you. That's got some sexy cash, doesn't it?"

"Sexy cash?" she asked, puzzled. "Oh, you mean *cachet*? Not really, Plato. I'm not in a position to make any investments like the one you want, and I have more than enough to worry about at the Scrapyard right now."

"Would you consider making a loan then? I have some collateral damage I can give you."

She forced herself not to laugh. "I'm sure you do, but I'm going to have to pass on the collateral damage."

"If I can get a loan from my brother, would you co-sign?"

"Only idiots co-sign on a loan, Plato. I don't want to hurt your feelings, but long ago I learned that no one should ever be a co-signer unless he's willing to make a gift if things go wrong. And things always go wrong."

"The thing is, I don't think I can stay open without more cash. I need a bailout."

"I guess this is the day for being blunt. If you can't make a go

73

of it the way you're managing the place now, Plato, more cash isn't likely to help. Something else is probably wrong. Your nut's too high -- ."

"What do you mean, my nuts are too high?" he asked, arresting the impulse to adjust himself.

Lexie choked back a laugh. "Your *nut*, Plato -- your overhead, fixed expenses like rent and payroll and insurance."

"Insurance?"

"Don't tell me you don't have insurance."

"I'll have to ask Petra."

"Well, back to the reasons for your troubles. Maybe your fees are too low, your competition's too strong, the location is wrong, something like that. Besides, I'm not in the business of saving faltering companies, and from what I've read bailouts never work without new, smarter management."

"Nobody's smarter than Petra. She's the manager."

"Well, there's your answer, Plato. If Petra is as smart as you say -- and I have no reason to doubt you -- then just keep plugging away. Something will happen. Either you'll get on the right track or close down. That's the way the business world works."

He clutched his stomach as if he'd been punched. "If I have to go to the hospital for awhile, which my doctor says I might, how am I going to pay for it? Who's going to take my place at the gym?"

"Oh, Plato, I'm so sorry." He looked so pitiful she had to do something. "I tell you what. I'll give you a ten thousand dollar advance on your services."

"You will?"

"But for the next twelve months -- ."

"But ten thousand only covers ten months," he protested.

"When you get money in advance, Plato, it's basically an interest-free loan, so you owe me more time than if I paid you monthly. I have to get some reward in exchange for trusting that you'll actually perform. You have to promise to be here five days a week, on time, no excuses -- and Petra comes in your place if you can't be here. In exchange, no more complaints or requests, no business talk at all."

"Can I have the money in cash?"

She hesitated. "Okay, but you have to sign a contract."

He was on the edge of tears. "I'll sign anything. It's very *magnananimous* of you, Mrs. Wright."

14

As the Spirits Command
Tuesday, March 20, 2012

March 20, the day of Mama Bee's Ostara celebration, was
very strange for Fort Wayne, almost one for the record books.
The temperature reached 84 degrees and only dropped to 60 by
evening. It was June weather, not March. Had she known, she'd
have planned the party for the gazebo, but it was too late for that.

In anticipation of the special reading tonight, Mama Bee
purchased three new decks of Tarot cards, two to practice with, one
to be left virginal for the party. The new deck would be untainted
with the energy from former querants and thus should yield an
authentically brilliant reading. Though she thought she should
probably just throw away the old Rider-Waite deck from which
the Fool was still missing, she found she couldn't do it. She placed
it in a miniature casket -- a souvenir of her youthful sojourn in
India, that exotic land of opulent palaces and street beggars -- and
hid it at the back of an étagère.

Two weeks earlier, when she examined the Fool card found
by the police and shown to her by Lieutenant Powers, it was from
an identical deck but was much newer than the one she'd lost.
Lieutenant Powers seemed disappointed, as if watching a promising
lead go up in smoke. She herself was shaken by a mixture of
relief that the card had nothing to do with her and unease at the
coincidence of losing the very card the police had found at a

murder scene.

She very much wanted to know who had been murdered, but Lieutenant Powers wouldn't say. She knew most murders in Fort Wayne were simply random, spur-of-the-moment shootings by boozed-up men quarreling outside of bars over women, drugs, and money. Some died trying to rob a convenience store or gas station or collect a drug debt. They died in streets and alleys, on front lawns and sidewalks, sometimes in their cars or in an emergency room, but only rarely at home and never where the murderer left a Tarot card and a jeering computer message.

By a process of elimination, having pored over a month's worth of newspapers at Fort Wayne's Central Library, she surmised that the dead man was one Alastair Rutherford Digby III. He had died at home. He was educated and rich, from an old Fort Wayne family, living alone. Nothing in the newspaper hinted at the murderer's motive or the manner of death other than a possible homicide.

The victim's name rang no bells with her. She'd never done a reading for him. He had never attended a group reading. She knew because she kept records.

Mama Bee did her best to put Mr. Digby out of her mind. For the last week she had practiced with two of the new decks: on herself, her daughter Ama, and four different friends, most women getting two or three readings. Before each practice session, she got on her knees and summoned the feathered serpent, the speaker of proud words, to cleanse her spirit and open her third eye to unseen spiritual dimensions. Once, she felt the flutter of wings near her cheek. And another time the scent of sulfur hung in the air, though perhaps it was only from the kitchen match with which she lit a candle.

On her quest to find the ideal reading, she tried various spreads -- the Celtic Cross, the Cross of Truth, the Nine-Card Spread, and the Life Spread. She also tried various shuffles, sometimes allowing the querant to do it, sometimes keeping control herself. She tried having the querant write out her question on a piece of paper, or not write it out but only verbalize it. For some readings, she suggested that the querant open her mind and relax, for others that she focus silently and intensely on the question as the cards were shuffled, in effect willing an answer. Sometimes she invited only a yes-or-no question, other times an open-ended one.

Her experiments did little to settle her mind as to how to conduct the special Ostara reading. It would come to her.

Now, in half an hour, her guests would begin arriving. As she stood before a mirror in her bedroom, adjusting the long white gauzy dress that hung to her ankles and then the crown of green laurel leaves gracing her cornrowed hair, she told herself to relax. Give up control. Stop trying to manage what cannot be managed. The party would progress as the spirits commanded.

She was wearing so many necklaces of bells and beads, she rang and rattled as she walked to the Crystal Cave.

15

Where's the Crystal?
Tuesday, March 20, 2012

Indeed, Ostara was celebrated as the spirits commanded.

The party started well. Because every guest knew at least one other, usually many others, there were no awkward moments of silence, no stray women too shy to join in the collective gaiety. At first, the rum-spiked green tea punch, infused with basil leaves, was pronounced by some guests as interesting or unusual, but it became more and more delicious as the punch bowl emptied and was refilled. Within an hour, the plates of green-frosted cream puffs and petit fours offered nothing but crumbs.

Mama Bee moved from cluster to cluster, not saying much, but smiling encouragingly, listening intently. The chatter was anything but spiritual. Clothes, concerts, restaurants, movies. Old feuds and surprise babies. Lost jobs and panicked men. Health problems and vacation dreams.

The women she hadn't met before intrigued her. Astrid, the Swedish bombshell, was unusually beautiful and lively, like a sparkler that never fizzled out. She was wearing a red wool string around her wrist. Mama Bee knew that Madonna wore a similar talisman. It was to ward off the evil eye, wasn't it? Astrid seemed to be in love with her boss, whose name Mama Bee didn't catch. The man was the handsomest and smartest man in the world. An excellent golfer. A seriously funny man. A tender father. The compliments rolled off her tongue. Didn't everybody agree? Instead of answering Grace Venable countered with her own catalog of praise for her darling dance instructor. The two women talked at cross-purposes, like speakers outshouting each other on soapboxes.

Then there was Petra Kuzmin, the little Russian dynamo, who had taken Shayla Soren aside for a lecture on the health benefits of regular workouts at Plato's Studio and the financial benefits of investing in fitness clubs. As Petra talked, she gestured with her hands, one sporting a huge green amber ring. Her black eyes darted around the room, reminding Mama Bee of a hungry cheetah scanning the savanna for fatter, slower prey. Shayla, a dull sort of girl, looked as if she was afraid of being on Petra's menu.

And, finally, there was Ivana Starr, dressed in a loose white sweater over narrow white slacks, white ballet slippers on her feet, her straight brown hair beautifully cut. She looked regal. Being thin and tall with regular features didn't hurt. Neither did the emerald pendant at her neck. Ivy, as she wanted to be called, moved from group to group, never saying much or staying long.

When it came time for everyone to take their places at the table in the Crystal Cave, a few women were baffled by the legends on the eggs and had to be helped to identify themselves so they could take a seat. Most of the clueless guests were amused and joked about their confusion, but one -- Doreen -- was not. She was offended that her name meant gift of God. Mama Bee found that puzzling. The woman, dressed in stiff white cotton garments that did nothing for her dull mauve complexion and bony frame, looked rather like a plowman in drag just in from a grueling day behind a horse. For a woman, she had big hands and feet. With so few obvious assets, why wouldn't she want people to think she was a gift from God?

Once the women were seated, Mama Bee turned down the lights, lit some candles, and took her seat. She let the chatter subside, then rang a bell and called for a few moments of meditation on the spiritual needs that had brought them to the Crystal Cave.

Then each guest was invited to open her egg -- not a real

egg, of course, but a hinged ceramic contraption -- to find a sprig of herb holding her soul-secret. Mama Bee had placed the magic crystal -- a chip of rose quartz -- in Cricket Grinderman's egg, entitling her to the special Tarot reading. She chose Cricket because she knew something about the girl, having met her several times before. She knew the girl was born in January, so a garnet -- or its cheaper substitute, rose quartz -- was appropriate.

A Tarot reading for Cricket should go well. Cricket was not a mystery. She was clerking in a liquor store. Her best friend was Trent Senser. Her sister had been murdered several years ago. Her father was a judge and her mother a former school teacher, now heavily involved in church work. Cricket had had two years of junior college, where she had been an indifferent student. She loved clothes and collected everything French, especially replicas of the Eiffel Tower.

Cricket was a simple girl, no doubt with the same dreams and terrors as all unmarried twenty-two-year-olds still living at home. Exploring her spiritual life was unlikely to require deep intuition.

Cricket was seated across the round table from Mama Bee. When Cricket opened her egg, she found a sprig of something and held it up. "I don't know what this is."

"Caraway," Mother Bee said, peering over her glasses. "It stimulates physical passion."

"That's my soul-secret?"

"Only you know that. I'm just telling you what the herb is for."

Cricket glanced at Trent, who was seated beside her. He patted her hand.

Time to lighten the mood. "Caraway is also good for digestion."

Everyone laughed, including Cricket, who rubbed her tummy and said she had no problems in that department.

"Now," Mama Bee said, smiling, "what else is in the egg?"

Cricket looked again at the two halves of the egg. "Nothing."

"Nothing? Look again. Did something drop on the table?"

With the help of Trent, Cricket felt around but found nothing.

Mama Bee's smile disappeared. She tried not to look panicked. What had happened to the rose quartz crystal? Was it still resting in a casket on her étagère? Had she mixed up Cricket's name with someone else's? Surely not. But what if she had? She wasn't prepared to give anyone else a Tarot reading.

16

The Moon and the Chariot
Tuesday, March 20, 2012

The woman beside Cricket -- Doreen, the plowman -- was opening her egg. Frowning, she held up a green sprig. "I don't recognize this," she said, sounding irritated, as if the herb had been placed there deliberately to make her look ignorant of the natural world she worshipped.

When she shook the herb, suddenly something dropped on the table. "And what's this?" She picked up the crystal and held it between thumb and forefinger as if it were a rabbit dropping.

"That stone is a rose quartz. It's one of the birthstones for people born in January."

"I was born then."

"You were?" Mama Bee said, with more surprise in her voice than she intended. "Well, that's the magic of the goddess." *If only the goddess could make that sparkly bindi between your angry eyes look anything other than ridiculous.* "And the herb you're holding is coriander."

"What's it good for?"

"If you burn it as incense, it promotes longevity. Otherwise, it's good for peace and security."

"So what's my soul-secret?"

Why must you ask in that sneering tone? Mama Bee composed her face. "Only you know that, but perhaps you're concerned about dying young. Or not having a peaceful life. Or running into trouble you can't handle."

"No, I'm not."

"Well, then," Mama Bee said, trying to stop the unraveling of her patience, "you'll have to dig deep into your psyche to decide what it means."

"My psyche or my soul?"

"Either. With the psyche, you use your reason. With the soul, you use your imagination, your intuition."

"I don't believe in women's intuition. That's a construct of a male-dominated culture to keep us believing that we women can't think for ourselves."

"Well, then, you'll use your reason."

Doreen looked around the table. "Did anybody else get a crystal?"

"No," Mama Bee said quickly, not wanting the remaining eggs opened except in the order she had planned. "The crystal is very special. All our goddesses will have their palms read, but the crystal entitles you to a full Tarot card reading." *If I can think of anything to say.*

Though Doreen protested that she wasn't a goddess and wanted no such distinction, Grace Venable jollied her into it with a challenge. "You don't want us to think you're afraid of something new, do you?"

Doreen didn't. But she would do it only if she could be first. She would have to leave before all the palms were read because she had a busy day tomorrow.

Though Mama Bee was concerned that her other guests would become restless waiting for their palms to be read, they were in fact mesmerized. The room became totally silent when Mama Bee took Doreen to a little table specially set up for readings.

"Now," Mama Bee said, looking straight into Doreen's shadowed eyes, "a reading like this is not like telling a fortune but an exploration of the spiritual forces in your life. So talking to me frankly and openly is the only way to get good results. Are you with me?"

Doreen, looking petulant, nodded.

"Tell me about something that is important to you. What would you say defines your life?"

"Nothing defines me. I define myself."

"Or how about a challenge you're facing."

"I'm not facing anything I can't handle."

Mama Bee sighed. "Most women are concerned with relationships -- husbands, children, bosses. Others have a question about money or health or a trip they're going to take."

"I am going to take a trip of sorts."

"For pleasure?"

"No. It's a journey to make the world better."

So that's what defines you -- saving the world! I wonder if Joan of Arc had big hands and feet? "That's very general. Can you be more specific?"

"I want to know if I'm going to get a stake in something."

"A stake? In what kind of thing?"

Doreen looked up at the ceiling. "A seat at the table. In an enterprise."

"That's still very general. Can you tell me about the table? or the seat? anything?"

"That's all I can say. If there weren't so many people around, I could say more."

"Do you want us to go my study where we can be alone?"

"No. Let's get this over with."

"So, before we start, would you state succinctly your question to the spirits?"

"Will I win my battle for a stake, a seat at the table, in an enterprise that needs me?"

"Do you expect the battle to be fought soon?"

"By the end of the week."

"Will it be a hard fight?"

"No doubt."

Mama Bee opened her new deck of cards, a gilded deck by Ciro Marchetti. The colors were electrifying, most figures resonant with hidden menace. She shuffled them this way and that, right

85

side up and upside down, a dozen times. Then she divided the deck into three piles, reassembling them so the bottom cards appeared on top. Then she asked Doreen to do the same.

When she began laying out the cards, she found herself using the five-card Cross of Truth again. It used the least number of cards and was the easiest spread to remember, but it yielded so few clues that a reading could be difficult.

She touched the card at the bottom of the cross, willing its meaning to penetrate her fingertips. "This card is called the basis, the starting point. It's where you are in your life before you start your battle. As you can see, it's the Ace of Swords in reverse. The sword is unsheathed. Does it mean anything to you?"

"An unsheathed sword, I suppose, means war. I'm ready for war."

"War! Not necessarily that strong a conflict, though you've used the word battle, so if in your mind it's a war you're facing, then it's a war. In this case, because the card is in reverse, I think it means you've been cautious in trying to attain your goal. Or you should be cautious."

Doreen grimaced. "Cautious! Is that a polite way of saying I'm a coward?"

Mama Bee hung on to her patience. "Not at all. Just that you're an intelligent planner. Have you thought long and hard about the battle you say is coming?"

"Yes."

"I thought so. Have you done everything you can to prepare for it?"

"Yes."

"Has it been long delayed?"

Doreen did not look up. "Too long."

Next, Mama Bee touched the card in the middle of the cross. "This is the card indicating your desires, the outcome you hope for. The Nine of Cups upright indicates that you very much wish a certain thing to come true."

"Who's the guy on the card?"

"The jolly innkeeper, holding one cup in salute; the other

eight cups are sitting on full barrels. This card is sometimes called the wish card because it promises abundance and cheer."

"Well, that's great for desires. But it doesn't mean I'll win my battle, just that I want to win it."

"We'll figure that out as we go, but try seeing the bright side. It's a card that should encourage you. Now this card on the right arm of the cross, the Seven of Wands upright, signifies what is helping you. The man in the doorway holds one wand against six others. He's defending something we can't see in the room behind him."

"What's he defending?"

"It might be something real like his family. Or something more abstract like his reputation or his ideals. He has energy and courage. As someone intent on making the world better, you do too, I assume. Notice that this is the *Seven* of Wands. Seven is the number of completion."

"What's he completing?"

"A cycle. Or a plan. An action that comes full circle. Now," Mama Bee continued, "the card on the left arm of the cross represents opposing forces. It's the Moon upright, showing dogs barking at it, a crayfish rising out of the water. The Moon controls the tides, both the water on earth and the water in us. When there's a full moon, strange things happen on earth -- lunacy breaks out. Lunar cycle -- lunacy -- lunatic -- you get the picture. Compared to the sun, the moon only dimly lights the scene below."

"You said the moon represents opposing forces, right?"

Mama Bee nodded.

"What opposing forces? Is my opponent a lunatic?"

"Very clever," Mama Bee murmured. *Clever, but not necessarily insightful. Perhaps you hope your opponent is a lunatic.* "Until we've looked at the last card, we won't know, but it seems to be a warning that you may have misjudged the obstacle -- the person or thing -- you have to battle. Moonlight is deceiving, you know. In moonlight we see distortions, shifting shapes and shadows. Could you have misjudged something or someone?"

"I doubt it."

"Perhaps this card is signaling that you must fight your battle in daylight, not at night. You say your battle is soon. There is only a waning crescent moon tonight but by the weekend there will be a waxing crescent -- a little sliver -- and the next night a little bigger sliver and so on." Mama Bee struggled to find a comforting interpretation. "So perhaps the force opposing you, like the moon, is not very powerful after all."

"Sure," Doreen said with a touch of sarcasm.

"And now we come to the top card indicating the outcome." And here Mama Bee faltered. It was the Chariot in reverse. Would anybody realize what she was doing if she covered it with her hand and surreptitiously turned it upright? But Doreen had already seen it, as had the women clustered around them. She hoped as she talked some positive idea would come to her. "Here we see a powerful woman in purple riding on the chariot, which is carried by two sphinxes, one gold and one silver." She tried to smile. "The Chariot is a card of triumph, of reaching goals."

"But it's upside down. What does that mean?"

"The two sphinxes indicate you might have some unconscious doubts or conflicting feelings about the battle ahead."

"I don't. I know what I'm going to do and it's the right thing to do. But you haven't said anything about the card being upside down."

Mama Bee wanted desperately to lie, but she'd already made a point about the Ace of Swords being shown in reverse. The plowman/Joan of Arc sitting across from her was far too sharp to accept at this late date a claim that a reversed card meant nothing. "If the card was upright, it would suggest victory for you, although not without effort -- not without reconciling your own inner conflicts first."

"So upside down means I lose."

"The cards never tell you your fate. They aren't that strong. They don't determine your destiny. The cards just reveal the spiritual forces you must confront. You can still prevail. Knowledge is power."

"How can I prevail? What power do I have?"

Mama Bee swept the cards with her eyes. A flash of something -- a flaming white banner on a sharpened pole -- passed like a floater just outside her peripheral vision, but when she snapped her head around, all she saw was a dark blue drape.

She returned her attention to the cards. The flaming white banner, the tricky moon, the opposing sphinxes, the overturned chariot -- altogether, they suggested that disaster lay ahead, but she couldn't say that aloud. Could she?

She tapped the five cards in turn. "Let's review what has been revealed to us. The Ace of Swords in reverse: you must use caution in your battle for power. The Nine of Cups: the power you desire is within your reach. The Seven of Wands: you have the energy and courage to get power. The Moon: your opponent is intent on deception, so you must see through the trickery if you want to prevail. If you do that, the Chariot will not be upside down. It will be upright. You will rise triumphant."

And then a dark thought slithered into Mama Bee's mind. Swaying as if buffeted by a stiff wind, she closed her eyes. Yes, she felt -- she knew, she saw -- what the problem was. Should she say so or not? She wanted the reading to end on a high note.

She opened her eyes and took Doreen's hands. She felt pity for the angry woman. "Your opponent -- the person you're fighting in battle soon -- isn't your nemesis. It's someone else. Someone else entirely. That's where the deception is. That's why you must not fight at night. That's why you must be cautious. You must not trust anybody."

"Who's doing the deceiving? Am I doing it to myself or is my opponent doing it to me?"

"That's an astute question, but only you know the answer."

Withdrawing her hands and pushing back her chair, Doreen peeled the sparkly green bindi off her forehead and tossed it onto the cards.

"Wait!" Mama Bee said. "Beware of fire. Look out for shape-shifters and white banners."

A snarky laugh burst from Doreen as she got to her feet. "I don't mean to be rude, but I'm just as skeptical now as when I sat down. I listen to reason, not to . . . well, not to this kind of . . . this kind of fantasy. I just don't believe in cards and spirits. But thanks. At least it was entertaining."

17

While I Have Breath
Wednesday, March 21, 2012

Wednesday night, Drago was waiting at the Fort Wayne airport for the arrival of a private plane from Detroit. It had been months since he had last picked up Mizz Royce to drive her home.

Drago had no trouble humbling himself to act as a chauffeur. He liked Mizz Royce. He was indebted to her for almost every good thing in his life other than his wife and mother. And he knew that keeping a boss indebted to you, even with small gestures, wasn't a bad thing. It balanced the scales.

The attendant allowed him to walk out on the tarmac to grab Mizz Royce's briefcase and tote as she deplaned. "Can you believe this weather?" he asked. He wasn't even wearing a light jacket, it was so warm.

"No. What do you think God has in mind, starting summer this early?"

"You think he has something in mind?"

"I've no idea really. It's just that I have strong premonitions about the year."

"Good or bad?"

"Earthshakingly bad. The doomsday predictions for 2012, the political discord, the sick economy, the global unrest -- it's all starting to accumulate in my mind like a garbage pile."

"Well, let's get you home. That'll restore your spirits. How was the book signing, by the way?"

"It went better than I expected because it wasn't in Detroit after all. It was near Bloomfield Hills. The women who came were mostly in their forties or fifties, usually college educated, fired from administrative jobs they'd had for years, some just before their pensions vested. A lot of their husbands are out of work or underemployed. Their kids are in college or back living at home. As you can imagine, they're looking to start their own home businesses and maybe my book will help."

Drago waited to talk about the Scrapyard until they were heading northwest on I-469. "So. Have you made any decisions now that Nate is gone?"

She smiled. "I have. You're the new operations manager."

"Really?"

"You're awfully young for the job, but the changes you've made in the last three years convince me you can do it."

"Thanks," he said, slapping the wheel. "I never wanted anything so much, know that."

"And I can tell that Trude is going to be right there, standing shoulder to shoulder with you. Not trying to insult you or anything, but she probably knows as much about the scrap business as you do. And she's not afraid of anything."

"That's true. The old gal has a brain in that head and a steel rod for a spine." He chuckled, glancing at her. "Like you . . . . except you're not an old gal, of course. Don't mean that."

Lexie laughed too. "We need to talk about compensation, of course. You'll be getting a substantial raise and a company truck. But there's a catch."

"There is?"

"You have to buy stock in the company. If you don't have a financial stake in this enterprise, I can't sleep at night."

"Does Trude own stock?"

"Yes."

"How about Nate?"

"Yes again. Non-voting, of course, but it's going to make his retirement a lot more secure than most people face. Therefore, a certain percentage of your pay has to be set aside so you're an owner with an owner's dedication to success."

"That makes me a real stakeholder, right?" He laughed. "Not like Doreen."

"Not like her at all, Drago. If the company goes bust, you lose your job and your savings -- ."

"Whereas she just moves on to the next company she doesn't like. I get it, believe me I do. Speaking of Doreen, she was the star of that crazy party Lucy went to last night."

"Trent called me this morning to say she's planning some kind of mischief in the next day or two, not later than the weekend."

"Lucy said the same thing. If that woman is dreaming of a union, she's barking mad. Trude and I have been talking to the workers, reminding them of how good they have it now. And Buck's gone, as you know. We kept Buck's brother Tig, but he's not saying a word. You'll never guess who's the maddest at Doreen's group."

"Who?" Lexie asked.

"Mick. He says he didn't lose a leg in Iraq only to be facing a bunch of thugs who want to tear down the place that gave him a job. If you armed our guys, there'd be nothing to worry about."

Lexie laughed. "I can't do that, but I've hired a security company to be around for the next week and alerted the police department to possible trouble. If you don't recognize a driver, you don't open the gates. Every load has to be inspected before it pulls past the gates. The protesters are to be kept off the property. We can't do anything about their occupying public property, of course, but the police can assert some control over property damage and personal assault if they're willing."

"What if the protesters throw fire bombs or something? What if they charge the gates?"

"Then we have a bigger problem than I'm anticipating. This is Fort Wayne, after all."

"So you think we'll survive?"

Time to buck up Drago's spirits. "Of course, we'll survive. I've been fighting off unions for years. It's true that the game gets rougher and rougher, the tactics more violent, the government less supportive of private property rights. Worse, I have family problems. My step-mother -- and this is strictly between us -- wants to sell the place, just to be done with the whole mess."

"You wouldn't do that, would you?" Drago asked.

"Not while I have breath in me."

18

Shape-Shifters
Wednesday, March 21, 2012

The house was quiet when Lexie entered through the garage. She ran upstairs to check on Lacey, who was sound asleep and well guarded by Henry, who got to his feet, licked her hand, and threw himself back on the floor with a loud chuff, reminding his owner that there was nothing to worry about here. He was the world's best guard dog, wasn't he? He earned every ounce of steak he consumed.

After tossing her bag into her closet and changing into sweats, Lexie went in search of Steve. She found him sitting on the side of the lap pool, talking to Astrid. Steve, his hair wet, had a towel draped around his shoulders. Astrid, who was also wet, had nothing draped around her; she was wearing a red bikini and sipping a glass of wine. The baby monitor was resting on a table nearby.

"Ah, this is a cozy scene," Lexie said, trying to keep the asperity out of her voice.

"Just talking about this and that," Steve said, hoisting himself up and giving her a kiss.

"I thought you couldn't pick me up because you had a meeting tonight."

"It's tomorrow," he said, wrapping the towel around his hips. "Sorry about that mix-up. But I'm sure Drago did the job just fine, right? Let me get you a glass of wine."

"Prosecco, please. And if there's some kind of snack in the refrigerator, I'll take that too. I didn't get dinner."

"Be back in ten."

Lexie pulled a lounge chair near Astrid. She was irritated with the girl, but no point in making an enemy of her. "So how was Lacey today?"

"Hungry. She's sleeping less, every day a little less than the day before. She's making lots of sounds too. I read somewhere a baby makes every sound anybody makes in any language. I'm going to teach her Swedish if that's okay with you."

"English first, with my accent. Swedish second with yours. And how was the party last night? I heard a little about it from Trent."

"It was hilarious. Mama Bee looks a lot like my mother, which is strange -- kind of plump and maternal -- except for all the necklaces. Do you know she jangles when she walks?"

Lexie shook her head. "I've never met her. I hear you all had your palms read."

"That was the best part. But first we learned what our names signify. Guess what mine means."

"Astrid," Lexie said, looking off into space for the answer. "Something connected with astral -- a planet or a star maybe?"

"No. Beautiful goddess."

Of course it does.

"Then we each opened an egg -- ."

"An egg?"

Astrid explained about the ceramic eggs. "The herb I found was cockscomb. Mama Bee told me it repairs a broken heart."

"And has your heart been broken?"

Astrid looked away. "Not yet. Maybe never, if I'm lucky." She gave Lexie a smile. "Anyway, she told me I had a secret admirer, an important man, and I would marry an American."

Lexie looked thoughtful. "I hope that's true." *But perhaps not the man you hope.* "What about Ivy? Do you remember anything about her fortune?"

"She should be careful not to spread herself too thin. Mama

Bee said she saw Ivy rising to heights no one could imagine."

"And how about Trent?"

"She'd given him a reading a few months ago, predicting he'd start a new adventure, which he said had already happened. She said it would be the making of him."

"And how about my step-mother, Matilda?"

"She shouldn't go on any fishing expeditions."

Lexie laughed. "Too late! She's already been on one with me."

"But Doreen was the star of the party. Mama Bee laid out five Tarot cards and told the woman not to fight at night."

"Really?"

"Because the person she thinks is her enemy isn't. It's somebody else. Moonlight is deceptive, she said. Have you ever heard of shape-shifters?"

"I think so. Don't some Native Americans believe people and animals can exchange bodies, especially at night? People become wolves and so forth."

"I never heard the term before. Anyway, Doreen was told to beware of shape-shifters."

"And what did Doreen say?"

"She thinks the whole thing is nonsense, so she just laughed and left. She was really a little rude, in my opinion."

"And what do you think?"

"It was a lot of fun. I'd do it again."

"I just noticed the thing you're wearing on your wrist. May I see it?"

Astrid held up her arm. "It's red thread, braided and tied. Everybody's wearing one now."

It's so proletariat it's pretentious. "Does it mean anything?"

"Somebody told me it has something to do with charity. It's mentioned in the Jewish Kabbalah as honoring Rachel, who charitably let her sister marry Jacob first."

"What do you know about Kabbalah?" Lexie asked, thinking the girl certainly understood nothing of the story of Rachel and Leah.

"Just that Madonna believes in it."

If she believed in jumping off a bridge, naked and drunk while yodeling Like a Virgin, would you do that too? Of course you would.

Fortunately, they were interrupted. "So, ladies, I come bearing gifts," Steve said from the doorway. Besides a broad smile, he was, to Lexie's relief, wearing a t-shirt and sweat pants. He set a tray of drinks and snacks on a table. "We've got Prosecco and scotch and what's left in the bottle of Santa Margherita. I found pita chips and hummus and a big jar of olives. So gather round, life is good. Astrid, you might want to put that shirt on again. It's such a nice night, I'm going to open these doors so we catch the breeze. Now tell me what you girls have been talking about."

The Prosecco did its job of lowering Lexie's tension, as did Astrid's donning of her shirt. Still, through narrowed eyes, she watched for any sign that Astrid's secret admirer, the American she hoped to marry, was her own husband.

19

Fizzle

Friday, March 23, 2012

"Damn the rain," Buck Tiddly grumbled. He was standing across the street from Summit City Metals and Scrapyard, glaring at the place where he used to work. Occasionally he spotted a worker crossing the Yard, moving from one building to another, but when he called out a taunt, they either ignored him or gave him the one-finger salute. No trucks entered or left; the gates stayed closed.

Doreen, wearing a rubber poncho, checked her watch, then eyed his wet mustache disapprovingly. "It's almost noon, Buck. Where in hell are all your friends?"

"Where are yours? Probably not used to rolling out of bed, especially when it's raining."

"If they could find a job, they would," Doreen said. "These signs you made, by the way, are pathetic. The cardboard's wilting, the ink is dripping, the wind is tearing them to pieces. Why didn't you use permanent markers and foam board?"

Buck just glared at her.

Maynard, always the peacemaker, spoke up, his voice gentle, his slightly bulging eyes magnified by the thick lenses of his old-fashioned eyeglasses. "You told us, Doreen, not to go to a printer because it would look too . . . what was the word you used? Too astroturf. You said printed signs look astroturf instead of grass roots."

"We are grass roots," Doreen snapped, irritated with Maynard as he ineffectually tried to swipe raindrops off his eyeglasses. Why did he have to wear lenses the size of pickle jar lids? He looked like a startled fish.

Maynard wasn't done. "I've got a flag, you'll notice, made out of sailcloth. And so does that woman over there."

"The flags are almost as bad as the signs, Maynard. They're so limp you can barely read what's printed on them."

"Not as limp as the other signs. How come the crowd's so small, do you think?" Maynard wanted to change the subject. "Where are the people who want a job? Where are the residents who hate the noise and dirt from truck traffic?"

Truck traffic. Now there was a sore point! Thursday night, the Kekionga faithful had scattered tin cans and soda bottles along Old Canal Street with the intention of blaming Summit City Metals for being a bad corporate citizen and trashing the place. In the morning, feigning outrage, Maynard would call various city departments to file complaints against the Scrapyard. Then he'd send pictures to the press.

To Doreen's and Maynard's dismay, however, no tin cans and bottles were in evidence this morning when they arrived. It wasn't until a few hours later they learned from someone in the crowd that scavengers had picked the street clean so they could earn a few dollars from Summit City Metals. Greedy vultures, Doreen thought, filthy cockroaches, politically naïve nitwits unable to take the long view.

"Have you counted how many people are here?" she asked.

"Twenty-three," Buck said, "including us."

"This weather is such bad luck," Lois said, shaking like a dog and spraying everyone in the face. "All week it's been sunny and warm, but wouldn't you know, today is miserable."

"Stop whining," Buck said. "It's at least sixty degrees out here."

"But the wind and rain make it cold. I'm shivering like a puppy."

Buck tried to bend back the corners of the tattered sign he was holding, then raised it high in his left hand. "Let's get a chant going," he suddenly yelled, making Doreen jump, "start walking. That'll warm us up."

Buck moved through the clot of people, commanding them to form a circle. He waved his right arm like an orchestra conductor and began to shout.

> "What's so hard about scrapping the yard?
> We want justice now!
> What's so hard about scrapping the yard?
> We want justice now!"

Slowly, the protestors formed themselves into a circle that looked like it had been drawn by someone with palsy. They dutifully trudged through mud and gravel, for the first ten minutes chanting at the top of their lungs and holding their wilted signs and flags high. Then, gradually, the volume dropped to their indoor voices and the signs and flags lay on their shoulders. Within an hour they looked as bedraggled as Army Rangers emerging from a swamp drill.

It was a sorry sight. Wishing she had a bullhorn and a cattle prod, Doreen glared at them from across the road. Where was their spirit? Where was their passion for justice? Why didn't they hate industry as much as she did?

Suddenly, despite Buck's protests, the little circle of dispirited demonstrators broke up, one by one straggling back across the road. Doreen heard mutterings. "We need food." "Where is the sandwich truck?" "Anybody got some coffee?" "Don't use the port-a-potty or you'll suffocate."

"You were supposed to bring your own food and drink," Doreen said through gritted teeth. "And somebody go clean the port-a-potty. You're not babies, are you? Where's your gumption?"

Again, she looked across the street. The huge metal sign hanging on the fence read "Summit City Metals and Scrapyard, Fort Wayne's Green Jobs." She knew the Labor Department now counted all jobs connected with reclamation and recycling as green, a ploy that in her mind had everything to do with politics and nothing to do with protecting Mother Earth. It was just like the hateful Alexandra Royce to turn Doreen's politics right back on her. Clearly, she was mocking The Kekionga Center for Community Justice.

Worse, nobody at the Yard was paying the least attention to the demonstration. Even the men in blue nylon windbreakers stationed at various points along the Yard's perimeter seemed to be staring into space instead of at the demonstrators. No TV trucks had pulled up to give Kekionga the publicity it deserved. No print reporters had come around, eager for an interview. The school bus of union supporters had not arrived. If any police were present, she couldn't spot them.

She checked her iPhone. Her husband had sent her a text. "Thought you'd want to know: religious liberty demonstration going on right under my window, 500+ people. Bible thumpers, right-to-lifers, seniors, Catholics, probably tea-baggers too. No bigwig politicians but despite the rain people are listening to speeches. Reporters & TV trucks everywhere. Miserable day. How's it going with you? ☺ "

She snapped her phone shut and retied the hood on her rubber poncho. Five hundred idiots downtown, twenty-three outside the Scrapyard! Where were people's brains? Didn't everybody know the world would be better off without religion? Didn't they know the only sure guarantor of their liberty was a government run by people like her who knew real justice when they saw it?

Doreen was prepared to direct a war from behind the lines, not coddle a bunch of whiny camp followers who couldn't march an hour in rain and wind, who dropped their tattered signs and flags wherever they stood. Camp followers too stupid to bring their own food, too uncouth to keep a simple toilet clean. Her supporters were nothing but brainless waterbugs.

She hated to admit that the ridiculous fortune teller was right. Her enemy wasn't Alexandra Royce. It was her own supporters.

20

I Get Your Point
Friday, March 23, 2012

Under a little copse of trees, about fifty yards from the Scrapyard, Buck dumped sticks of wood and paper, including the stakes from the ruined signs and flags, into a 55-gallon drum and lit a fire. It was now dark, not just because the sun had set but because the Scrapyard's floodlights had been turned off, no one was sure why. Normally, Buck knew, they burned all night for security. The rain had diminished to a light drizzle but the wind hadn't let up and the temperature had dropped. The trees, dripping glistening beads of rain, hardly provided any shelter at all, but it was better than nothing. He'd backed his pickup into the copse so they could have a tailgate party.

Only three demonstrators besides Buck were left: Doreen, Maynard, and Lois.

Doreen was berating Lois for not informing her about the religious liberty demonstration.

"What does it matter?" Lois protested. "Of course, I knew about it, but I didn't think it would be so big, and besides anybody who cares about religious liberty wouldn't have been here anyway, so it didn't change the number of our protestors."

"I have to know about these things or I can't do my job," Doreen said. "We're competing with every selfish asshole in the world for media attention, you know." She shook the hood of her

103

poncho. "How the hell did I get so wet under this thing? If I don't end up with pneumonia, it'll be a miracle."

"You don't believe in miracles," Lois said.

"Oh, shut up."

Buck was roasting hot dogs over the fire. "Put your back to the fire, Doreen. You'll dry out."

"What used to be in that drum?"

"Water-based lubricant."

"Did you clean it first?" Doreen asked. "You're probably going to poison us with chemicals. I hate chemicals. They should all be banned."

"I power-washed it. It's fine. Speaking of chemicals," he said, handing her a charred wiener on a stick, "get some food in you. You'll feel better."

"I sent pictures of us to the paper," Maynard said, brandishing his cell phone. "We might get some notoriety; you never know."

"We don't want *notoriety*, Maynard. Do you even know what that word means?" Doreen scolded. "We want fame, the good kind. We want publicity -- publicity that's sympathetic to our cause."

"It could happen," he said stubbornly. "I got a good shot of Buck's sign: Scrap Is Crap. It's catchy. They might want to run that."

"Why didn't you point your truck the other way, Buck," Doreen asked, "so we'd have some light?"

"Didn't think of it." The question irritated him; there was no pleasing the woman. "But at least you can sit on the gate so you're facing the fire. Check the cooler. There should be some beers in there. The ice is gone, I suppose, but they should still be cool."

They continued arguing and eating charred hot dogs washed down by tepid beer for another hour. "I've got to get home," Buck suddenly said.

"It's only a little after nine," Doreen protested.

"We're spinning our wheels this time of night. Nothing's going to happen."

Maynard spoke up. "If you're leaving, then Lois and I have to go too. You're our ride."

"So I'm going to be left here all alone in the dark, is that it?" Doreen asked, a whimper creeping into her voice.

"Some of us have a life, you know," Lois said.

"If your husband wants to give me a ride home when he picks you up," Maynard volunteered, "I can stay with you, but I can't stay too late. The wife is waiting up."

"Go," Doreen said in exasperation, windmilling her arms. "All of you."

"You want me to put out the fire before I leave?" Buck asked.

"Are you crazy? It'll be the only light and heat I have," Doreen snapped. "Get out of here before I lose it."

"Why isn't your husband here?" Lois asked.

"He'll come get me when I tell him to."

"What difference does it make if you stay or not?" Maynard asked. "Nobody's around to notice. Why don't you just call it quits too?"

"Because I never call it quits, that's why."

"Is your phone working?" Maynard asked.

Doreen checked it, then nodded at him.

Doreen watched them pull out onto the road, then returned her attention to the fire. The flames were no longer leaping above the rim but quickly dying to embers. If she didn't collect some more wood, the fire would soon go out. Then, because there was only the tiniest sliver of moon, she'd be alone in deep darkness.

She felt sorry for herself. When she was a little girl she would stand on the porch in bad weather, pretending she was an orphan, saying things like "Poor little girl. All alone. No one to love her." Her parents thought she was nuts, talking about herself in the third person like that, ignoring the blessings of food and shelter and a loving family.

When Doreen heard something rustling just beyond the light cast by the fire, she wasn't alarmed. It was probably just a raccoon who'd smelled the bits of food she and her companions had dropped on the ground. The rustling stopped, then started up again. A twig snapped, then another. Was that a woodpecker hammering into a tree? at this time of night? She squinted into the dark copse.

When a hooded figure suddenly appeared in the penumbra of the firelight, she was startled but quickly regained her composure. The figure gave her a friendly wave. The firelight glinted off a large pair of glasses.

"Oh, thanks for coming back. But where did you find that flag?" She laughed for the first time that day. "Is that the white flag of surrender? Are you telling me it's time to call it quits?"

There was no answer. "I get your point, Maynard," Doreen said. "Let me put this fire out first, then we'll go."

21

Smoldering Barrel
Saturday, March 24, 2012

As Dave Powers sped toward Old Canal Street, he checked the time. 2:29 am, Saturday. A man had called 911 just before 2 am, identifying himself as Dallin Kawzy. He'd found his wife head over heels in a smoldering barrel, a flag protruding from her neck. It was the strangest description of a scene he'd ever heard.

Dave was inured to disgusting murder scenes, but this one would live in his memory. A fire truck, two squad cars, and an ambulance were already present. Dallin Kawzy was standing by a smoldering barrel, yelling something, tugging on the feet sticking out of it. A police technician was taking pictures. The firemen were trying to move Kawzy aside so they could get the body out.

They laid the burned body on the ground. An EMT felt for a pulse, but anyone could see from the condition of the woman's head and upper torso that she was either dead or would want to be dead. Dave walked over to the flag, which had been removed from her neck. It was sailcloth, soggy wet but scorched along the bottom edge. The message was barely readable: NOW YOUR A STAKEHOLDER. Ungrammatical and enigmatic. The wooden post to which the flag was attached had been weaponized with a bloody roofing nail inserted at the bottom. Had the woman died from being stabbed with the nail before being pushed into the fire? He could only hope so.

"That's your wife?" Dave asked the distraught man.

"I'm sure."

"What makes you so sure?" Dave asked, noting that her face was burned beyond recognition.

"The yellow poncho, the gray running shoes. I recognize the wedding ring. She never takes it off."

Wanting to distract the man while the emergency workers and police did what they had to do, Dave led Dallin toward a squad car. "Want to get in here where it's warm and dry and talk to me a few minutes?"

"I should be with my wife."

"Nothing you can do for her, I'm sorry to say. We won't let her be taken away without telling you first. If you'll answer a few questions, maybe we can get justice for her."

"It wasn't an accident, was it?" Dallin asked as he slid into the car.

"I don't think so," Dave said wryly, "given that flag stuck in her neck. Why wasn't she at home with you?"

"She led the demonstration out here today. Her friend Lois called around midnight asking if I'd picked her up yet. I told her Doreen gave me strict instructions not to come out here till she called and she hadn't called me yet. Doreen doesn't like being rushed. I dozed off awhile. When I woke up, I called her cell phone but went to voice mail. That worried me, so I got in the car and raced out here."

Dave looked down the street toward Summit City Metals. "Are you talking about the Kekionga demonstration against the Scrapyard?"

"That's the one. Doreen was out on Old Canal Street all day."

"Does she have enemies?"

Dallin snorted. "Everybody's who already got it made and doesn't want to share. Every company she's ever picketed. All the other community organizers competing for money and attention."

"Why was she out here in these woods alone?"

"She wasn't alone at first. She and her friends stayed awhile after the demonstration was over. They had to wind down from the excitement of the day, show they weren't defeated. Lois said she and Maynard left with Buck because he was their ride, but my wife wouldn't go with them or call me. Doreen told Lois she wasn't quitting."

"You'll need to give me her friends' full names, but I still don't understand why she stayed alone in the dark, in a deserted place, so late at night. She must have been tired, don't you think?"

"You'd have to know her to understand that."

A little late for that now. "What's that barrel doing here?"

"It was probably a way to keep warm. Her group's done that before late at night after a demonstration."

"Hate to ask this, but any problems in your marriage?"

Before Dallin could answer, one of the technicians stepped up to the driver's side of the car. Dave put his window all the way down. "We found this nailed to that tree," he said pointing a few yards to the south.

The card, now inside a plastic baggy, depicted a woman in a purple gown, on some contraption supported by two strange creatures. The legend read, "The Chariot."

"I can't believe this," Dave said.

"What?" Dallin Kawzy leaned over to see the card. "What is it?"

Dave held the baggy toward Dallin without letting go of it. "I think it's a Tarot card. Know anything about Tarot?"

"No," Dallin said. "But my wife had her cards read Tuesday night at a party on the other side of town. She thought it was bunk."

"What party? Who read her cards?"

"Some kind of crazy celebration of spring with a fortune teller. The woman was named . . . not sure, maybe Mama -- ."

"Mama Bee?"

"Could be."

"Out on Huguenard Road?"

"Don't know."

They sat in silence a few minutes. "Did your wife ever know a man named Alastair Digby?"

Dave got no answer, for Dallin saw that his wife's body was being loaded into the Coroner's truck. He leapt out of the squad car and promptly collapsed on the ground. Dave watched as Dallin was rolled onto a stretcher and loaded into an ambulance headed for St. Joseph hospital.

Had Dallin Kawzy killed his wife? If not, how about the people who said they left her alone in this dark, deserted area? Just how many enemies did Doreen have because of the causes she took up, and who were they?

And did she have any connection to Alastair Digby? Their deaths were eerily similar: a controversial victim stabbed in the neck at night. In each case, the murderer had left an enigmatic message -- "You'll never hurt anyone again" on Alastair Digby's computer screen, "Now your a stakeholder" on the soggy flag rammed through Doreen Soren-Kawzy's neck -- together with a Tarot card. He had his work cut out for him.

Part Two

Whoever loves discipline loves knowledge,
but he who hates correction is stupid.

Proverbs 12: 1

"All knowledge lies in the Void, and the Void is in me."

Mama Bee

22

The Chariot Is Missing
Saturday, March 24, 2012

When Mama Bee saw the black sedan pull into her driveway late Saturday morning, she wasn't nervous. She rather liked Lieutenant Powers, a handsome gentleman with a badge. This time she asked if he wanted a cup of herbal tea, maybe a glass of pomegranate juice. He politely declined.

The photograph of the Tarot card nailed upside down on a tree was jarring. "Doreen Soren-Kawzy, you say. She's your victim."

Dave nodded.

"I must confess something, Lieutenant. I did a little research after I left the police station a few weeks ago. My guess is that your first victim was a Mr. Digby. Am I right?"

"Good investigative work," he said. "Did you know him?"

"No. I looked at my records. I never gave him an individual reading. He was never part of a group reading and never came to one of my special parties."

"How about Doreen?"

Her hand flew to her heart in a gesture of shock and sympathy. "Such a coincidence! She was here on Tuesday for my Ostara party celebrating the spring equinox."

"What did you think of her?"

"Not a pretty woman, not very feminine, but smart. She seemed angry."

"At what? Or at whom?"

Mama Bee shook her head, puzzled. "That's the thing. Nothing, no one specific. Just kind of mad at the world. You know what I'm talking about?"

"I do. Everyone knows somebody like that."

"A very strange thing happened that night with Doreen."

"Tell me about it."

"I intended to give a special Tarot reading to one of the young guests I knew, but the marker somehow ended up with Doreen. The marker was a tiny crystal, a chip of rose quartz, the birthstone for January. Even though I didn't want Doreen to get it, she did, and you know what? The birthstone was actually her birthstone, like it was meant to be. I still can't explain how that happened. I'd never met Doreen before. I could tell right away she didn't believe in anything I was doing."

"Does that happen a lot?"

Uncomfortable, Mama Bee smoothed her skirt. "People who come for individual readings accept that I can see their fate in the cards or their palms or in a crystal ball. If they didn't, they wouldn't pay for my services. But people who attend a party with friends -- well, some are skeptical. They're just here because their friends decided to come. Anyway, Doreen didn't want her cards read but the other ladies teased her into it. . . . Do you mind if I get my notes?"

"All the better."

Mama Bee returned in a few minutes, a little breathless, and took her seat again. She paused a minute to review her notes. "She asked the spirits if she'd get a stake in an enterprise, win a seat at the table. She said she was in a war with somebody."

"What did that mean?"

"I wasn't sure. She said she was on a journey to save the world. The first four cards were pretty encouraging, but the last one was the Chariot in reverse, just like this," tapping the photograph of the card nailed upside down on a tree, "signifying she might fail. Because of the Moon card -- the card signifying the forces working against her -- I told her not to fight at night. I told her that her enemy wasn't who she thought it was."

"Who did she think was her enemy?"

"She didn't say."

"Who did you think it was?"

"I didn't know, but it didn't matter if I knew or not, only that she did. It was up to her to figure out the specifics. After the reading, for just a moment, I saw a flaming white banner out of the corner of my eye -- ."

"Tell me about that."

"Nothing more to tell, really. The reading was done but I had -- I guess you'd say I had a vision. A flaming white banner on a sharpened stake suddenly appeared before my mind's eye, just for a second. It flashed past so fast I can't describe it any better. I didn't know -- I don't know -- what it meant." She touched his arm. "Do you?"

"I might," Dave said, picturing the flag reading NOW YOUR A STAKEHOLDER, largely intact but scorched by the fire, limp from the rain, and fitted with a lethal roofing nail. "Can you show me the deck you used?"

Suddenly, Mama Bee was on alert. "The card in this picture can't be from my deck. I know that because Doreen suddenly got up from the table and practically ran out of the house, even before the other women's palms were read. She never touched the cards. All five were still on that little table over there when I cleaned up the next morning."

"I wonder if you'd humor me anyway."

Mama Bee slowly walked over to her étagère, debating whether she could get away with a lie -- the deck had been lost, she'd given it away, it was nowhere to be found. No. The polite but sharp-eyed detective would see through the ruse. "It's a new Ciro Marchetti deck," she said, holding out the box without opening it. "The only time it was ever used was for Doreen."

After a few moments, waiting for her to return to the table, Dave said, "I'd like to see the card."

Reluctantly, Mama Bee took her seat again and laid the pile of cards in front of her. She nervously straightened the edges. "Like

115

the Fool, the Chariot is part of the Major Arcana. It indicates major trends, big spiritual issues in a querant's life. It comes right after the Lovers."

"And it means what?"

"Triumph -- but failure when it's in reverse. Sometimes a last minute loss you didn't see coming. A defeat."

Carefully, one by one, she laid aside the first seven cards of the Major Arcana: the Fool, the Magician, the High Priestess, the Empress, the Emperor, the Hierophant, and the Lovers. But the Chariot wasn't the next card.

Not again! She couldn't believe it. As she had the last time Detective Powers visited her, she sorted through the cards, a little frantically at first, then with painful care, ensuring that no card was stuck to another. The Chariot was simply not in the deck.

It wasn't anywhere.

23

Guard the Nest
Saturday, March 24, 2012

Early Saturday afternoon, Lexie was in the atrium, reading *I've Got Your Number*, the latest Sophie Kinsella novel. It was light and funny, her favorite kind of book on a lazy afternoon. Lacey was napping in her basinet; Henry, who had triangulated himself between the baby and Lexie, was dozing, now and then opening an eye. Lexie felt cozy and relaxed.

And then Steve called from the Club. "I just talked to Dave, said he couldn't play golf today, even though the weather's not that bad. How often do we get to play in March? Anyway, you know what he told me?"

"No."

"Doreen was found dead early this morning."

The book slipped from her hand as she leapt to her feet. "How? Where?"

"Across from the Scrapyard. Upside down in a burning barrel, a stake through her neck. Her husband found her."

"What do you mean, a burning barrel?"

"A 55-gallon metal drum. She and her friends made a fire in it, cooked hot dogs and warmed up."

"A stake through her neck? How is that possible?"

"It had a flag on one end, a nail on the other, but Dave hinted the message on the flag probably wasn't one her supporters showed up with."

"So what killed her? The stake or the fire?"

"Don't know yet."

"Who would do such a thing?"

"Dave says no one's been identified yet but the field of suspects is so big it would fill the Coliseum."

"I don't get it. Why that many?"

"He didn't say. But my guess is the cops will start with the usual: her husband. Then the people she was last seen with. The rest of her supporters. The people she irritated with her demonstrations."

"Like me?"

Long pause. "Like you. Dave didn't mention you specifically, though he did say she was demonstrating outside of the Scrapyard yesterday."

"I know that. Hold on. Todd's waving at me from the patio; he's carrying a shovel."

"What's he doing there on Saturday?"

"I don't know, but I'll find out." Lexie opened the French doors. "What is it, Todd?"

As Todd stepped into the atrium, Lacey woke up and began to fuss.

"This morning, drinking coffee with Phyllis and talking about the week, I suddenly remembered I left some tools out by the creek, so I came out to get them before they're ruined by the humidity, and guess what I found on one of the trees?" He held out a folded piece of white paper.

"Don't tell me," Lexie said, taking it from him.

"Yes, ma'am, another one of those poems, and I read it, I did, just to be sure it is what I think it is. Not signed."

Lexie put the phone back to her ear. "Steve, let me call you back."

"What's going on?"

"Another sucky note. Everything's happening at once. Lacey just woke up and I want to read the note, then talk to Todd a minute, so I'm hanging up." She unfolded the note and read:

I guard the nest
of my little dove
so she can rest
in the arms of love

Lexie looked up at Todd. "I'm a dove again. Wasn't that how I was described in another note?"

"You talking about the one you gave to Phyllis for safekeeping, the one Plato found on the auto gate?"

She snapped her fingers. "That's the one. And why does my nest need to be guarded?"

Puzzled, Todd shook his head.

"Lacey just woke up and needs some attention. Let me pick her up, then let's walk out to the creek so you can show me the tree."

"Can I carry her out there? I hardly ever get to hold her."

Lexie smiled. "Of course. You really like babies, don't you?"

"You bet I do. Never worked anywhere before where I could see a baby every day. I made a mistake, not having any of my own, yes, I did, that was a really big error. Nothing I can do about it now. But at least I get to play with Drago's boys and cuddle this little one," he said, adjusting Lacey's blanket and kissing her forehead.

Lexie smiled at the sight of Todd, a stocky guy who looked like he could wrestle bears, delicately carrying the baby. Lacey never took her bright blue eyes off his face.

"You know what, Miss Royce? I think she just smiled at me. Could be gas, I suppose, or just a reflex, but I think that was a smile. I'm no baby expert, I'm just sayin'."

"I don't know why I'm walking out here, Todd. The grass is so squishy I'm ruining my shoes and there's probably nothing to see anyway."

"I don't know about that, no sir, I don't. I've found stuff out here before, you know."

Neither Lexie nor Todd was willing to dwell on the lost jewelry he'd found by the creek a year before, jewelry that implicated two different people in murder. "So," Lexie said, "where exactly did you find the note?"

"See where the spade is laying under the big old oak tree? About five feet up on the creek side of the trunk."

"How was it affixed?"

"With a nail. I put it in my pocket. Here, take Lacey and I'll show you." He dug into his pocket. "It's just a common roofing nail. Nothing special."

"What's that on the ground?" Lexie asked, pointing a yard away.

Todd bent down and picked up the thing. "Looks like the stub of a movie ticket. *Hunger,* it says."

"Short for *Hunger Games,* I'll bet. Cricket's reading the books and can't put them down. The movie opened last night at the Carmike, so Trent and Cricket were planning to go. I heard a lot of other people were eager for the movie to open too."

Todd looked at the wet stub. "This thing might not have anything to do with the note that was nailed on the tree, of course, but if someone was digging in his pocket to pull out the note and the nail, maybe the ticket stub got pulled out too. What do you want me to do with this stuff?"

"Let's go back to the house. We'll put them in the cubby with the other notes. I'll talk to Steve about what to do."

He pocketed the movie stub and roofing nail and held out his arms for the baby. "Let me carry her back. I'll come back for the rest of the tools later." They began squishing through soggy grass back to the house. "You'll never guess in a million years, I know you won't, where Phyllis is making me go tonight."

"No, I won't, Todd."

"To see *Sleeping Beauty* at the Auer Center downtown. It's ballet, dancing done on a stage, I hear. Lots of fancy costumes and high-class music. Have you ever seen something like that?"

"I have."

"Well, I haven't, didn't even know Fort Wayne had such a thing. We're even going to the champagne reception afterwards. Phyllis is a wonder, she is. She said if she has to go rock-hunting with me, I have to do some cultural things with her. Would you have guessed she liked ballet?"

"She's never mentioned it before."

"You think I'm going to like it?"

Lexie laughed, picturing dancers mincing and prancing around in tutus and tights -- not so different, really, from baseball players striding around in spandex pants, spitting and adjusting themselves. "I doubt the dance troupe will replace the TinCaps in your mind, but I want to hear every last detail Monday."

24

On Top of Things
Monday, March 26, 2012

Monday morning, Lexie crossed the courtyard to her office, where Ivy was already hard at work, seated at Jean's desk rather than her own. She looked up all smiles. "Oh, Miss Royce, so nice to see you. That's a beautiful dress. I've made coffee but I see you have a mug already."

Lexie took the guest chair. "Where's Jean?"

"She won't be here this morning. She said she's not feeling well and is going to try to get in to see her ob-gyn first."

"I'll give her a call later. Anyway, that's why you're here, Ivy. To make sure the office is covered."

"Do you want me to put a note in Jean's file so we can keep track of her sick days?"

"No."

Ivy looked a little chastened. "Okay. How about for the other women in this office?"

"Yes for you and them, but not Jean. My relationship with Jean isn't strictly about work, but that's a long story."

Ivy sipped her coffee. "Plato won't be here this afternoon either. He had to go to the hospital Friday night, or was it Saturday? Apparently he got into a fight with somebody and broke his hand. He's been discharged, of course. Petra will come in his place."

"Who did he get into a fight with?"

"Petra didn't give me any details but something she said made me think they were at a bar. Did you know Plato has a record for assault and battery?"

"How did you find that out?"

"I've been doing a few background checks on the people in this house. Apparently the old fights were in a bar too. The charges were knocked down to a misdemeanor. Plato also has some odd gaps in his work history. When he was just out of high school, he was fired from a job in a fitness center and then wasn't employed again for over a year. My guess is he was caught with his hand in the till."

"Why is that your guess?"

"I'm basing it on my work experience at the hotel. You can't believe how many employees are fired for stealing. Of course, I won't say anything about Plato to anyone else. I'm not trying to hurt him and I'm not one for gossip -- not like Trent. But I thought you ought to know about Plato."

"Who else in this house have you done background checks on?"

"I'm just starting to take a look at Astrid. Did you know her father is on trial in Sweden for fraud? He's a commodities trader, covered some of his losses using his clients' money. Or at least those are the allegations. It's been headline news over there."

"Ivy, I think I understand what you're trying to do -- ."

"I hope so, Miss Royce. I just think you should know everything you can about the people who work for you."

"I appreciate that, but let's hold off on that. No more background checks."

"Really?"

"Really."

"If you don't mind my asking, why not?"

"Why not?" Lexie asked, stalling for time. "Cold hard facts are helpful, but sometimes people change so the old facts about them are stale and out-of-date. Or the facts you find in a public record are selective and don't tell the whole story. Would you want a more thorough background check done on you, for example?"

"I'm clean as a whistle, so it wouldn't bother me a bit."

"I can believe that, but for now we're not going to do any more digging into people's pasts."

"Well, okay. You're the boss and I recognize that you know what you're doing. I just want to help. . . . It's shocking, isn't it, what happened to Mrs. Soren-Kawzy?"

"Horrifying. I never liked her but I never wanted her dead. Have you found out yet when and where her funeral will be?"

Ivy jotted a note on her laptop. "I'll try to find out as soon as we're done here." She glanced up at Lexie. "Do you know how many times Doreen was arrested for trespassing on private property, blocking public streets, demonstrating without a permit, that kind of thing?"

Lexie gave Ivy a thoughtful look. "Matilda told me about some of the trouble Doreen got into as a community agitator, but I think it went with the territory. From my point of view, it was a foolish way to live a life, but Matilda admired her niece and nobody in Doreen's family ever thought less of her. In fact, given their political views, I'm pretty sure they admired her courage."

"She was very determined in our meeting at the Scrapyard. As fierce as a dragon. I think she even intimidated Miss Weide a little."

Lexie laughed. "Intimidated Trude? I don't think so. When I was younger, Trude scared even me, so you might have misread the situation."

"So what's going to happen now?"

"With what?"

"The Kekionga group's efforts to unionize the Scrapyard."

"We'll have to wait and see. I don't know if there's anyone to take her place."

"Didn't you say your step-mother wants to sell the business?"

I never said anything to you about it, so you must have overheard my conversation with Matilda. "No, I didn't say that, so where did you hear it?"

Ivy closed her eyes as if trying to remember. "I can't recall. Trent maybe."

"As you can imagine, I don't want a rumor like that to spread.

. . . I know you went to the same party Trent and Astrid did, the one at Mama Bee's. Tell me about that."

"I don't believe in that fortune-telling stuff, but I went because it was something to do and everybody else was going, so it was a chance to be with friends. It was kind of fun, more fun than I expected, hearing what Mama Bee had to say to everyone. She had the most to say to Doreen, of course, and since then I've done a lot of thinking because it's a little uncanny how things turned out for that poor woman. Her chariot ended upside down, that's for sure."

"Astrid told me Doreen was warned not to fight at night. But I hear you got a great reading."

Ivy smiled modestly. "I did. But just because Mama Bee predicted a great future for me doesn't mean I believe her, of course. I'm not that gullible. But she did make it sound like I'll rise to great heights. I assume she means the career ladder."

"You're certainly on top of things, Ivy, so she's probably right."

"By the way, I'm still waiting for Trent to turn in his personal receipts for your trip to New York. He's a great stylist, I'm sure, but I don't think he pays much attention to bookkeeping details."

Lexie got up and started toward her glass-enclosed private office. "Trent can't have had many personal expenses other than a few cab trips, maybe a fee to get into a sample sale or a designer's showroom, but I'll remind him this afternoon. It's in his interests, after all, to pay attention to his expense account. Now, come along with the files on the wind farms and my travel arrangements for the Kentucky Derby."

25

Justice or Liver
Monday, March 26, 2012

For once, being interviewed at the police station didn't make Drago uncomfortable. He knew nothing about Doreen's death other than what he read in the paper, and having met her only twice, knew very little about her. He didn't care one way or another whether she lived or died, though in fact he felt a small measure of satisfaction that she'd gotten justice -- not the kind she wanted but the kind somebody must have thought she deserved. When he was a young scoundrel, dealing drugs for the arrogant and lazy Rolie Royce, his own mantra was "There ain't no justice in the world, know that," but now he knew that anyone who was hot to trot for justice probably didn't intend to give it to anyone else.

With respect, he watched Detective Powers enter the little gray room and take a seat. Who could deny that a badge and a gun gave a man importance? And the man was in shape, that was for damn sure, not like some doughnut-hog cops. Drago used to despise black lawmen as homeboys pretending to be something they weren't, but he didn't feel that way any more. He had now joined Dave Powers on the right side of the law, making it straight in a tough world and doing a pretty good job of it.

After Dave Powers took a seat, he let the silence grow. Drago's eyes crinkled in amusement. He recognized the detective's technique, waiting for the other guy to speak first.

Finally, Detective Powers opened with a few words about the cemetery thief Drago had caught the year before. Drago recognized this technique too. He was being warmed up to spill his guts. Fortunately, there was nothing to spill.

"Okay," Dave said, opening a folder. "I understand you had a meeting on March 7 with the Kekionga group and Doreen Soren-Kawzy was there. Is that right?"

"Don't remember the exact date, but we had a meeting all right. Trude Weide, the office manager and bookkeeper, and Ivy Starr, Mizz Royce's assistant, and I were there. Doreen had two people with her, a guy named Maynard and a woman named Lois."

"How'd it go?"

"Doreen and Maynard did most of the talking. Doreen said she wanted the Scrapyard to go union. She and her friends gave speeches about stuff like diversity and justice and then handed Trude and me a wad of papers, which we gave to the boss. Mizz Royce has been fighting union organizers all her life."

"What did you think about it all?"

"I'm the new operations manager, so I'm not going along with anybody's agenda but Mizz Royce's, and if she doesn't want a union, then I don't either. It's that simple."

"I take it you'd do anything for your boss."

Drago hid his amusement at the trick question. "Anything legal."

"Were you at work on Friday when the Kekionga group was demonstrating?"

"You bet your ass I was. I haven't missed a day of work since I started. Stayed in the Yard, mostly in my office, watched the whole thing on a monitor. Mizz Royce told us not to provoke them. Let them do what they were going to do unless they charged the gates or started throwing firebombs or something wild like that. We had plenty of security if something crazy happened. Mizz Royce said she didn't think it would get that bad though, this being Fort Wayne, but we weren't taking any chances."

"I hear the floodlights were turned off when the workers went home. Who did that?"

"I did."

"Why?"

"A judgment call. I could have gone either way on that. Keep the lights on so the cameras record any property damage, if that's what the demonstrators have in mind. Turn the lights off so the crazy people can't hang around. It was my call and I made it."

"I still don't understand how you made the call."

"Did you get a look at the Kekionga group that day?"

"Not in person."

Drago rubbed his chin. "Pitiful group. Very few people, kinda tired looking, couldn't make a formation to save their souls. Their signs were so wet you couldn't read what was on them. They looked like they wanted to be anywhere but out there in the rain, holding signs and chanting. Nothing about them worried me. In fact, I almost felt sorry for them. If they weren't trying to put us out of business or bring in a union, I'd have sent coffee out.... So, I gave the poor bastards darkness, a reason to leave."

"Were the cameras recording after the work day ended?"

"I didn't turn them off, so I suppose so, but I haven't checked to see what they picked up, if anything. They don't record all the time, you realize, just when they detect motion."

"I need to know where you were and who you were with after you left work Friday night."

"No problem. My in-laws took Lucy and me and the kids out to dinner in Auburn. We ate at the Mad Anthony Brewery. Ever eaten there?"

Finally, Dave smiled. "Last summer, my wife made me go to an art fair in Auburn, so, yeah, I've eaten lunch there. Good wings and a lot of special beers to choose from. So where'd you go after dinner?"

"We drove by a liquor store the Flowers are thinking of buying. If they do, my wife, Lucy, will run the one here in Fort Wayne and the Flowers will run the new one in Auburn. In my wife's mind, that'll make her the Liquor Store Queen."

"And you're the Scrapyard King."

"I don't go around saying any such thing, know that."

"And the rest of the night?"

"At home. We put the boys to bed, watched the eleven o'clock news, and then went to bed ourselves. That was it."

Dave pushed a piece of white paper and pencil toward Drago. "I want you to print out four words: Now You're a Stakeholder. Use all capital letters."

Drago frowned. "What's that got to do with anything?"

"Humor me."

Drago snorted. "Some joke. Well, here goes." He printed "NOW YOU'RE A STAKEHOLDER" and pushed the paper back to Dave.

Dave eyed Drago with new respect. "Perfect spelling. I take it you did well in your English classes."

"Not bad. Mostly got at least Bs. Didn't do that well in a lot of other classes, but I had a good English teacher. Mrs. Watts. A little on the fat side, kept a tissue in her sleeve. Looked jolly enough but she ran a tight ship. She made us keep a daily journal, at least a paragraph every day. For some reason, I got into it -- probably because it was all about me. I was running track in those days, and was mad at my dad for just about everything, so that's what I wrote about. You ever have a teacher like that?"

"I did. Mine was Mr. Potgetter, taught history and civics. Didn't think I'd like civics, but he made me want to run for office someday."

"I don't always use good English, as my mom tells me just about every time we get together. I got into some bad habits when I was workin' the streets a few years ago . . . talking about grammar here," winking, "nothing else. Now I've got to start sounding like I deserve to be the boss, so I try to watch it."

"You have any idea about who might have wanted to kill Doreen Soren-Kawzy?"

"Probably anybody who met her."

Dave frowned. "What do you mean?"

"My mouth got ahead of my brain. I just mean, she wasn't as nice a person as she wanted you to think she was. She came to the

Scrapyard to get justice for me even if I don't need it or want it. And if I don't go along with her, she'll eat my liver." Drago made his hands into balance scales. "Justice or liver. Take your pick. Sort of like your mother saying, as she whacked your bottom, this is for your own good and it's hurting me more than you. Know what I'm talking about?"

Dave laughed. "I have a mom like that." *And everybody I've talked to so far says pretty much the same thing about Doreen.* "I'd like to see the SD cards from the Yard's cameras along Old Canal Street."

"Let me talk to the Big Boss first, okay? But I'm sure it's fine with Mizz Royce. If she says okay, I'll have somebody run them over to you this afternoon."

Dave stood up. "Thanks for coming in."

Drago stood up too. "If I hear anything, I'll let you know. None of us is happy about what happened, believe me. Makes the Scrapyard look bad, even though we didn't have anything to do with what happened to Doreen What's-Her-Name. Mizz Royce don't . . . oops, see what I mean about old habits? . . . Mizz Royce *doesn't* take kindly to negative publicity, know that."

26

Lady-in-Waiting
Monday, March 26, 2012

"So," Lexie said Monday afternoon, greeting Jean as she walked into the atrium and took a chair, "how are you feeling?"

"Better. I'm taking some new pills for my blood pressure. I think I'm a little old for a first pregnancy."

"Oh, come on. We're the same age and I did fine. You will too. The first couple months are the hardest."

"I'm kind of excited about going to the Kentucky Derby. I just hope I'm feeling okay by then. Who else is going?"

"Sheila and Dave, Jessica and Ed. Ed, who likes a good sports bet, has volunteered to prepare information sheets on all the horses and trainers and jockeys. He'll have all the odds calculated to a decimal point. . . . Where are my manners? Do you want something to drink?"

"Phyllis' famous raspberry lemonade, if you don't mind. What are you wearing to the Derby?"

Lexie held up a finger while she buzzed Phyllis and requested lemonade and cucumber sandwiches. "Don't know yet. Trent is working his very well tailored butt off finding me exactly the right dress and hat. You'd think we were meeting the Queen of England. I'm sure he'd be happy to do the same for you. Jessica has already requested his services, which has given Trent no end of importance. If you have a little bump by then, you'll need something new anyway. And keep the weather in mind. Todd assures me that he's consulted the Farmers' Almanac and learned the weather will be warm and dry. He's no meteorologist, he's just sayin'."

They laughed. Then the conversation turned to Doreen. "Were you as shocked as I was to hear she's dead?" Jean asked.

"Shocked and horrified. Not just that she died but the way she did. You won't be surprised to know I've heard from Matilda."

"What'd she have to say?"

"She screamed at me for ten minutes."

"Screamed at you? Why?"

"If I'd met Doreen halfway, she said, this wouldn't have happened. If I'd taken the time to understand her, we could have compromised. I told Matilda I understood Doreen thoroughly, which is why I'd never agree with her. She wanted a piece of my business; I don't want to give her a piece. Where's the compromise? Divide the baby by agreeing she can have half? That's like reaching a compromise with Hitler: killing Jews is wrong, but in the interests of compromise and unity we'll let him kill only half."

"What did Matilda say?"

"She didn't respond to a word I said but just went on her with diatribe. I'm too stiff-necked for my own good. We should sell the business while we can. Doreen wouldn't have had to demonstrate in the rain if I'd just been willing to talk to her. If she hadn't been so discouraged by the day, she wouldn't have stayed behind and been vulnerable to attack. Doreen's mother is going to send me the bill for the funeral and if I don't pay, I'll find out . . . ."

"Find out what?"

"Matilda didn't finish the threat, but I'm guessing I'll find out what a she-bear she is. . . . Oh, yeah, how could I forget? She even hinted that maybe I hired somebody to kill Doreen."

Jean looked horrified. "She didn't!"

"She did."

"She's completely irrational. Giving her niece control over the family business wouldn't have helped her."

"I pointed that out."

"You want to know my theory?"

"Of course."

"Matilda's been mad at you ever since Rolie died, as if that was your fault. She had to find somebody other than her son to blame for his stupidity, and you're handy. She's so angry she'll say anything to wound you."

"I shouldn't have brought her up. Just thinking about her gives me a headache. . . . By the way, did you know that Ivy's been busy getting background information on everybody in this house?"

Jean sat up a little straighter. "What do you mean?"

"She found out Plato has a criminal record, assault and battery. Then he got in a fight this weekend and broke his hand. From a gap in his work history, she suspects he stole from his employer. Astrid's father is some kind of con man in Sweden. Trent's sloppy with his expense report and gossips too much."

"How about you and me? Are we subject to her detective work too?"

"I told her to stop."

Jean lowered her voice to a whisper. "What about Drago?"

"It won't matter to me what she finds on him. I know his history as well as anybody's. I think it's just part of her personality. She's showing me how efficient and loyal she is."

"I don't care what you say. She worries me."

"How?" Lexie asked.

"First of all, she's using the oldest technique in the book to tie you to her. She warns you about everybody else's faults so you begin to think the only buffer you have from your enemies, the only source of information you have about them, is Ivana Starr. She's like the lady-in-waiting the queen depends on for court gossip."

"Forewarned is forearmed. And second?"

"I might have hired my very efficient, totally loyal replacement."

"Don't be silly. This morning she wanted to know if she should put a note in your file to keep track of your sick days. I told her no. She doesn't understand our relationship, that's all. But in time she will."

133

"She's given me an idea."

"What?" Lexie asked.

"I'm going to do a little background search on her. How about that?"

Lexie smiled. "You'll probably find, to your chagrin, that she won the Nobel Peace Prize at fifteen and turned down the ambassadorship to Britain at nineteen."

Jean got to her feet. "Then you'll never hear a word from me about it."

27

Captain Moonpie
Wednesday, March 28, 2012

"Captain, you wanted to see me?" Dave stood in the doorway of his boss' office.

Captain Schmoll signaled him to come in and take a chair. "Any progress on the Barrel Murder, Detective?"

Dave could never quite get used to the Captain's enormous neck and many chins, as if a smaller face had been sloppily pasted on a bigger one. Behind his back, the Captain's nickname was Moonpie. Dave laid his folder on the desk, opened it, and focused on his notes. "I've interviewed a fair number of people. No real leads yet."

"So what's your theory?"

"The oldest one in the book. Who benefitted from Doreen's murder?"

"Same theory for that old poof on Forest Park, right? The Ice Pick Murder."

Dave winced. The younger cops didn't use terms like poof, at least not openly. "Yes. But let's look at the woman's death first."

"You can't ignore the husband, Detective. They're always our best suspects."

Dave bristled at the implication he'd ignored the husband. "I *started* with him -- Dallin Kawzy. He's out of the hospital and doing fine. Just had a blackout from shock. He's a tall, thin guy, low blood pressure, has a history of blackouts if he stands up too fast. Dallin was alone at home during the time his wife was murdered. Fell asleep, didn't call anybody, so his alibi can't be corroborated, but if he had a motive to off his wife, I haven't found it. No domestic battery complaints, no debts other than a mortgage and car loan, no life insurance." He looked at the Captain. "Who doesn't have life insurance these days? Anyway, neither one had a honey on the side. No criminal history. He comes across as a nice guy, maybe a little hen-pecked -- ."

Captain Schmoll snorted. "Pussy-whipped, you mean. The pussy and the whip are gone now, so there's a benefit."

Dave tried not to smile. Was Captain Moonpie pussy-whipped? "A very minor one. Dallin doesn't think he's better off with his wife dead, so I'm putting him aside."

"Don't cross him off the list."

"I never cross anybody off the list until the case is solved, but I have to prioritize our resources."

"What about the old man? Who benefitted from his death?"

"At the time of his death, Alastair Digby had no wife, no children, no partner. He was briefly married in the Sixties, had a son who died at the age of six from meningitis, then got divorced, lived with a male friend for thirty years. When his friend died, Alastair moved back here, where he was born, and has lived alone ever since. His brother Desmond says the trust reverts to the family; the life insurance and other assets will be divided between him and Carleton, the third brother. That's the way the Digbys have always done things; money stays in the family. But Desmond and Carleton are both well off in their own right, so I don't see money as a motive. And both have solid alibis."

"So your theory of benefit doesn't go anywhere, Detective."

The theory isn't mine, you big bucket of rancid fat. And you know damn well that's where we always start an investigation. "It still might. Both Alastair and Doreen had a lot of enemies outside of their family circle. Alastair had apparently made a fool of the wrong person; we just don't know which one, but I'm having an assistant compile a list of the authors he insulted. According to Drago Bott,

Doreen wanted a stake in Summit City Metals and Scrapyard, hence the pun on the flag that was stuck in her neck, so I'm going to interview more people at the Yard. Getting rid of Digby and Soren-Kawzy benefitted somebody."

"Just one person or two different ones?"

"Good question." *Obvious question, but flattering you won't do any harm, so let me pretend it's a good one.* "I haven't found a meaningful connection yet between the two victims, so that suggests two different people who wanted them dead. But the time and manner of killing -- fatal stabs to the neck at night -- and the messages and Tarot cards left at both murder scenes suggest the same murderer with the same MO."

Captain Schmoll stood up and straightened his tie. "I've got a meeting in two minutes. These cases have gotten national attention, you know. The Chief calls me every hour for an update and I don't have shit to give him. The stupid media is pumping them up to be more sensational than they are and the Chief don't like it. So I suggest you put your thinking cap on and get to work."

I've gotten about ten hours' sleep since Saturday, so what do you think I'm doing, you condescending old fart? Twiddling my thumbs? Dave rose too. "Cap's on, motor's running. I'll keep you posted."

Dave hadn't reached the Captain's doorway when he was called back.

"Detective!"

Dave turned, keeping his face impassive. "What?"

"I know about your friendship with the socialite who runs the Scrapyard. Don't go easy on her. She ain't likely to have had warm and fuzzy feelings about the dead woman."

"Socialite? Are you talking about Alexandra Wright?"

Captain Schmoll nodded.

"With respect, sir, I don't think Mrs. Wright thinks of herself as a socialite, but you have my word, I'm not ignoring anybody."

"We're taking all this incoming flak, Detective, might as well return some. Wouldn't it be a kick in the pants if it turned out the rich bitch did the dirty deed? Now, there are headlines to sell newspapers. Rich Bitch Stakes Her Future on Death . . . Local

Heiress Barrels Ahead . . . Scrapyard Queen All Fired Up . . . well, you get the idea."

How long have you been plotting to work that schtick into the conversation?

Dave returned to his desk, stung by the Captain's taunt, which landed too close to the mark. The last thing Dave wanted was to implicate the Wrights in something like murder. His wife, Sheila, formerly a middle school teacher, was working with Lexie to found a private college preparatory academy with the idea of franchising the business nationwide. If it succeeded, Sheila would have the job of a lifetime, not to mention fame and wealth. He and Steve Wright had been best friends from high school, where they were both star athletes, Steve a baseball pitcher, Dave a quarterback. Every year they spent a week in Arizona to watch Spring training and play every round of golf they could fit into a day. They hunted pheasants in the Fall and spent the occasional weekend with their wives watching the best *noir* films of the Thirties. He and Sheila were part of the group the Wrights were taking to the Kentucky Derby, all expenses paid. Friends as entertaining and generous as the Wrights weren't easy to find.

Dave wanted to punch something. Instead, he opened one steel desk drawer after another, as if he were looking for something, then slammed each one shut as hard as he could. He knew it was a stupid thing to do, but somehow it was satisfying. He pictured a startled Moonpie in the Chief's office, one face slipping back and forth over the other as he tried to figure out who was shooting who in the bullpen.

Then, working from the notes Mama Bee had happily given him about her readings for the last month, Dave began making calls.

28

Stupid Word Zapper
Friday, March 30, 2012

Friday night, Trent Senser was in his element. Lucy Bott had persuaded her parents to install a little deli market in a corner of their liquor store featuring exotic cheeses, patés, cold cuts, jams, olives, crackers, and other delicacies from around the world. Trent had come up with the name: Bourbon Street Charcuterie. The play on words was delicious for a liquor store. Lucy's father objected to "charcuterie" because no one would realize it meant deli and was too foreign for Hoosiers to pronounce. But because Lucy agreed with Trent, and because Louis Flowers could deny his only daughter nothing, the Bourbon Street Charcuterie was now a name in neon lights.

Lucy had decided that on opening night, she would pair cheeses and wines, but knowing nothing about such pairings, she asked Trent for help. Knowing as little as Lucy did about such delicacies, Trent had, for two months, studied everything he could find on the Internet. By the time of the opening, he was not an expert but he figured he knew more than anyone else who would attend.

Lucy had also taken Trent's advice about the staff's uniforms: black jeans, white dress shirts open at the neck, long white aprons, and red berets. A red, white, and black striped awning hung over the deli corner and colorful hot-air balloons bobbed from the ceiling. In the expectation of hordes of Francophiles, a lifelike mustachioed French waiter greeted customers with a tray stacked with wine menus, and black wrought-iron park benches allowed them to rest between tastings.

Long tables draped with starched white linen held a dozen bottles of French wine, each labeled and paired with a different cheese. Eiffel Towers from Cricket's collection were scattered among the bottles. At six o'clock, there were only a dozen customers in the shop, rendering Trent so nervous he couldn't stop chattering. But by seven, there was standing room only and Trent was busy for the next three hours, chatting up the customers and opening bottle after bottle. The clerks behind the counter sliced meats and wrapped slabs of cheese until their arms were numb. The stock boys lugged cases of wine to the checkout desk. Lucy's parents, Denise and Louis, who were acting as cashiers, were exhausted by the time the last oenophiles straggled out the door.

"I don't know if you'll keep getting this kind of business," Louis said to his daughter as he removed his apron, "but that went a hundred times better than I expected." His swarthy face was flushed dark red.

"That's because there's no other deli like this in Fort Wayne," Trent said.

Louis held out his hand to Trent. "I thought the berets were a little over the top, but I have to hand it to you. People like them. I took mine off for a few minutes and now it's gone."

"Maybe you should start giving one away with every case of wine somebody buys. It would be a big draw."

Louis, looking doubtful, repositioned the few strands of black hair covering his scalp. He was built like a cannon-ball wrestler, Trent thought, a man you might underestimate until he had you in a headlock. "It's not in my nature, but I'll think about it." He hugged Lucy. "Anyway, kid, your mother and I are exhausted, so we're going home."

"Go," Lucy said. "I'm too excited to go home. Drago's got the boys, so I'm not on a schedule."

While the clerks straightened up, Lucy, Trent, and Cricket

took chairs around a little umbrella table. They spent the next half hour comparing notes about which wines people liked and which cheeses smelled too strong for Midwestern tastes. They played wine pong with olives. Eventually, the conversation turned to Doreen's murder.

All three had been interviewed by Detective Powers. All three were shaken by the experience, feeling vaguely guilty without knowing why. They were completely stumped by the request to print out "NOW YOU'RE A STAKEHOLDER." Each had spelled the last word differently -- one word, two words, hyphenated.

"Are you worried?" Cricket asked Trent for the umpteenth time.

"A little. The detective kept asking me if I'd taken the Fool card as a souvenir when Mama Bee read my cards a few months ago before I started working for Mrs. Wright, or if I might have mistakenly taken the Chariot card at the Ostara party. Or if I had my own decks of Tarot cards."

"And you said what?" Cricket asked, knowing full well what he'd said but never tiring of the subject.

"I've never stolen anything in my life, including a souvenir . . . except the complimentary toiletries at the hotel a few weeks ago, but everybody does that so it doesn't count. And I don't even know where to buy Tarot cards."

Lucy held up a bottle of white Bordeaux. "Let's finish this off so I don't have to re-cork it. . . . We know from being at the party the bad card Doreen got was the Chariot, but the newspaper accounts of Doreen's death never mentioned Tarot cards or anything about a stakeholder, so what's it all about?"

"From the way I was questioned," Trent said, "I think both the Digby murder and Doreen's involved Tarot cards. When I was in New York with Mrs. Wright, her agent told us about the Fool card found near Mr. Digby's body. Maybe the Chariot card was found near Doreen's."

"Did you tell the detective about how when Mama Bee read your cards before you got the job with Mrs. Wright, the Fool card came up?" Cricket asked, knowing he had.

"Not only that but I told him about Mrs. Lazare's joke about how her investigator found Digby after he was dead. If he'd been alive, she'd have told him to put a sock in it, but since he was dead, she'd gotten revenge without even trying. She thought it was funny as hell."

"Did Mrs. Wright laugh?"

"No."

"Did you?"

"No! I couldn't take my eyes off the woman's enormous bosom."

"You didn't really tell the detective about the revenge joke, did you?" Lucy chided. "That makes it sound like Mrs. Wright was the one who orchestrated the man's death as revenge for the bad review he wrote about her book."

"You think?"

Lucy gave him a schoolmarm look. "You and I both know that. The man who made fun of her book is dead. The woman who picketed the Scrapyard is dead. The detective probably didn't connect Mrs. Wright with Digger -- ."

"Digby, not Digger."

"He didn't connect *Digby* and Mrs. Wright until you repeated the joke."

Trent put his head in his hands. "My mouth!"

Cricket got up and hugged him from behind. "Don't blame yourself, my handsome *sommelier*. Time to take me home. We'll think about it in the morning."

Lucy smiled. "So how's the apartment hunt going?"

Trent, grateful for the change of subject, pushed back his chair. "So far, we like the Three Rivers apartments best."

"So you two are going to be roommates. Who would have thought?"

"When we were in high school," Cricket said, "we vowed to get married if at thirty we were both still single."

"That's a long way off."

"Too many years to keep living at home," Cricket said. "If I don't leave the nest soon, I think my parents are going to give me a little shove whether I can fly or not, so it's time to see where my wings can carry me. Now that Trent's working for Mrs. Wright and I'm working for you, I think we can catch the thermals and stay aloft."

"Very poetic."

"We'll each have our own room, of course," Trent said.

"Of course." Lucy turned serious. "You'd better hope you haven't hurt Mrs. Wright saying what you did about that New York woman's joke. You aren't going to stay aloft if she hears about it."

"Don't remind me. Somebody should invent a machine that takes your words back."

"Now there's a brilliant thought."

"I can see it," Trent said with a thin laugh. "A heat-seeking missile zaps your stupid words right out of the air. Everybody gets brain freeze, remembers nothing."

"The Stupid Word Zapper. Get on it, Trent. You'll be a hero, make a fortune.... Not trying to open old wounds, but how often have I told you to stop gossiping?" Lucy asked, walking them to the door.

Cricket frowned but Trent looked chastened. "I'll never gossip again, and that's the truth."

The women giggled all the way to Trent's car.

29

Here Comes the Witch
Friday, March 30, 2012

Lexie had never been escorted out of a place by a security guard before. It was humiliating.

Friday night, together with Jean and Ivy, she dutifully drove to D.O. McComb & Sons for Doreen's visitation. Dallin was standing by the closed casket, greeting mourners. A large foam board on an easel bore the title "Doreen the Activist." It was covered with casual photos of Doreen with various members of her family, even group pictures of demonstrations she had led and a few reprints of newspaper articles about her. Floral arrangements were displayed on wire stands near the casket. No one else was in line.

Lexie held out her hand to Dallin. "I'm so sorry for your loss." She knew the words sounded hollow but what else could she say? Looking numb, Dallin mumbled something.

Then the three women took seats in the second row of mourners and looked around. There were only a few people in the first row, one man sitting alone in the back row.

"The bouquet of roses I ordered isn't here," Ivy whispered. "I wonder why not. Armstrong never lets us down."

Lexie patted her hand. "Never mind. I think that's a plainclothes guy in the back row."

"Probably trying to see if he can spot the killer," Jean whispered.

"Why would the killer be here?" Ivy asked.

Jean smiled. "It's been known to happen. You ever watch *The Sopranos*?"

"I don't see Abigail or Matilda," Lexie said.

Jean nodded toward the door. "They were standing with Doreen's sister Shayla and a couple of women I don't know in a little knot at the end of the hallway when we came in. I don't think they saw us."

"How long do we have to sit here?" Ivy asked. "I've never been to one of these things before. Are we supposed to look like we're praying or something?"

"Respectful and sad will work just fine," Jean said dryly.

And then Matilda and Abigail entered the room. Abigail, Doreen's mother, said something to Dallin, patted his shoulder, and gave him a little push in the direction of a chair. When she turned to face the room, she spotted Lexie and whispered something to her sister Matilda, who turned around. When she too saw Lexie, Matilda's lovely peach skin suddenly darkened to the color of a bruise. Her gray eyes narrowed to gun slits, her teeth slammed down like a portcullis barring entry into a castle.

"Oh, God, here comes the witch of Endor," Jean said. "I swear there's smoke coming out of her ears."

Matilda leaned over an empty front row chair toward Lexie, looking like she was about to spit fire. "What are you doing here?"

"Paying my respects," Lexie answered, trying not to focus on the spittle on the side of her step-mother's mouth. "We all are. I'm sorry -- ."

"Leave now."

"But we just got here," Ivy whined. "Where's the floral arrangement we sent? Those roses cost a fortune. It was a bigger bouquet than any others up there."

Matilda took her time answering. "There's a dumpster outside, you stupid girl. Take a look in it. Now all of you, get out."

"That's a great suit. You buy that specially for the funeral?" Jean, smiling wickedly, couldn't deprive herself of the joy of poking the witch. "You don't look like you've cried, though."

"Oh!" a strange woman exclaimed, turning around to glare at

Jean.

The three women rose, heads up -- Jean defiant, Lexie embarrassed, Ivy puzzled -- to make their way to the end of the row, but that wasn't enough for Matilda. She crooked her finger at a man they hadn't noticed before. He was wearing a navy suit, a black arm band, and a steel-trap jaw. "Take them out, Doug. Make sure they get in their car and leave."

"No need for that, Matilda," Lexie said. "We're going."

But Doug was not to be deterred. He walked behind them to the car, one hand in his jacket pocket as if holding a gun on them. Looking triumphant, he stood his ground until they pulled away.

30

Omen
Monday, April 2, 2012

Monday night, Lexie was hungry and exhausted when once again Drago met her at the Fort Wayne airport.

She'd been in Iowa all day, walking around her wind farms and inspecting a synthetic fuel operation in which she had invested heavily. The walk-arounds weren't strictly necessary, but she never felt comfortable that she really understood an operation and its value unless she took a close personal look. Besides, she liked getting out of the office and talking to the people who ran things.

"How was Iowa?" Drago asked. "Never been west of the Mississippi myself."

"Windy and flat. The horizon stretches a hundred miles in every direction, almost no trees, and the soil is the richest, blackest stuff you've ever seen, not like Indiana clay. No wonder it's the bread basket of the world."

"Didn't know it was."

"Kind of a sad place in some ways. We landed in Mason City, a county seat that's losing population, just like all the little towns around it. An abandoned farmhouse here, a shuttered school there, a grain elevator burned to the ground. The rural way of life isn't what it was, as everyone kept telling me. Young people leave for the cities. It makes me think of what it must have been like to live in some French city rich with trade when the Roman empire collapsed and the Roman roads with it, or some little English town after the plague swept through and there was no one left to plow the fields. You know things are changing all around you, not for the better, but there's nothing you can do about it."

"Roman roads and English plague! I wish you'd been my history teacher. Maybe I would have liked it."

"I almost got killed today, Drago."

His head snapped around. "What do you mean?"

"I was standing on a road looking at a wind farm when two blades suddenly whirled right off the tower and flew to the ground. One of the blades landed in a plowed field, the other not ten yards from me. The third blade was still hanging by a thread when I left. Everything -- the whole damn farm -- had to be shut down, of course. The engineer who was with me was stunned into silence, finally said he didn't think it could happen. He got right on the computer and couldn't find any other instance. So now I've got two lawsuits on my hands. The landowner's probably going to sue my company, and my insurer is no doubt going to sue the manufacturer of the windmill, who in turn will sue some poor subcontractor. God, I hate litigation."

"Are you okay?"

"Every time I picture what happened, I practically go into shock again. It feels like a bad omen." She laughed shakily. "And I don't even believe in omens."

But the word omen came back to her with new meaning an hour later. After checking on Lacey and then changing into sweats, she was prepared to run back downstairs to the lap pool when she heard what sounded like crying from the far end of the hallway. Not Lacey's cry. Astrid's?

Astrid's door was slightly ajar. She pushed it open. There was Steve, sitting on Astrid's bed, holding her in his arms, stroking her hair, and murmuring something. They didn't seem to hear her.

As she pushed the door wide, she asked in an acid voice, "What's going on here? What in hell are you two doing?"

Steve shot to his feet, his freckled skin blotchy embarrassment. He held his arms wide to show they were empty.

"It's not what you think."

"What do I think?"

He ignored that. "Astrid's father was just found guilty of fraud. He's going to prison."

"I'm sorry to hear it, but do you have to be in her bedroom? Do you have to hold her in your arms?"

The rest of the evening was a mess, full of tears, accusations, and protests. Astrid stayed upstairs, presumably crying herself to sleep. Steve followed Lexie around the kitchen as she poured herself a glass of Prosecco and found something to eat, reassuring her there was nothing going on, Astrid's father really was going to prison, and he was only trying to comfort a young girl who was broken-hearted and all alone in a strange country.

Lexie believed him but for a few hours was too sore to say so. By the time she told him about the broken windmill in Iowa and he expressed the proper shock and gratitude for her escape from death, they were almost back to normal.

31

Heads Up
Friday, April 6, 2012

Friday evening, Dave was in civilian clothes. He looked vaguely uncomfortable. "Thanks for letting me come over, guys."

Steve led Dave into the library. Lexie walked in behind them with a tray of mixed nuts and mini pretzels, closing the door behind her.

"What'll you have?" Steve asked, walking to the wet bar and pouring himself a scotch.

Dave took an armchair near the enormous limestone fireplace. "I'm off duty, so a beer is fine. In the bottle, if you don't mind. And the fire feels good."

They talked a few minutes about the weather, always a safe subject in Fort Wayne. It had been unseasonably warm in March and now, in April, was yoyo-ing between unseasonably cold and unseasonably warm. Every living thing was confused. Most of the bipeds had allergies.

When there was a lull in the conversation, Dave looked around. "Is anybody else in the house?"

"Just Astrid," Steve said, "upstairs with Lacey. Henry, of course. Everybody else has left. The house is locked up for the night."

"I'm sure you've guessed why I'm here."

"Sheila's absence is a big clue," Steve said wryly. "It's about Doreen's murder, right?"

"And Digby's."

"Digby's?" Lexie asked.

"Afraid so."

Steve walked over to his humidor. "I have some new Opus X Arturo Fuente cigars. Under the circumstances, would I be in danger of a bribery charge if I offered you one?"

Dave laughed. "I can't be bribed, you know that, but I think you can be charged with changing the subject." He held out his hand. "Bring it on. What did these beauties set you back?"

"Fifty-five dollars each, so enjoy."

"Last month you smoked one at the Old Stogie Club, if I remember right," Dave said with a chiding smile. "You didn't share it then."

"So maybe I *am* trying to bribe you."

Dave snorted.

"So, don't hold us in suspense," Steve said, taking the armchair on the other side of the fireplace. Lexie snuggled into a corner of the sofa so she could watch the fire and both men's faces.

"The way we typically start a murder investigation is with the question of benefit. Usually it's the spouse, sometimes a teenaged child, who benefits -- concealing a debt or a girlfriend, preventing an expensive divorce, maintaining control, speeding up an inheritance, something like that. But that doesn't seem to be the case with either Digby or Soren-Kawzy."

"Just so we're clear," Lexie said, "I know something about Digby's murder -- more than the newspapers have reported. My literary agent told me."

"I heard about that."

"You did?"

"Trent . . . ."

"Trent Senser," Lexie said.

"I forgot his last name. Anyway, he told me."

"Ah."

"Since then I've talked to your New York agent, Mrs. Lazare, and her investigator."

"And?" Lexie asked, riveted to hear what was coming next.

"The investigator swears he had nothing to do with Digby's death, and there's nothing to suggest he did, but the idea of a conspiracy isn't off the table."

"And the conspirators would be who?"

Dave closed his eyes a second too long. "I'll get to that."

"Why do you think there's any conspiracy at all?"

"Benefit. Mrs. Lazare was gleeful he's dead because of the way he demeaned her agency. If you look at the Digby case the way my Captain does, you benefitted too, Lexie. Your book sales took a hit a few days after Digby's review was published."

"His death doesn't increase them."

"That's a matter of dispute. The national notoriety has boosted the sales of every book he trashed. I've done my research."

"I didn't know that. . . . But you can't possibly think I had anything to do with his death."

"The Captain's theory is not that you personally ice-picked him but hired somebody to do it."

"Oh, for heaven's sake, that's crazy. And what about Doreen?"

"According to her supporters and your step-mother -- ."

"My step-mother?" Lexie exclaimed. "She's been talking to you? She has her own ax to grind, you know."

"She called me and even came down to the station. She said her niece was a thorn in your side. If I look at it from her point of view, Soren-Kawzy was using extortion to get you to unionize. Getting rid of her means you get peace and a non-union shop at the Scrapyard."

Lexie's heart was beating just a little faster. "You've known me for almost twenty years, Dave. Do you really think I'd kill anybody, let alone my step-mother's niece just so she'd quit picketing the Scrapyard? You know I've never shied away from a battle and I fight them fair and square . . . and I've won the battles without murdering anyone."

"No, I don't think you're a murderer. That's why I'm here, off the record, as a friend. But the Captain is eager to believe you would kill an enemy -- again, not personally but through someone you hired."

"Same reason I'd want to kill Digby, I suppose."

"The same. Furthermore, the murders are eerily similar. We tried to keep the significant details secret, but with the interviews I've had to do, they're leaking out, so you might as well hear it from me. A Tarot card was found at both murder scenes: the Fool beside a computer at Digby's house and the Chariot nailed to a tree in the woods where Soren-Kawzy died. In both cases, there were also enigmatic messages left behind: "Fool, you'll never hurt anyone again" on Digby's computer, "Now Your a Stakeholder" on the flag stuck in that poor woman's neck." Dave did not explain the spelling of "Your." "For that reason, we think there's a connection between the two murders, odd as that seems. From all I can find out, the two victims never met each other in life, had nothing in common -- other than hurting you, Lexie."

Steve, agitated, stood up and began to pace. "Tell me about the Tarot card nailed to a tree."

"As I said, it was the Chariot, a card that a fortune teller turned up when Soren-Kawzy had a reading."

"Astrid told us about that," Lexie said. "She mentioned that it was upside down."

"That's the way it was on the tree too."

"You do know, Dave, I didn't attend that occult party the girls went to. I've never touched a Tarot card in my life."

Dave said nothing.

Steve glanced at Lexie. "Time to tell him about the messages you've been getting."

Dave sat up a little straighter. "What messages?"

Lexie got up from the sofa. "I'll go get them. They're in my cubby off the kitchen."

When she returned to the library, she opened a manila folder and began laying out the messages on the big round library table near the curtained window. There were seven, all written on white half sheets, folded in quarters, childishly printed in pencil.

Dave walked over to look at them. "Did you keep a record of when and where they were found and who found them?"

Lexie picked up the first one. "I wrote my own little

handwritten note on the bottom of each. Take this first note: 'January 26, 2012, Jean found on her car seat when she got home from work; gave it to me the next day.' It reads:

> I dream of Jeanie
> with the light brown hair,
> but it's her boss
> who is so fair.

Sort of clever." Lexie smiled grimly. "And very strange, don't you think?"

"Not signed," Dave said. "And not threatening. Furthermore, the handwriting -- I should say, the printing -- is obviously disguised, so anybody could have written it."

"Steve found the next one in February on his office door; it has my name at the top so that -- I'm guessing here -- he didn't get confused and think it was for him. Phyllis found the next one on her porch chair, also in February and again with my name at the top. Then Todd found this one on my car, which was in the garage, on February 29. Next, Ivy found this one about a dove on the courtyard gate on March 2. Then we get to this one, also mentioning a dove, which Plato took out of his duffel, saying he'd found it on the auto gate on March 19 before one of my training sessions. Five days later -- the day after Doreen was murdered, you'll notice -- Todd found this one nailed to the oak tree by the creek. In this little baggy is the nail that was used and a movie ticket stub we found on the ground."

Dave rubbed his chin. "No Tarot cards?"

"None."

"I suppose a lot of people have handled these notes without worrying about fingerprints."

"Never thought about it."

"The nail too?"

"Yes."

He picked up the nail to examine it. "A common roofing nail. Just like the one that pinned the Tarot card to the tree where

Soren-Kawzy was found. And like the one inserted into the end of the stake."

"If it's a common roofing nail, that doesn't say much, does it?" Steve asked.

"Maybe. Maybe not. I'll bet you have nails like this in your garage. I know I do."

"Probably." Steve said. "Todd keeps tons of stuff in a little workshop he's put together on the side of the last bay, but I don't go in there much."

Dave looked at Lexie. "Why didn't you tell me about these notes a couple months ago when the first one showed up?"

"What would I have told you? Somebody's leaving me mash notes? Not a police matter, you would have said."

"Possibly. But now, in light of what's happened, they make it look like you have a stalker." He pointed to the note Plato found. "Who's your trainer again?"

"Plato Jones. He runs Plato's Studio in a strip mall on Dupont."

"I'm acquainted with him. You think he might have written it?"

"Unlikely. But Ivy thought he wrote the one she found because of all the misspellings. If you know Plato, you know he's not the sharpest tool in the drawer, especially with regard to the King's English. His malapropisms are so entertaining I've thought of collecting them for a bedside book of humor."

"I'd like to take all this stuff back to the station, if you don't mind."

Lexie hesitated. "I want copies for my own records."

"I'll make sure you get them."

When they were again seated, after an awkward silence, Steve asked, "So where do we go from here?"

"I'll hold off the Chief as long as I can, but if he demands that I ask for your phone or bank records -- ."

"Bank records?" Steve was flushed with anger.

"He'd be looking for big cash withdrawals, payoffs to hired guns."

"You're kidding."

155

"Afraid not. Anyway, if he demands records or a handwriting sample or a statement or something else, I'll give you a heads up."

"A heads up! Thanks," Lexie murmured. "I think."

32

Flipping Liver
Saturday, April 7, 2012

Plato was in a back room of his fitness studio with a salesman hawking the latest protein supplements when he got a call from a man whose name he recognized, Detective Powers. Plato was a tough guy with marshmallow innards. Panicked, he slipped into the unisex restroom and locked the door so the salesman couldn't hear anything. "What's this about?" he whispered.

The detective answered the question without really saying anything. He just wanted to talk to Plato about the weekend. Which weekend? The detective was vague. Plato looked at his hand, still in a cast. Had the guy he floored at the Breakpoint Bar complained to the cops? In the emergency room, he'd explained that his hand got broken when his Kawasaki fell over as he was repairing it, but Petra had heard the bar rumors and, furious, recited them daily as evidence of his stupidity. She was sure he'd be arrested.

Then came the clincher. If Plato didn't come down to the station within the hour, the detective said, a squad car would come to Plato's Studio to pick him up. That would be bad publicity, wouldn't it? What would his girlfriend think about that? Plato was sure he felt his poor liver flop to the other side of his body. He agreed to be there in an hour.

He told the salesman to leave, then called in Lenny, one of his trainers, to help him cut off the cast. Plato whimpered like a baby at the pain. Then the box-cutter slipped and he ended up with a gash that wouldn't stop bleeding. He wanted to kill Lenny. He filled a towel with blood, then poured superglue on the gash and wrapped his hand in strips Lenny tore from a t-shirt.

His hand hurt so bad he couldn't change from his workout clothes, so he slipped on a pair of nylon pants and a sweatshirt. Obviously he couldn't drive his Kawasaki, so, since the studio was largely empty anyway, he ordered Lenny to drive him to the police station. Lenny was sworn to secrecy. Petra could know nothing about this visit.

The interview was a nightmare. To Plato, Detective Powers looked like Darth Vader.

"You assaulted a guy named Dicky Dickson, isn't that right? At the Breakpoint Bar around 1 am on Saturday, March 24, 2012."

"No. I wasn't even there."

"You sure?"

"I'd remember that. I was home with my girlfriend."

"So Dicky is lying."

"He's a piece of shit."

"You do know him then. But you aren't friends."

Plato didn't know what to say.

"Your hand was broken, I hear. You got emergency treatment at St. Joe."

"Yeah, but only because I cut my hand on my motorcycle. It wasn't broken."

"What's that bloody stuff wrapped around your hand?"

"Just reopened the old cut an hour ago."

"Is there a cast under there?"

"No. You wanna see?"

"Yah."

Wincing, Plato unwrapped the stained bandage and held out his hand. He let out a little yelp of pain when the detective grabbed his fingers and twisted just a little.

Detective Powers looked at Plato's eyes instead of his hand. "That cut looks new."

"It's the old one, I swear."

"What's your relationship with Alexandra Wright?"

Plato was flummoxed at the change in subject. "I'm her trainer. I go to her house five afternoons a week. I designed her workout room. You should see it."

"I have. You look a little sick, by the way. Why that yellow color?"

Plato's head was spinning. "My doc says I got a liver problem from the supplements I'm taking. Heavy metals, he says. You ever heard of heavy metals?"

"How's business at your fitness place?"

Plato's liver, like a gigged fish, flopped over again. What was all this about? He couldn't keep up. "Great. Never better. I'm always looking for investors, though." He tried to smile. "You looking for a place to put your money?"

"What's your impression of Mrs. Wright?"

Why didn't Darth Vader ever stay on the subject? "She's a rich lady. I like her."

"What's Mrs. Wright pay you?"

"Fifty dollars an hour, works out to about a thousand a month."

"She pays you how -- weekly, monthly?"

"Monthly."

"In cash or by check?"

"By check. But she just gave me a big advance so I can cover a few bills."

"Check or cash?"

"Cash."

"Why cash?"

"Because . . . ." He didn't want to admit his bank account was overdrawn and a check would have been eaten up. "Because I asked for cash."

"How much?"

"Ten thousand."

The detective whistled. "That's quite an advance."

"Mrs. Wright is *magnananimous*. You have to give her that."

"You call it an advance. An advance on what?"

159

"The usual. Helping her get rid of the *postpartnumb* baby tummy. Get back to her old self."

The detective smiled. "Nothing else? Nothing special?"

"You mean, like I'm shagging her or something like that? She's not my type, I can tell you that, and I don't think she'd go for a little sumpin' sumpin' on the side. All I want is to keep working for her."

"What was your relationship with Doreen Soren-Kawzy?"

"Who?"

"How about Alastair Digby?"

"Digby? I've heard that name. What's he look like?"

"About five-seven, slender, sixtyish, a pencil mustache, horn-rimmed glasses. Kind of an English accent. Always dresses like a professor about to give a lecture. Sometimes carries an ebony cane he doesn't need. Smokes a big white pipe; the bowl is carved into a man's face."

Plato snapped his fingers. "I'll bet that's the guy who hangs out at The Cornjerker. He tells great stories. Haven't seen him in months, though."

"You hang out at The Cornjerker?"

Plato flushed. "Not often. I'm not a fag, of course, but I know a lot of them. Fags aren't *social leopards*, not in my mind. Sometimes I go with my friend Lenny. Good for business, that's for sure, so I hand out my card. Get a lot of customers from there. Thanks to Hollywood, the pretty ones like to stay in shape."

Plato thought the interview would never end. By the time he was allowed to leave, he was vaguely aware that Darth Vader suspected him of something much worse than clocking Dicky Dickson. He hoped it wasn't being a fag.

33

Surprise Party
Friday, April 13, 2012

Friday night, Lexie surprised Steve with a birthday party at the Gretna Green clubhouse. He'd been gone for two days, looking at property in Hilton Head, so Trent had been able to decorate the entry hall and main dining room without tipping off the birthday boy.

The theme was Monopoly in honor of Steve's profession as a property developer. Trent had devised a game, on the order of Bingo but involving Monopoly squares, the winner to receive a three-month membership in the Gretna Green Golf Club. Second prize was a season's pass to the TinCaps' baseball games, another of Steve's passions. Third prize was an Embassy Theatre gift certificate, suggested by Lexie. Guests were instructed not to bring gifts, but if they did, only a joke gift.

The band was in full swing, pounding out rock-and-roll hits personally selected by Trent and Cricket. The lead singer was a plump, pretty blonde who looked and sounded a lot like Stevie Nicks. Lexie had been a little doubtful about a group named the Roach Masters, but Trent assured her she'd like them. And she did. Even so, she kept an eye on the musicians, adorned with various arrangements of facial hair and punk hats, just to be sure no roaches of any kind crawled out of their pockets.

The birthday cakes Trent designed in collaboration with

Courtney's Bakery were spectacular too. One depicted the 19th hole with a tall sugar flag on top, surrounded by bite-sized golf balls and beer mugs -- all edible, of course. The other was topped with a sugar Monopoly board surrounded by edible tokens, dice, and cards. Even with two cakes, Lexie wasn't sure there was enough to feed a hundred people.

The dining room had been cleared for dancing. Little round bistro tables hugged the perimeter, without chairs so the crowd would keep moving. The bar was open, keeping four bartenders working non-stop. One table in the foyer was piled high with joke gifts for Steve; the other was loaded with goody bags for the guests.

Best of all, Steve was definitely surprised. He kept hugging Lexie and patting Trent on the back and then circulating again like the good host he was. He circled and circled, growing more rather than less animated as the evening wore on. Trying to stuff down her irritation, Lexie watched Astrid, who was wearing her blond hair up with tendrils framing her face and a skintight electric blue cocktail dress, hovering at his elbow, moving as he moved, occasionally running to the bar to refresh his scotch and water. Apparently Astrid had recovered from her sorrow over her father's imprisonment.

When Ivy introduced her companion, Matt Beasley, a baby-faced man a few inches shorter than his date, Lexie hid her surprise. Ivy had never mentioned a boyfriend. "Matt's in my class at IPFW. He's an accounting whiz."

Matt smiled shyly. "I've heard a lot about you, Mrs. Wright. Ivy's learned so much at Royce Enterprises, she thinks you're the eighth wonder of the world. Especially that book of yours."

Lexie made a pooh-poohing gesture. "Not everyone agrees about that book, as you may have heard."

"Oh, you can't listen to the critics. This is a great party, by the way. Maybe I shouldn't admit it, but I'm hoping to win first prize. I love golf but on my salary I can't afford a membership, so that would make my year." He laughed. "Or at least the summer. But I've never won anything in my life, so . . . ."

"Well, then, I hope you do win, Matt. Have you met my

husband yet?"

"We're just making our way over to him," Ivy said. "We'll follow the nanny's bright blue dress and then see if we can push her aside long enough to squeeze in an introduction."

My thoughts exactly. Try pushing the nanny in the bright blue dress out the door, would you? "I don't think Astrid's found a boyfriend yet. You have a brother, Matt? A cousin?" *An American father who's rich and important?*

"I have two brothers, both married, but I've got a friend I could set her up with."

She might prefer the married ones. As Lexie watched Ivy and Matt make their way toward Steve, she felt an arm around her shoulder. "Oh, Dover." She gave him a peck on the cheek. "How's the expectant father?"

"Well, my breasts are swelling and I've gained a few pounds. Other than that, just fine."

They both laughed.

"Is that a new hairdo, Dover?"

His green eyes twinkled. "*Haircut,* please. Men have haircuts -- even pregnant ones. Long hair was okay when I was a school counselor, but as the Club's golf pro, I think a military look is convincing evidence of my dedication to sport. What do you think?"

"I'm convinced." Lexie looked around. "Where did your lovely wife go?"

"Jean's in the ladies' room. She wanted me to find you and ask you to join her."

"Is she sick?"

"No. She just wants a private moment."

The private moment, it turned out, was about Ivy, so to be sure they weren't overheard, they retreated to Steve's office and shut the door.

"I won't keep you long," Jean said, turning on a table lamp, "but remember when I said I was going to do a little background research on Ivy?"

Lexie nodded.

"She never finished her degree at IU."

"Are you sure?"

"Nine credits short."

"Do you know why?"

"No. But that's not important. She lied on her résumé."

"Maybe that's why she's taking night classes at IPFW."

"Maybe."

"If you'd known she hadn't finished her bachelor's when you interviewed her, would it have made any difference?"

Jean sighed in exasperation. "No. But that's not the point, is it? She lied and then has the nerve to check out everybody else."

Lexie sighed too. "Ivy's the least of my worries right now. If she's performing the way you want -- and from my point of view she is -- then I say forget about it. At least for now."

Jean stood up. "Did you notice Astrid's clinging to your handsome husband like a limpet?"

"I forget. What's a limpet?"

"A snail. You want me to take her out?"

"Out how? Just walk her outside or something else entirely?"

Jean laughed. "I haven't decided. If she's here, who's taking care of Lacey?"

"Sadie. She volunteers every time Astrid's got time off and we're occupied."

A knock on the door startled them both. It was Ivy, of all people, summoning Lexie back to the party. The prizes were about to be awarded.

And then the unthinkable happened. Trent announced, with a rim shot from the Roach Masters' drummer, that Dave Powers won the golf membership. Lexie watched from the sidelines as Steve and Dave hastily conferred with Trent. Looking awkward and confused, Trent announced that a mistake had been made and the first prize winner was really -- rim shot -- Matt Beasley. Matt looked like he'd just seen the Archangel Gabriel. Dave looked like he wanted to disappear. Steve -- his face almost as red as his hair -- looked flustered.

Trent recovered enough to award the second and third prizes

as if nothing strange had happened. But the rest of the guests whispered as if trying to figure out the meaning of the final blackout scene in *The Sopranos*.

At a signal from Trent, the Roach Masters began playing Stevie Nicks' version of *Fall from Grace,* a song Lexie had never liked. With a sinking heart, she knew what that awkward scene with Dave signified. Awarding anything to him would look like a deliberately orchestrated bribe in the guise of a random lottery ticket. People went to jail for things like that.

So Captain Schmoll still thinks I conspired to murder two people. I have indeed fallen from grace.

Tomorrow she would call Duke Simmons, the best criminal defense lawyer in northeast Indiana. She'd consulted him before but never on her own behalf.

34

Traps
Sunday, April 15, 2012

Steve and Lexie spent all of Sunday with Lacey. They'd taken her with them to The Chapel for the eleven o'clock service, where the nursery attendant reported that she slept peacefully the whole time. Then they ate lunch at Biaggi's, where Lacey was wide awake but didn't fuss. At home, however, Lacey was anything but peaceful. She wanted her bottle; then she had gas and needed burping; she couldn't fall asleep. She cried for no reason. In between walking Lacey around the house to soothe her, Steve and Lexie snatched a few minutes here and there to watch the last of the Nick and Nora movies and play cribbage.

Their idyll ended late in the afternoon, as they were snacking on leftover roast chicken. Astrid, wearing a fetching hot-pink track suit, suddenly walked into the family room. She looked like she'd been crying. Even with red eyes and Heidi braids, she was stunning.

"What's the matter?" Steve asked, standing up but checking the impulse to hug her. "You look like you've been crying."

"I have a favor to ask," she sniffled.

"Shoot."

"I just got off of Skype with my brother. Mamma's having a breakdown and Sven wants me to fly home for a week or two."

"Not a problem," Lexie said, trying not to sound as pleased as she felt. "Sadie will fill in."

"Sadie can't clean the house and take care of Lacey too," Steve said.

"We'll figure that out, but if Astrid needs to see her family at this difficult time, then we have to let her do it."

Astrid sat down on the edge of a chair and wiped her eyes. "There's a problem."

"There is?" Steve asked.

"I don't have any money for an airplane ticket."

"Why not?" Lexie exclaimed. *We pay you well and you live free here, so how can you have no money?* "Don't you have a savings account?"

Astrid shook her head. "And I've reached the limit on my credit card."

"Which is what?"

"Two thousand dollars."

Lexie was ready to scream. "What did you spend all that money on?" *How many spandex shorts and cocktail dresses are in your closet?*

Steve signaled Lexie to stop, then turned to Astrid. "But your parents have money."

Astrid, shaking her head, choked on a sob. "All of it went to lawyers. Now there's a big fine to pay. Sven says Mamma has lost the house. She's trying to find an apartment and a job."

"I thought the much-vaunted safety net meant nothing like that could happen in the socialist paradise known as Sweden," Lexie said acidly.

Astrid looked puzzled. Steve looked angry. "This is no time to make her feel worse." He turned his attention to the distraught girl. "Go upstairs. My wife and I will talk about this, but I promise we'll find a solution. Don't you worry about it."

Once Astrid left the room, Lexie gave her husband a searching look. "I'm confused, Steve. You want her to go home to see her family, or you don't?"

"If we work out the care of Lacey, sure."

She looked dubious. "So what's the solution you promised?"

He gave it a few seconds' thought. "You gave Plato an advance. Why not give her one too, big enough to pay off her credit card and buy a round-trip ticket to Sweden?"

Lexie snorted. "Why am I always the sucker?"

"Then I'll do it."

Lexie got up to pour herself a glass of Prosecco and a tumbler of scotch for him. "You realize that what's mine is yours and what's yours is mine, so whatever money we give her comes out of the same pot."

"Then why did you call yourself the sucker?"

Time for a different tactic. "Just feeling angry and a little sorry for myself. Maybe a tad jealous."

"Of what?"

"You have a soft spot for that girl, admit it."

"Not that kind of soft spot." He grinned. "Besides, if I had the wrong kind of feelings for her, 'soft' wouldn't be the right word, would it?"

She laughed. "Here's my proposal."

"Oh, God," Steve groaned. "Why am I married to somebody smarter than me?"

"We buy her a one-way ticket and we give her enough severance pay that her credit card is working again."

"One-way ticket, you say."

"That's what I say. Sadie is just itching for the nanny job. And Phyllis will find us another maid in a week."

They nif-naffed back and forth awhile before Steve was convinced. He got up to kiss his wife. "The solution is so reasonable, how can I argue about it?"

"You can't. I'll even be so *magnananimous* -- Plato's brilliant word -- that I'll let you go upstairs alone and tell Astrid what we've decided. You can say your good-byes without me." She looked at her watch. "Fifteen minutes should do it."

Grinning again, Steve stretched out on the sofa. "Woman, I may not be as smart as you, but this fox don't fall into no traps hidden in the ground, so you do it. Otherwise, I'll be eating my own foot off to get out."

"Fine. *I'll* be back in fifteen."

35

Suspects
Friday, April 27, 2012

Dave Powers was frustrated. He was making progress on the Barrel and Ice Pick Murders, measured by the thickness of the binders he'd assembled, but he had no answers.

If Captain Schmoll was right that Alexandra Wright had orchestrated two murders -- revenge for a bad book review and a hostile demonstration at the Scrapyard -- then two possible suspects stood out.

Just repeating to himself the Captain's theories about motive made him want to laugh and cry at the same time. In the end, the bad book review didn't seem to have hurt sales much, and the Kekionga demonstration lasted ten hours at most and generated no significant publicity. He knew in his gut that Lexie wasn't the kind of person to kill anyone. Even if Captain Moonpie didn't have the same gut instinct, couldn't he see that in these circumstances murder was so disproportionate to the offense as to make no sense? Who risked a fortune, a marriage, and new baby to get rid of two losers?

Still, he took another look at Drago. He'd gotten a promotion. Was that a reward for killing two of Lexie's enemies?

But his alibis checked out. He knew Doreen but not Alastair. He didn't misspell "you're." Nobody other than Buck Tiddly had a bad word to say about him. He hadn't gotten into any trouble since Rolie Royce died. He ran a clean Scrapyard. He lived in a highly respectable neighborhood with a working wife and two little boys. Neighbors described him as quiet but helpful when needed. His wife had attended the Tarot card party before Doreen died but was believable when she denied meeting Doreen before or knowing anything about Tarot other than what she saw that night.

And Drago -- presumably with Lexie's approval -- readily handed over the SD cards from the Yard's cameras. All they showed the night after the demonstration was the occasional passage of a vehicle on the lightly trafficked Old Canal Street. None of the vehicles looked like Drago's or his wife's. The film was grainy and dark and the camera range didn't include the woods where Doreen's body was found, so in the end the film didn't tell much.

Next was Plato Jones. A character on the make but without the brains to succeed, possibly a little iffy as to sexual identification, Plato was acquainted with Alastair but didn't know who Doreen was. Petra Kuzmin, his girlfriend, did, but like Lucy Bott, she wasn't helpful.

Something was fishy about his wounded hand, but what? Maybe Plato removed the cast that St. Joe confirmed it had placed on his hand so he could deny he'd broken it in a bar fight with Dicky Dickson. Plato had a record, after all, for several earlier offenses and might have been afraid of jail time. It would be just like a bozo like Plato Jones to think that showing up for a police interview without a cast would collapse the case against him. Dave laughed to himself. Plato could have saved himself the trouble of cutting off the cast if only he'd known that Dicky had no intention of filing a complaint or testifying against his old drinking buddy.

Though, as far as Dave knew, Plato had never been implicated in anything as serious as murder, still he had a record for violent offenses. And then there was the little matter of the ten thousand in cash, supposedly an advance on future services at fifty dollars an hour. Was fifty an hour really the going rate for a fitness instructor? And why would Lexie pay for ten months' of services in advance? Plato couldn't be trusted to do anything he promised to do in the next hour, let alone for the next ten months. Until he got Lexie's bank records, however, Dave couldn't confirm Plato's story.

And then there was Plato's printing of the legend on the flag: NOW YOUR A STEAK HOLDER. "Steak" was so funny Dave laughed out loud and asked Plato how often he held a steak while eating it. But he couldn't ignore the fact that Plato was the only witness -- or suspect -- to get "you're" wrong. Did it mean anything or not?

Finally, he couldn't stop thinking about the anonymous notes Lexie had started getting in January. Was there some guy in her orbit who was secretly in love with her? Would he murder to impress or protect her? Lexie seemed genuinely to have no clue.

Anybody could have printed the notes. The writing was obviously disguised. All were left in places with public access, except possibly the one Plato took out of his duffel, depending on whether he told the truth about finding it on the auto gate.

The note that actually bothered him the most was the one Todd Fingerhutt found nailed to the oak tree the afternoon of Doreen's murder. Dave had sent the original notes out to the fingerprint expert, but he found a copy in his binder and read it again:

> I guard the nest
> of my little dove
> so she can rest
> in the arms of love

Was someone confessing he'd killed Doreen to protect Lexie? Was he a free-lancer or had he been paid by Lexie? Or could Lexie herself have put the note on the tree to deflect attention? Maybe she wrote all of the poems to make Steve jealous or cause the police to chase phantom rabbits. Was that level of deviousness and cruelty even possible? He hated himself for such ugly thoughts, but as a detective he had no choice. No one, not even his gracious friend, could be struck from his list.

Dave began filling out warrant requests for Drago's and Plato's cell phone and bank records. He already had their fingerprints. Then, with a certain amount of reluctance, he filled out the same forms for Lexie.

Before he left work, he once more returned to the Scrapyard film, which he'd already studied a dozen times. Something on it caught his attention: a light-colored pickup -- apparently a Dodge Ram -- heading toward the woods and then a couple hours later heading back the way it came. On each door was lettering that read "BBB Enterprises," though he could find no such business in any directory. The bed appeared empty except for a flagpole sticking over the end -- a pole that had disappeared on the return trip. The truck was heavily dented on the passenger side, the driver's side headlamp was on low-beam, and it was the only vehicle that traveled both directions that night. It looked like there were two people in the truck; the passenger seemed to be wearing huge eyeglasses. He wished he could read the license plate.

36

Dark Corners
Friday, May 4, 2012

A little after noon on Friday, Lexie, Jean, Jessica, Trent and Cricket returned to the Brown Hotel from their private heritage tour of Louisville, all but Jean a little buzzed from the premium bourbon tastings at the Jim Beam Distillery.   Steve, Ed, and Dover exited the van at the Louisville Slugger Museum, where they planned to immerse themselves in baseball memorabilia until closing time. Trent knew he was supposed to stay with the men, but baseball was so boring. Whatever the women were going to do next, he was sure he'd like it better than standing around the world's biggest bat, trying to think of manly things to say about it.

Lexie was vaguely uneasy at the absence of Dave and Sheila. It was like attending a family reunion where one sibling was absent. The absent one became the focus of attention.

"I'm sorry, we can't go with you after all," Sheila said a week before departure for the Kentucky Derby. The reason for her visit was to discuss the progress she'd made on Summit Academy, the private college preparatory school she and Lexie planned to open in the Fall, but once their business had been concluded, they always detoured from the professional to the personal. "Dave says that under the circumstances, it would look . . . ."

"Corrupt?" Lexie asked, dismayed at Sheila's hesitation. She supplied the harshest word she could think of. "Like a bribe?"

Sheila shook her head, her glistening curls bouncing, her beautiful brown eyes embarrassed. "Just wrong, that's all. Captain Moonpie would have a fit."

"Captain Moonpie?"

"I shouldn't have said that. It's Dave's nickname for his boss, Captain Schmoll. He's been ragging Dave about going too easy on you. I know this is last minute, so if there's a penalty for canceling our reservations, we insist on reimbursing you."

Lexie waved her hand dismissively. "Not a problem. It'll be easy to find someone else who wants to go . . . Trent and Cricket maybe. But you don't know how sad this makes me."

"And worried too, I'm sure. Probably I'm speaking out of turn here, but just so you know, Dave doesn't suspect you of anything. For the sake of keeping Captain Schmoll off his back, though, he has to look like he's treating you like everybody else."

"In my opinion, a court order to cough up bank records isn't going easy on me. . . . I suppose I should be glad Captain Moonpie doesn't have the power to put me on the rack. I feel like a criminal and I haven't even done anything."

Lexie had handed the problem of records over to Duke Simmons, a criminal defense lawyer she knew well, but still she couldn't put aside the disgusting, unfounded suspicion she now labored under. Duke urged her to hire a private investigator, giving her the name of an ex-FBI man whom she would interview next week.

Seated in the Grand Lobby of the Brown Hotel in Louisville with her entourage, Lexie did her best to look bright and cheerful, as if focused on them instead of herself. Though only half-listening, she kept her eyes on Trent, who had never met a silence he couldn't fill.

"My goodness, girls, you all look like southern belles," Trent exclaimed. "I never dressed grand southern ladies before, but I love it. So Fifties, the gathered skirts and floral prints, the mile-high stilettos. Wouldn't it be fun to put on a charity ball in Fort Wayne with an antebellum theme?"

Jessica laughed. "And just what charity would fit that theme,

Trent? Heat Stroke Awareness? Swamp Fever Advocacy? And how about the dress code? I can see it now: Black Tie -- Pith Helmet and Mosquito Net optional."

"Well, then," Trent responded, not to be deterred, "a Kentucky Derby party at the Club for the poor schlubs" -- laughter -- "who can't make it to Louisville in person."

"Now that's not a bad idea, Trent," Lexie said. "In fact it's a good one. Big-screen TVs, mint juleps, beautiful hats, private betting. It could be fun. I'm sure Steve would love it." She wanted to support Trent so he didn't think he was under judgment. The evening after Sheila cancelled, she asked if he and Cricket wanted to go to the Kentucky Derby. He looked unexpectedly tentative. "I realize it's short notice, of course," she added.

"It's not that."

"Well, what is it?"

"Mrs. Wright, I have to confess something."

"What?"

"After you hear me out, you might want to retract the invitation."

"I doubt it, but go ahead."

"I told Detective Powers about what Mrs. Lazare said about finding Mr. Digby dead and getting revenge without even trying."

Lexie put her hand over her mouth, not sure what to say next.

After a long pause, Trent soldiered on. "Lucy says he'd never have connected you with Digby if I hadn't said what I did."

"Well, that isn't true. Dave found my name on the list of authors Digby had trashed, so the connection was easy for him to find. The revenge part, however, ..."

"I know, I know. I should have kept my mouth shut."

"Talking about revenge might have planted a seed in Dave's mind, I suppose, but it's such a natural, especially in view of Doreen's death, he'd probably have thought of it anyway." Lexie patted Trent's knee. "It's okay. You were just telling the truth and you couldn't foresee the consequences. I'm not afraid of the facts."

"You don't hate me?"

Lexie laughed. "Of course I don't hate you. Now, how about

the Derby? If you come along, you can inspect all the dresses you selected for us before we leave the hotel for Churchill Downs, make sure we meet your impeccable standards. It'll be fun and no point letting a valuable reservation go to waste."

He hugged her. "Divine. I can't wait to tell Cricket. I'll have to find something for her to wear too."

Lexie's reverie about Sheila and Trent was interrupted by Jean, marveling at the magnificent hotel lobby. "The gold chandeliers, the arcade effect, the paneled walls and ceiling -- I've never seen anything like this before," Jean said. "But I'm getting tired. I need a nap."

"Before we scatter, let's talk about the race tomorrow," Jessica said. "Has everybody decided what horse to bet on?"

"I don't understand win, place, and show," Trent said. "And what are odds exactly?"

"I can explain that," Jessica said.

Lexie abruptly stood up. "Why don't we all go up to my suite so we can order some lunch and get comfortable while Jessica illuminates the dark corners of horse racing for us? Jean, you can nap on my bed. I've got a little gift for each of you just in case it's cooler than expected -- Pashmina shawls all around."

"Really?" Cricket asked. "I've never had one of those."

"With Jessica's help, we can decide what horses we're betting on," Lexie said, moving toward the elevator. "With my luck, they'll all be losers, of course, but no harm in giving it a try. That's why we came, after all."

Her friends looked stunned.

Now where had that cynicism been hiding all her life?

37

Honored Guest

Friday, May 4, 2012

Ivy was angry. Jean and Trent got to go to the Kentucky Derby with their significant others but she and Matt weren't invited. How did that happen?

She was the perfect employee, better prepared than a Girl Scout, well-dressed without being showy, polite, ready to take a bullet for Miss Royce. She always did something extra for her boss: making sure Starbucks treats were on the private plane before Miss Royce took off for one of her day trips; being her boss' eyes and ears at the Scrapyard meeting with that dreadfully plain, foul-mouthed Doreen; doing Internet research on every little thing so the recommendations she made could be backed up with facts. She looked the other way when Astrid, encased in shameless spandex and coquetry, threw herself at Mr. Wright. She never scolded Trent for his endless gossip or obsession with trivialities. She pretended Jean Pitt was as smart as she was. She had read Miss Royce's book three times and made sure everyone knew it.

Friday afternoon, while the Wrights and their friends were no doubt luxuriating at the Brown Hotel in Louisville -- which she had recommended and booked -- she once again read the letter directed to Miss Royce from her step-mother, Matilda Royce. The words were so hot she was surprised the paper didn't spontaneously combust. What would Miss Royce do when she read it?

"You're a selfish, greedy woman. . . . Your indifference to your own family resulted in the deaths of my son and niece. . . . Nobody but a person as conniving and deceitful as you could have arranged to kill both a poor old man who had the nerve to call your silly book what it is and a brave activist whose noble mission in life was to improve the lot of the workers you so harshly exploit. . . . Denying me the chance to endow a chair for studies that will benefit all of mankind is symptomatic of the narcissism that has corrupted your soul. . . . You have my sincere word that I will do everything I can to bring you to your knees, preferably in a solitary cell in prison where your false prayers will simply evaporate in darkness, heard by no one. . . . Selling the Scrapyard is the only way I will ever be able to separate my life from yours so that I can heal from the malignancy that entered my life thirty years ago when I married your cold, critical father who had the soulless temerity to favor one child over another. . . . If you think I haven't talked to the police about my suspicions, you are as usual self-deluded to the point of insanity." And on and on, three single-spaced pages written in a flourishing calligraphy without a single line-out or correction.

Ivy was filled with both shock and admiration for the vindictive rant. Shock that anyone was so foolish as to be this candid. Admiration that anyone had the guts to be this candid.

A hundred times she'd wanted to write the same thing: to her childhood friend who taunted her that she might be smart but would never pass fourth grade, to her mother for nagging her to stand up straight, to her father for having no ambition, to her older sister for her passivity, to the boy who pulled her pants down in fifth-grade recess, to her seventh grade teacher on whom she had a school-girl crush, to her high-school math teacher who wouldn't give her an A and her speech teacher who chided her for talking with her hands, to the sorority girls that never gave her a bid, to her college sweetheart who dumped her just before her fourth-year finals, to all the engaged women who rejected her proposals to hold their weddings at the Conrad Hotel, to her new apartment neighbors who ignored her in the elevator.

Fortunately, she never quite found the courage to put her most hateful thoughts into words, the way Matilda Royce just had. Words were, in the end, a bit cowardly. And, if discovered, they could hang over your head the rest of your life like the sword of Damocles. She wondered if she should show this letter to Miss Royce when she returned Monday or burn it now, pretending it had never arrived.

She walked out to the courtyard to pace and think. Was there some way she could mollify Matilda Royce? Maybe, if the old lady just had a chance to spew her venom to another person -- especially a sympathetic listener -- she'd get it out of her system and make up with her step-daughter. Not that Ivy was ever truly sympathetic, but she was good at dissembling. Somehow, she'd make things right between Miss Royce and her step-mother. Blessed are the peacemakers and all that cant. Then next year she would be the Wrights' honored guest at the Kentucky Derby.

When Ivy returned to the office, intending to call Matilda, one of the staff told her that a Belinda Cripps was holding on the line.

"Who's that?" Ivy asked. "What's she want?"

"I asked if you'd know who she was and what this was about. She wants to talk to Miss Royce. When I told her she's not here but maybe you can help, she said all right, you'd know who she was. You were her guest at a party a few weeks ago and she's calling about an overturned chariot."

"Mama Bee!" Ivy exclaimed, taking a seat at her desk. "I've been thinking about her."

38

Loyal Servant
Friday, May 4, 2012

Friday night was warm for early May. A full moon rose through wisps of clouds. The air was completely still, redolent with the earthy scent of fertile soil and new vegetation, perfect for Mama Bee's purpose. She told Ivy to wear something white and feminine. She'd bring everything they needed.

The woods where Doreen died were deserted, but wilted flowers, faded ribbons, plastic wreaths, one-eyed teddy bears, a paint-flecked statue of the Virgin Mary, and other homely treasures were still heaped against a new 55-gallon drum, an informal memorial. Mama Bee didn't know the precise location. Ivy said she didn't either, though she'd heard from office gossip that it was less than a block southeast of the Summit City Metals and Scrapyard in a little woods off of Old Canal Street.

Mama Bee was the first to arrive. Slinging a Native American woven bag across her chest, she got out of her car and let her eyes adjust to the darkness. She mentally reviewed the upcoming ritual until Ivy pulled up.

"You look very -- what's the word?" Mama Bee said. "Very royal in that white caftan. You have the posture of a queen."

After exchanging a few pleasantries, they proceeded to the drum.

"What are we doing?" Ivy asked.

"Saging the place. Getting rid of the negative energy."

"I saw that on TV once. I thought it had to be done in a closed space."

"It works anywhere. . . . What's that religious statue doing here? I don't like her watching us. Let's put her in the drum before we start." When that was done, Mama Bee continued with her explanation of the ritual of saging. "Now I've got two torches for us, both made of sage and cedar twisted together. Once they're burning, we'll move our arms clockwise, like this, and let the smoke permeate everything in the area. I'll be invoking the spirits. Then," she said, reaching into her bag for two large white chicken feathers, "we'll drive the smoke and negative energy away with these."

"What spirits are you invoking?"

Mama Bee took on the tone of a born teacher, generous with her knowledge. "The spirits in the Great Void, the spirits that animate the world. The Great Mother who gives life. The Torch-Bearer who provides the light of reason while we visit the earth. The Supreme Lover who gathers all spirits back to him for eternal bliss. The Feathered Serpent who rules them all."

"Are we asking the spirits to come to us or driving them away?"

Mama Bee was startled. *Why don't other people know this?* "We're asking the spirits to come to us and then *they* will drive away the negative energy. All the power lies in them."

"What is negative energy? Does it have a name?"

Mama Bee hid her irritation. "It doesn't have any other name. It's just what it sounds like: a bad connection between the visible and invisible. Neg-a-tive en-er-gy."

"I'm not sure I understand."

"We're going to replace the bad connection with a good one."

Ivy took a deep breath. "Should I be saying anything?"

"No. I'll do the talking. If you don't know the spirits, they'll hear you but not listen or do what you want. But you can pray silently."

"To whom? About what?"

"To anything you want -- a god you like, the force, the universe

182

-- or to nothing. Pray about driving out the negative energy."

"So why am I here? I don't mean I don't want to be here, but you could have done this by yourself, couldn't you?"

"You're a witness. At the Ostara celebration, I noticed how regal you are. I immediately recognized you from another life as a very intuitive woman, a temple priestess perhaps, ministering to mortals in need. Maybe you were even once the Corn Queen who renews life after killing the Corn King, dismembering his body, and scattering the parts in fallow fields to renew their life-producing energy."

Ivy shuddered. "Surely not that."

"We were all goddesses once, you know. With time, we will be again. You noticed, didn't you, that everything I predicted for Doreen came true."

"The upside down chariot?"

"The fire, the flaming banner in her neck, her body upside down in a barrel. I've learned she thought the woman you work for her was her enemy, but I know Mrs. Wright didn't kill Doreen."

"How do you know that?"

"I just do. Like you, I'm intuitive. I hear Doreen died without a struggle, so she must have thought the enemy who was about to kill her was her friend -- a shape-shifter. Just as I warned, she was deceived by the moon."

"You really saw all that in her cards? The fire, the banner, the shape-shifter, the upside-down finale, the sliver of moon?"

"I did." *And I'm as astonished as you are. Where did the knowledge come from?* "The negative energy we're going to get rid of is the suspicion Mrs. Wright is under and Doreen's skepticism about what her cards told her. That's why I wanted your boss here with me, but I can tell you're a loyal handmaiden, as keen for justice as I am, so you'll be her stand-in."

"I'm honored."

"When we're done, we'll have a little wine somewhere and toast the spirits. Saging is a very draining exercise. Perhaps a bite to eat too. I'm hungry."

39

Therapy
Monday, May 7, 2012

"How's Petra working out?" Steve asked the night after he and Lexie returned from the Kentucky Derby. They had swum a few laps in the pool and were now wrapped in terry cloth robes, relaxing on lounge chairs, savoring their nightly refreshment, Prosecco for Lexie, scotch for Steve.

"She's as good at her job as Plato was. The only problem is she keeps telling me about all the amber jewelry she can get from Russia. Wouldn't I like some? It's rare and a bargain to boot, very beautiful and sophisticated. She has connections, so everything I buy will be at wholesale prices. She needs money to help her family rotting in the Ukraine. Next time she'll bring over some pieces for me to look at."

"And?"

"I could have told her that at present I have no need of more jewelry, but I know that line of reasoning will just lead to more argument, so I told her that unless Trent approves, I don't buy anything, and I don't think he likes amber."

"Is that true?"

Lexie laughed. "I have no idea, but putting up a barrier to a transaction, even a false one, ends the discussion, at least for awhile. If she continues, I'll make the same threat I made to Plato."

"Has she given you a hint where Plato is?"

"No. He seems to have disappeared. . . . But there's one person who hasn't."

"Oh? Who's that?"

"Astrid."

Steve tensed. "What do you mean, Astrid?"

"Jean said she saw Astrid in Macy's today in front of a perfume counter, but when she made her way through the clutch of women watching a Christian Dior demonstration, she couldn't find the girl."

"Then she can't be sure she really saw Astrid. Isn't she in Sweden?"

"I'd have thought so. Maybe she never left or maybe she's come back."

Steve looked doubtful. "Or she's not here at all. Spotting someone in a crowd and then not finding her -- well, that sounds like Jean's having hallucinations. Or caught in a hormonal hurricane."

"Tomorrow I'll ask Todd if he saw Astrid check her luggage and go through security the day he took her to the airport. . . . You're sure there's nothing going on I should know about?"

Steve rarely got angry, but he was angry now. "Don't even go there, Lexie. There was never anything going on between us and there isn't now. Astrid Wikfelder means nothing to me. Never did, never will."

"Sorry, I shouldn't have said that."

"No, you shouldn't."

"Meanwhile, what do I do about Matilda's letter?"

Steve recovered himself. "That woman belongs in a loony bin."

"You think I should show the letter to Dave?"

"I leave that to you. . . . Or better yet, show it to Duke first. He successfully fought the release of your bank records, so he might view the letter very differently from the way we do. Maybe it's irrelevant. Or maybe it's *too* relevant."

"What do you mean?"

"You just better hope nothing happens to Matilda. Digby

condemns your book; he's dead. Doreen threatens your business; she's dead. Matilda blames you for everything that's ever gone wrong in her life and demands the sale of the Scrapyard; we don't want her dead."

It took a few minutes for Lexie to digest that statement. "My bank records wouldn't have helped Dave anyway. I took the cash I paid Plato from my office safe."

"Which in itself looks suspicious, you know."

"Suspicious or not, it's a fact. I have the contract Plato signed. I haven't paid him since and won't until he works out the terms."

Steve snorted. "What's that contract prove? That you and Plato conspired to disguise a fee for murder as merely a fee for fitness training. Dave would assume, if he knew you had that kind of cash on hand, that you'd planned Digby's and Doreen's deaths well in advance."

"I didn't pay Plato until several weeks after Digby died and a week before Doreen did."

"Which only proves how clever you are. Plato didn't get paid until he'd killed Digby. Then he got an advance on Doreen. That's how the cops will see it."

"I have enough cash and gold on hand," she protested, "to be sure we can eat and gas up our cars and pay our staff for a year in case there's another stock market crash, so ten thousand is nothing."

"Which won't endear you to the cops, who don't make in two years what you have stashed away. Or persuade them you aren't hiring goons to do your dirty work."

Lexie put her head in her hands. "How did things come to this? I can't stand it."

"So how's Sadie working out as a nanny?" he asked, knowing the answer but in need of a new subject.

Lexie smiled. "That's the brightest spot in this household. All Sadie has to do is start singing a hymn or a lullaby and Lacey looks like a subject of hypnosis, eyes soft, body relaxed, all crying replaced by cooing. Sadie's teaching her to crawl too. You should see them in the playroom, Sadie with her long skirt hiked up, Lacey in her onesies, Henry fetching balls, thinking it's an exciting game on his level."

"You realize, don't you, that Sadie was the only one to bet on the winning horse in the Derby? She gave me ten dollars to win. Sadie the Mennonite betting on a horse! Who would have thought?"

"How'd she choose I'll Have Another?"

"She said that's what her younger brother always said when he was allowed to buy an ice cream cone. 'I'll have another, please.' Ed is so mad. Though he studied all the racing sheets, he lost thousands on Bodemeister, the favorite, whereas Sadie won $150 because the horse's name reminds her of her brother."

"That's life as I know it. You can do all the planning in the world, inform yourself to the point of brain glut, be the best expert there is, and still lose."

Steve slid to one side of his lounge chair and opened his arms toward her. "Come here, woman. I think you're in need of a little therapy, and not the retail kind. Or even the talking kind. I know just what you need."

40

The Evil Eye
Wednesday, June 20, 2012

By nine o'clock, Mama Bee's guests had arrived for her summer solstice party. It was still very hot, so every woman was fanning herself with a bedazzled fan in an Indian motif created by her daughter, Ama. The guest list was the same as for her Ostara party but with two additions to replace the absent Astrid and the dead Doreen: Petra Kuzmin's cousin, Olga, a yoga instructor who was as startlingly blond as Petra was brunette; and Sheila Powers, a woman with poise and presence who looked like she was taking mental pictures of every aspect of the celebration.

Mama Bee had given Mrs. Wright a personal invitation by telephone but had been politely refused. The whole family and some of their friends would be spending ten days in Hilton Head, so it wouldn't be possible for her to attend. Mama Bee couldn't tell from Mrs. Wright's tone whether she would have accepted otherwise.

The gazebo was dazzling. White scrim fluttered gently between the pillars. Fairy lights twinkled above long divans slipcovered in white and piled with colorful cushions. An Indian trio with sitar, tabla and flute serenaded the gathering from a pile of larger cushions in one corner. Underwater lights illuminated the koi flashing about in the pond below, and incense pots burned at either end of the bridge. A buffet table offered a variety of shrimp, oysters, and crab legs, on ice, from Sam's Club. Another table offered a gigantic punch bowl of Pimm's Cup, which she informed her guests was a gin-and-lemonade drink favored by British expats in colonial India. The seafood surely justified the doubling of her fee.

This time the color theme was blue. Each guest received two gifts: a blue bindi to be pasted between her eyes and a long necklace made of woven ribbon from which hung a pendant inset with the evil eye, a talisman fashioned of concentric blue and white circles. All the women were wearing saris in shades of blue with glittering metallic trim, just as she had instructed. The younger women, most with spray tans and buff bodies, bared their midriffs and arms and pulled their hair into a bun, sometimes adding some decoration around the forehead. The older women, white as pastry, covered everything and left their hairdos and foreheads alone.

Pleased, Mama Bee listened to her guests' happy chatter and laughter about the difficulty of finding saris, wrapping them to look right, and walking in them. They kept fingering each other's evil eye and wondering what it was about. Grace Venable, a dedicated world traveler, said she knew but she'd let Mama Bee explain when the time came. Then she heard with dismay Grace laughing about Mama Bee's warning at the Ostara party to Matilda Royce that she shouldn't go on any fishing expeditions. Mrs. Royce had apparently installed a natural water feature, including a waterfall and rock pond for koi -- and she and Grace were setting sail in a few weeks on a Greek cruise where fresh fish would be on the menu. Grace's theme seemed to be that these parties were a hoot but shouldn't be taken seriously.

Mama Bee's chance to explain the evil eye pendants came just before ten, when Ama -- an unsmiling and silent ghost -- had refilled the punch bowl for the third time, taken away the empty seafood platter, deflected all compliments on the colorful palm fans, and once again disappeared into the house.

Mama Bee clapped her hands for silence. "I'm sure you're wondering about the pendant. Some call it the evil eye. In India, it's called Buri Nazar or Dishti. It has power. When you glare at someone too long with envy, you've giving them the evil eye. With the pendant you can impart a curse."

When Cricket raised her hand, Mama Bee frowned. Cricket asked too many questions. "Yes, Cricket."

"What if we don't want to give anyone the evil eye?"

"Or," Ivana Starr interjected, " we want to ward it off?"

"If you don't want to give the evil eye to someone, don't wear the pendant at all. Or if you do wear it, think positive thoughts. People who don't believe in the power of talismans simply ignore the evil eye or treat it as a curiosity. Others who aren't sure about the evil eye cross their index fingers like this when they see it."

As if hypnotized, everyone crossed their fingers.

"Or you can wear a turquoise bead instead of the evil eye. Many people in the Middle East do that just in case someone tries to curse them. And Madonna wears a red string bracelet to ward off the evil eye. Astrid wore one, remember?"

Cricket wasn't done. "I saw a YouTube video claiming the red string bracelet is part of devil worship."

Mama Bee was momentarily stumped for a response. She herself put a lot of credence in YouTube videos. "I haven't seen that one. But celebrities are much too aware of their image to associate with the devil. So the meaning of the bracelet is the opposite of what you've heard.... I'm not here to curse anyone or worship the devil. Nor am I encouraging you to do that."

"Then why give us this thing?" Cricket murmured, holding up the evil eye.

Ignore that. "Now I want each goddess to close her eyes as I pass around this bowl filled with stones. The one who pulls out a chunk of lapis lazuli will get a Tarot card reading. The rest of you will have your palms read."

Mama Bee was thrilled when Ivy Starr drew out the special stone.

She'd learned quite a bit about Ivy. After saging the site of Doreen's death, they drove to Chop's Wine Bar for tapas and wine flutes. There, Ivy became talkative. Her mother was depressed, sitting all day in a rocker, saying nothing. Her father had somehow managed to be demoted at the Post Office. Her older sister still lived at home, pretending to be the good child while endlessly complaining about her lot. Her boyfriend, Matt, was very nice but the two of them had no chemistry. By the time she was thirty she wanted to own her investment company. She admired Alexandra Wright more than any other woman she'd ever met and hoped someday soon to be her executive assistant or even her partner. Alexandra and her husband Steve were mismatched. Anybody could see he had a thing for the nanny they'd sent back to Sweden. Every last person on Miss Royce's staff other than her was not up to the job.

The theme of Ivy's life was ambition modeled on her boss' success.

"You're a very blessed woman, Ivy. Lapis lazuli is a special stone, used by the ancients for jewelry and decoration. 'Lapis' is Latin for stone. 'Lazuli' is Persian for heaven. You can see it's as blue as the sky. Therefore, it's known around the world as the stone of heaven. . . . Remember how I told you last time that you'll rise to great heights?" Mama Bee smiled. "This stone confirms that prediction."

After all the palms had been read, Mama Bee took Ivy to a little table. First, she rubbed the lapis lazuli between her palms, then rang a silver bell to summon the spirits. Before touching the cards, she took Ivy's long, slender hands, which were tense and cold, and asked her to close her eyes and meditate on her spiritual question.

"Now," Mama Bee asked, "what is your question for the spirits?"

"When and how will I rise to great heights? What must I do to get there?"

Mama Bee had no idea what the cards could possibly say about that. Covering her doubt and stalling for time, she shuffled the cards this way and that. Finally, she began laying out the five-card spread known as The Cross of Truth. Over and over, she said to herself, *You can do it. You did it with Doreen. You have the power of the spirits. Let the spirits enter as they will.*

Touching each card in turn, bottom, center, right, left, top, she willed meaning to enter through her fingertips. She stared at the cards, letting the images connect as they would. Suddenly, she felt light-headed, unable to believe what she saw. Afraid she would levitate out of her chair, she grabbed the edges of the table and glanced again at Ivy, but it wasn't Ivy she saw. Ivy's face had morphed into someone else's, a pretty face bloated and drained of blood with unseeing eyes. She looked down at the cards again and back at Ivy, willing her vision to clear, her body to stop lifting off like a balloon.

Then the cards blurred into a horrific vision, a short, jerky, silent film of disaster. Her heart began knocking against her ribs, her head filled with stars flashing like semaphores in a black void. She swayed as if buffeted by a violent wind. Suddenly unable to breathe, she bolted out of her chair, pushed the scrim aside, and leaned over the railing, gasping for air. The screams behind her came from another world, one that had nothing to do with her.

She felt herself falling, floating, falling as if from a great height and then the cold weight of water pressing on her face. Her sari coiled around her body like a serpent, around and around, tighter and tighter, the final, strangling embrace of a shroud. She stopped flailing. She let herself sink as if into the arms of a lover. Something was nibbling at her feet.

41

Don't Be Koi
Saturday, June 23, 2012

"Aren't you afraid your neighbor's cat will eat the koi?" Grace asked, chuckling at the thought.

Matilda's eyes didn't leave the fish pond. "Look at that red one! Isn't she beautiful?"

"She?"

"I'm guessing. The way she swims is so feminine, like a water dancer. I've named her Sofia -- the Greek spelling in honor of our upcoming vacation."

Grace snorted. "I don't think Sofia cares if she has a name, much less how it's spelled."

Matilda ignored the jab. "Do you know what kind of fish the koi are?"

"Expensive. Demanding. Useless."

Matilda made a face. "You know what I mean."

"Catfish?"

"No. Carp. Isn't that strange? I always think of carp as gray and disgusting, but these little swimmers are beautiful."

"I don't think about fish at all except in a good seafood restaurant."

"In Japanese, the word koi sounds like the word for love, so koi are symbols of love and friendship. They're frequently chosen for tattoos in Japan. Did you know that?"

193

"Not until this moment. You're quite the school teacher today, Matilda." Grace backed away from the pond and took a seat in a comfortable chair. She sipped her iced tea and fanned herself with the colorful palm fan from Mama Bee's party. "Are you hinting we should get matching koi tattoos on our ankles?"

Matilda laughed and took the other chair. "We're a little old for that."

"I beg to differ with you. I have dancers doing the tango tattooed on my left buttock. Got it three years ago in Argentina when I was there with Rafael."

"You didn't!"

"Fortunately, I wasn't quite drunk enough to have his initials tattooed on the other cheek. Jaime would be upset."

"But you're willing to leave Jaime for six weeks while we cruise through the Greek islands."

"Never get too attached to a man. They come -- which is good. They go -- which is good too."

"You're so heartless, Grace. Why can't I be heartless? It would be so freeing."

"Maybe Jaime has a friend he could set you up with. Then you and I could take our boy toys along on the cruise. Remember that rich old lady who claimed to be a countess on the Caribbean cruise? She always had her handsome, perfectly tailored escort at her side, pretending he was her nephew."

"I thought he *was* her nephew. Or a servant. He looked too gay to be anything else."

"Gay or not, he wasn't her nephew, silly. Maybe a servant of sorts. A bit like that stylish guy at the party who pulled Mama Bee out of the pond. What's his name again?"

"Trent Senser, Lexie's stylist. . . . So hifalutin, don't you think, Lexie having a stylist? The way that woman spends her money makes me sick. I could spend it better."

"I watched him and Cricket at the party," Grace said. "I'm not really sure he's all that gay. I think it's an act so he looks like he knows more about fashion than anybody else. Who hires a straight guy for that kind of job, after all?"

They mused awhile about Mama Bee. What had happened to make her throw herself off the gazebo into the pond? Had she seen something in the cards or not? Or perhaps she just had a sudden break with reality. Her daughter, Ama, was certainly strange. Matilda's sister Abigail said she was glad Mama Bee hadn't died, but she wanted her money back anyway. The younger girls simply enjoyed the drama.

Grace looked at her watch. "I'm going to go home to shower and change for the Club. What time is our reservation?"

"Seven-thirty."

Grace stood up and pointed at the boxwood along the property line. "There's that cat again. She looks hungry and sneaky. I'm telling you, Matilda, you'll be lucky if those fish survive a week."

"The guy from the koi pond place is coming to rearrange some of the stones at the top of the waterfall, so I'll ask him what I can do about the cat."

A few minutes later, Matilda was kneeling by the pond, trying to entice the fish toward her wiggling fingers, when out of the corner of her eye she saw a figure in overalls, wearing oversized sunglasses and carrying an armload of tools, round the corner of the house.

"You're early. It's a hot day for outdoor work, isn't it?" she asked without taking her eyes off the graceful Sofia, who seemed to be responding to her voice.

When she heard tools clatter to the ground, she started to look around but before she could turn more than a few degrees, she felt something sharp and cold dig into her neck, thrusting her into the water. She couldn't get away from the cold thing, which as it pushed deeper and deeper, set her blood on fire, a missile intercepting her voice in mid-scream. Mercifully, the trident, aided by the water, did its work very quickly.

It wasn't long before the neighbor's cat, just as stealthy as the human intruder but in no need of manmade tools, used its claws to work the same trick on Sofia.

Part Three

Be sure of this: The wicked will not go unpunished,
but those who are righteous will go free.

Proverbs 11: 21

"If a loving God really created the earth,
he wouldn't have added humans."

Doreen Soren-Kawzy

42

The Spider and the Fly
Saturday, June 23, 2012

It was still light when Dave arrived in Sycamore Hills. He and Sheila had been having a very fine dinner at the Catablu Grill with friends when he got the call. Sheila, who said she'd get a ride with her friends, promised to have his strip steak boxed up and waiting for him when he got home.

"Is that the murder weapon?" he asked one of the crime scene technicians.

"Yeah."

"It doesn't look like a normal pitchfork."

The technician, a farm boy and fisherman, smiled. "You a city boy?"

"I suppose you could say that."

"This isn't a pitchfork. You can tell because it only has three prongs. Pitchforks have more. My brother-in-law and I use a thing like this, called a gig, for spear fishing." The technician then walked Dave over to a maple tree. "We left this in place for you to take a look at before we take it down and bag it."

Another hand-printed note, another poem.

> I hate you,
> said the spider to the fly.
> Trembling in my web

Pretending to be koi.

I hate you
said the spider to the fly.
The fish will find
You taste as sweet as pie.

I hate you,
said the spider to the fly.
With cunning joy
I watch you as you die.

An irreverent thought took hold. What grade would Sheila give the poet? In the first stanza, "fly" and "koi" didn't rhyme but "koi" rhymed with "joy" in the third. Weren't they in the wrong lines? Was the repetition of the first two lines good or bad? Is joy ever cunning? And how about the pun on "coy?"

Dave shook himself. That wasn't the point. The poem was stunning in its hatred of the poor old woman kneeling by the pond, face down, her head bobbing on the surface, the gig still stuck in her neck. She probably never saw what was coming. Who would she trust to get that near her with a tool used for spear fishing?

"Somebody find a way to turn off the waterfall," he said, surveying the scene. "What's that?" he asked when he spotted another technician rounding the corner of the house from the street. He was holding a crumpled, dirty piece of paper by the corner.

"An IPFW RiverFest band schedule. Found it out in the street in front of the house. There are tire marks on it."

"The RiverFest. When was that?"

"It's going on today, runs till midnight."

After taking a brief look at it, he said, "Probably has nothing to do with this scene, but bag it."

When an older woman suddenly emerged through the back door, Dave asked out of the side of his mouth, "Who's that?"

"The woman who found Mrs. Royce. Her name is Grace

Venable. She was hysterical when we got here, so we let her go in and lie down a minute."

He introduced himself and asked Grace to have a seat on a decorative stone bench.

"Mrs. Royce is your friend, I take it."

Grace wiped her eyes and nodded.

"How'd you find her?"

Dave was startled by her voice. In his experience, old women didn't sound sexy or look so flirtatious. It was unnerving, like seeing a mermaid in a junkyard. "I came by around 7:15 to pick her up. We were going to eat at the Club. When Matilda didn't answer the door, I let myself in. We have each other's keys; you know how it is with old ladies who live alone. When I couldn't find her, I decided to look out here. She's in love with those stupid fish." Grace put her hand on his knee. "Sofia's missing."

His knee involuntarily jerked, but Grace didn't remove her hand. "Sofia? Who's that?"

"Her favorite fish, the red one she said moved like a water dancer."

"You think it was stolen?"

Grace laughed grimly. "Look for the neighbor's cat and open it up. I'll bet you find Sofia there. . . . I don't know if I did the right thing or not, but I found this on Matilda's chair. I was afraid it would blow away."

"What is . . . . oh, crap, another Tarot card."

"Another?"

Never mind. "I take it you weren't worried about fingerprints."

"Oh," Grace said, lightly slapping her cheek. "I never thought about it. Anyway, this is the same card that turned up at a reading at Mama Bee's Tuesday night." She gave him a speculative look. "The African-American woman, Sheila Powers -- that wasn't your wife, was it?"

"She was there. She told me about Mama Bee's . . . ." He fumbled for words.

"Her incident. I'd call it a fugue state. I'm not a psychiatrist, but I used to write romances for Harlequin and I know about fugue states. They're very handy when you're writing drama where characters do inexplicable things and then can't remember them."

"I'm not a psychiatrist either. What's a fugue state?"

Grace looked off toward the trees at the back of Matilda's property. "It's a rare thing where a person for a short time loses all sense of identity and does something strange, like blacking out or wandering away. As I remember, it's called a dissociative state. When the person recovers, she often has amnesia, unable to recall what happened."

"What causes it?"

"Something stressful or shocking. Seeing someone you think is dead; that's the plot point I used in one of my books. But usually the person can't remember either the fugue state itself or what led up to it."

"Can it be faked?"

"I suppose so." When the detective sat in silence, she began, as a way of illustrating a fugue state, to tell him the plot of *All Night Long*, the second in her series about Dudley Longstaffe, an aristocratic rogue famous both as a cad for seducing King George III's cousin and a hero for rescuing political victims from the French guillotine.

Dave found himself listening, but just as she began the hottest seduction scene, he cut her off by abruptly standing up. "So if I go talk to Mama Bee, she probably won't remember throwing herself into the pond."

"In my book, she wouldn't."

He signaled a technician to come over. "We'll put this in a bag." He took another look. "The Lovers, I see. Did Mama Bee say what it meant?"

"It was upside down, by the way, at the top of the spread. When Doreen's cards were read, the top card was the outcome. In her case it was the upside down chariot. Mama Bee didn't say, but my guess it means someone crossed in love."

"Sheila told me the woman whose cards were being read was Ivy Starr, who works for Alexandra Royce."

"That's right. A pretty girl, very poised. The strange thing is, a few days ago Miss Starr called Matilda, asking to meet her somewhere, but Matilda refused."

"Do you know why your friend refused?"

"She thought the girl was a nobody, meddling where she shouldn't. The girl said something about healing the breach between her and her step-daughter -- an idea Matilda scoffed at. Who was a stranger to try to do something like that?"

"So the first time the girl and your friend met was at Mama Bee's party."

"I don't think they even met there, not formally. The instant Matilda spotted her, she moved away and turned her back."

"Did Mrs. Royce happen to go to the IPFW RiverFest today?"

"No. Much too hot. Anyway," she said dismissively, "we've been there, done that."

"Was Mrs. Royce expecting anybody this afternoon?"

"As a matter of fact, she was. I was here for an hour or so around four to admire the fish. Then I left to get ready for dinner. She said a guy from the company that designed the pond was coming over to rearrange some stones at the top of the waterfall."

"Was there a truck on the street when you left? Or when you returned?"

Grace shook her head.

"Back to the party. Sheila said Mama Bee laid out the cards but never actually gave Miss Starr a reading. But by then Matilda's palm had been read, I understand."

"That's true. Miss Starr never got her reading. Once the cards were on the table, everything went to hell before a word was spoken. Earlier, Mama Bee read all our palms, not just Matilda's. She told me I'd soon meet a tall, dark, and handsome stranger -- which now I've done." She winked at him. "She told Matilda the voyage she was undertaking would last longer than she expected."

"What did that mean?"

"It's obvious, isn't it?"

"Not to me."

"In two weeks Matilda and I were leaving on a long cruise to the Aegean islands. I've been there before -- you know, Mykonos,

Santorini, Patmos, Hydra, Crete. Have you ever been there?"

Dave shook his head. *Not on my salary.*

"I especially like Crete. The palace of Knossos is something to see, believe me. You don't see Bronze Age ruins everyday, not in this part of the world anyway. It was all going to be new for Matilda, so she was very excited." Grace gazed out at the fish pond where the EMTs were wrapping her friend's body. In the twilight it was hard to see exactly what they were doing. "A long voyage indeed! If I were still writing books, I'd write about this, only with a different ending. Matilda finds a lover, not a killer."

43

The Spider and the Fly Redux
Sunday, June 24, 2012

After playing nine holes of golf, Lexie, Jean, and Jessica retired to the Harbour Town Grill in Sea Pines for salads and iced tea. Their husbands, having risen much earlier to play eighteen holes, would soon join them.

"This is my favorite part of the world so far," Jean said, "though I haven't seen all that much of it yet. The ocean breezes, white sand beaches, palm trees -- what's not to love about Hilton Head? And I could happily eat outside every day of the year."

"How are you feeling?" Jessica asked. "It's not easy to play golf when you're five months' pregnant."

"Better than I have since getting pregnant. I've already pretty much forgotten the misery of the first few months."

"That's the brilliance of the maternal mind and body. You forget the morning sickness and swollen ankles, the heartburn and then the contractions, and a few months after the birth you're ready to do it all again."

Jean made a face. "Well, that's going a little too far, given where I am, but thanks for the encouragement." She cocked her head at Lexie, who was reading a text message on her iPhone. "What's that look?"

The blood had drained from Lexie's face. "A message from Phyllis. Matilda was found dead yesterday evening."

After a shocked silence, the questions and speculation began. Where? How? Why? What time? Who would do such a thing? Who had a motive? How was she found? Now what?

"Now what indeed!" Lexie said, restating Jean's last question. "Now I'm really a suspect. Digby aka Atticus Solon sneers at my book and he dies soon after. Doreen makes unreasonable demands and tries to embarrass me and she dies soon after that. Matilda threatens me every which way from Tuesday and now she's dead."

"Could she really have forced you to sell the Scrapyard?" Jessica asked.

"No. She could make my life miserable but she couldn't force me to do anything. I have control. Furthermore, under the terms of Dad's trust, if she consented to the sale, she'd get a small lump sum from the proceeds but wouldn't be entitled to any further income, so it was never in her interests to demand that we get rid of the Scrapyard."

"Then why did she say what she did to you?"

"I don't know. She must have been confused or never consulted her lawyer. I was insulted by her demands, especially the way she planned to aggrandize her own legacy at Dad's expense, but I wasn't worried I'd really have to sell the Scrapyard. . . . So if the cops think I had any motive to get rid of her, they're on the wrong track. . . . Hold on. My phone's beeping." She read the screen, then looked up. "Phyllis says she's sending me a picture of a note Todd found this morning on the pool house. They both went over to the house just to check on things. Let me read it:

I love you,
said the spider to the fly.
You're the apple of my eye
but I will not tell you why.

I love you,
said the spider to the fly.
Why are you so shy?
Help me be less sly.

I love you,

said the spider to the fly.

I wait for your reply

so you don't have to die."

Lexie made a gagging gesture. "Is this disgusting or what."

"What a mixed message," Jessica said. "The writer is the spider and you're the fly. He secretly loves you but if you don't love him back, he'll kill you."

Jean reached for Lexie's phone to read the note for herself. "How many notes does that make?"

Jessica, looking shocked, unceremoniously grabbed the phone from Jean and studied the screen. "Are you saying this isn't the first note you've gotten like this?"

"Since the beginning of the year I've gotten at least half a dozen. Always poems, printed by hand on plain white paper, never signed, left in all kinds of different places. Not as threatening as this one, though."

"Like where were they left?"

"Phyllis' porch. Jean's car. The courtyard gates. My car. A tree near the creek behind our house. Even Steve's office."

"So it wouldn't have to be a member of your household or someone close to you? Anybody could be leaving these notes."

"Maybe I'm being followed -- again." Lexie shuddered, remembering how her own half-brother had hidden a tracking device in her car for months before he died.

"You have a stalker, my dear, someone who knows your life well," Jessica said, as if her pronouncement settled the matter. "I take it you've gone to the police."

"I showed the notes one evening to Dave."

"And he said what?"

"Almost what you said: I *might* have a stalker. But he gave me a funny look, like maybe I've written them myself or I know who it is but won't say."

"That's absurd," Jessica said. "Isn't it?"

At Lexie's hurt look, Jessica patted her hand. "Just kidding. But I suppose that's the way a cop thinks. Suspect everybody, believe nobody."

Lexie retrieved her phone from Jessica. "I've got to make some calls, starting with the charter jet company. Can we be ready to leave in three or four hours?"

"Whatever you say," Jessica said.

"Sadie's probably still on the beach with the baby but she needs to start packing up herself and Lacey. Duke needs to see this note and make sure Dave gets it. And maybe I should call Grace to find out if she's making plans for the funeral."

After lunch, the six vacationers disconsolately returned to the five-bedroom beachside villa Lexie and Steve had rented and prepared to return to Fort Wayne.

44

Methane Sludge
Sunday, June 24, 2012

Astrid and Ivy were strange roommates. Neither really liked the other.

Astrid had spent the last two weeks of April in Malmö with her mother and brother, but Sweden's third largest city was no longer the paradise of beauty and security she had believed it to be only six months' earlier. The Middle Eastern population, half of which was unemployed, was hostile and growing, committing violent crimes in full view of the police, who did nothing. Her best friend had been raped. Her high-school crush, a Jewish boy, had been struck with a bottle in a demonstration. Her mother, who had lost weight for all the wrong reasons, was as bitter as the tea she brewed to cleanse the blood. At first, Sven welcomed his sister's presence but grew increasingly angry at supporting two women.

Worse, by the American standards of comfort Astrid now thought of as normal, the apartment her mother took was cramped and ugly, with no elevator to make the climb up four floors bearable. Why did pipes have to be exposed and the water heater hang in a corner the bathroom? Why couldn't radiators be covered? Why did kitchen counters have to be made of chipped melamine instead of gleaming granite? Her father's prison cell was roomier and handsomer than her mother's minimalist bedroom.

For two weeks, Astrid slept on a divan that was too narrow and too short for a good night's sleep. She woke up to white walls and bare floors, a television the size of her makeup bag. There was no money for shopping. New clothes and a round of golf were as out of the question as a trip to Mars. She no longer liked the food either. Having grown used to Phyllis' rich and satisfying hot dinners, Astrid gagged on her mother's plain boiled potatoes and cold open-faced sandwiches of smoked fish.

The city of her birth had always been boring; now it was boring, cramped, and scary.

When Ivy texted her to come back to the States, Astrid couldn't believe it. They hadn't been friends. Why, then, would Ivy lend her money for airfare and offer her a place to live? All Ivy would say was that Astrid had been unfairly treated. So American, Astrid thought, a stranger's concern for her welfare.

Astrid needed very little persuasion. Neither her mother nor Sven argued with her.

Though she had looked forward to the coziness of living with a roommate in a familiar American city, things did not turn out as she hoped. For most of every day she was left alone. Without a car, there was little she could do for entertainment. Ivy worked long hours five days a week and sometimes went to the office on Saturday. She also left many evenings to listen to the odd lecture -- without inviting Astrid to tag along. Ivy was taking yet another class at IPFW and at least once a week went to dinner or a movie with Matt. Astrid was surprised, and a little hurt, that Ivy never tried to set her up with a date.

Astrid was growing restless. She did little favors for Ivy, but she needed a real job so she could repay her debt to Ivy, buy some new clothes, meet people, and have an interesting way to occupy the hours. She didn't want to be a nanny again, she was firm about that, but a job at Macy's perfume counter might be fun. Or clerking at TJ Maxx, where she'd get a discount on top of a discount. Event planning sounded glamorous too, though she had no precise idea what it entailed. Perhaps there was an opening at a country club, where, dressed in the latest fashions and deploying her charming accent to maximum effect, she could meet prosperous American men on an almost equal level. The club she had in mind was Steve Wright's, and Steve was the American uppermost in her mind, but she wasn't sure how to approach him without alerting his jealous wife, who would probably try to deport her.

Tomorrow, however, she was determined to take action. She would answer an ad for a shampoo girl in a little salon near Georgetown. It didn't pay much but it would be better than nothing. Perhaps the owner was looking for a young blond wife. Or an admiring customer would introduce her to a handsome nephew with a big trust fund.

Better yet, Steve Wright would pop in for a haircut and rescue her with the swipe of his credit card. Perhaps he'd reveal that his wife had bolted with another man, or lost all her money, or better yet died of a horrible disease. Astrid never gave voice to such fairy tales -- except to Ivy, of course, who was most sympathetic -- but they were always there, fermenting at the bottom of her soul like methane sludge.

She pushed thoughts of Steve aside. First, she had to ace tomorrow's interview by demonstrating her technique, though the only hair she'd ever washed before was her own. So she found a YouTube video, GorgeousLooks, to see how shampooing was professionally done. She was astonished at how complicated a simple, everyday act could be made.

Before retiring to the bathroom to try out the new hair washing technique, she decided to check her e-mail, an account that Ivy had generously set up for her.

"What is this!" she exclaimed aloud when she saw sswrightcons@comcast in her in-box. The tone of the message alarmed her. "What the hell are you doing back? And why did you send those pictures to my wife?"

What pictures was he talking about? She hadn't sent any pictures to anyone. She didn't even remember Mrs. Wright's e-mail address. Puzzled, she got out of e-mail to check her downloads, and there she found some photos she didn't remember being taken. A shot of her at JFK walking out of the customs area, pushing a luggage cart and wearing a fetching knitted cloche over her long blond hair, a mini-skirt the size of a cummerbund, and high heels that made her legs look a mile long. Another shot of her in profile, holding out her delicate wrist at Macy's for a perfume spritz. A third, faintly pornographic, showed her pretending to eat a hot dog at RiverFest.

Though she knew Ivy took a lot of pictures of her, she'd never been shown the finished product. Ivy must have sent them then. But why? Surely Ivy didn't pay to get her here only to arrange for her to be returned to Sweden like so much unclaimed luggage.

Astrid stood up and stretched, then went to the kitchen to steal another Cadbury ice cream bar from the freezer before trying out professional hair washing.

What was Ivy up to? And what would Steve do now? Was he really angry, as his message suggested, or secretly thrilled, as her fantasies suggested?

Facing the bathroom mirror while running her hands through her hair to remove loose hair and dust, the way the video instructed, she smiled confidently. She was young and beautiful. She was Swedish but spoke perfect English. Everything she ever tried on looked smashing on her athletic body. She was the stuff of every male fantasy. Any man would be lucky to have her.

Of course Sterling Steven Wright was thrilled to have her back.

45

Power Vacuum
Monday, June 25, 2012

"Have you seen Astrid?" Lexie asked, not bothering to sit down.

Ivy looked up, shocked. "No. Isn't she in Sweden?"

Lexie held out her phone. "Take a look at these pictures. She sent them to me."

Ivy took the phone to study the screen. "Is there a date on these pictures?"

"There's a date on the message: 'I thought Steve would like to know I'm back.'"

Ivy looked skeptical. "That picture in the airport could have been taken the first time she entered the country."

"The first time? You're thinking there's a second time then?"

"I didn't mean that. Just a . . . ." *Just a slip of the tongue.* "Just a figure of speech."

"What about the RiverFest picture? She wasn't here last year for that."

"She wasn't?"

"No."

"Maybe it's photoshopped," Ivy suggested.

"Do you have any reason to think she's that good with photoshopping?"

"I don't know that much about her."

213

"Has she contacted you?"

"No." *I contacted her, so strictly speaking I'm not lying.* "But if she does, I'll let you know right away."

Ivy watched Lexie walk to her office, turn her desk chair so her face couldn't be seen by the staff, and start making calls. Astrid didn't deserve Steve Wright, but getting him out of Miss Royce's life would create a power vacuum that Ivy was ready to fill.

46

Words Get in the Way
Monday, June 25, 2012

Ama led Detective Powers across the bridge to the gazebo, where a fan had been set up to cool the recumbent body on the divan. "Excuse me if I don't get up," Mama Bee murmured, adjusting her long skirt.

"Please," he said, taking a seat at right angles to her, "stay where you are. How are you feeling?"

"I'm not myself." She looked up at her daughter. "Bring us some iced tea, would you? That's a good girl."

Dave watched Ama waft back across the bridge to the house. He wondered what her voice sounded like. "You've heard about Mrs. Royce, I assume."

"Poor woman. I hear she was killed with a pitchfork in her koi pond."

He smiled. "Not a pitchfork. A three-pronged tool. My tech calls it a gig; he and his brother-in-law use it for spearing fish."

"Three-pronged? Long handle?"

"You've got it."

Mama Bee raised herself on an elbow. "Well, then, it is a gig, but I call it a trident, the symbol of Neptune, the Roman ruler of freshwater, or Poseidon, the Greek ruler of the sea. It fits."

"Fits with what?"

"Everything I saw in that poor woman's hand. I told her not

to go on a fishing expedition. Her friend Grace mocked that. Then I said that her voyage would last longer than expected. I didn't see death exactly but I couldn't see her returning to the place she started."

"Another Tarot card appeared at the murder scene."

Mama Bee looked wary. "Don't tell me."

"The Lovers. Does that mean anything to you?"

She sighed with relief. "No."

"Are you sure?"

"Why wouldn't I be sure?"

"Mrs. Royce's friend says the card called the Lovers appeared at the top of the spread you laid out for Ivana Starr."

"Ivy Starr," she murmured, looking off into space. "She's a good girl. She helped me sage the place where the plowman died."

"The plowman?"

"Oh, forgive me. Doreen, the woman who died near the Scrapyard. She had the hard, bony look of a farmer, very big hands and feet, dusty-looking skin. In my mind, she was the plowman. But I don't remember the Lovers at all. I can't even remember giving Ivy a reading, and I was looking forward to it."

"My wife says you didn't read the cards. Both she and Mrs. Venable said everything went to hell as soon as you laid them out."

"I'm not sure what they mean by that. There's a big hole in my memory between finishing the palm readings and the sensation of being cold and wet. I thought I was dying."

"Fortunately, one of the guests pulled you out of the pond."

"Ama told me that. The young man leapt right in."

She paused while Ama set a tray on a little table and then, without being asked, adjusted the oscillating fan to catch both Mama Bee and the detective. She raised an eyebrow at Dave. "Thanks," he said. Once again, Ama slipped away without a word.

"I do remember something, though," Mama Bee said.

"What?"

"I was floating down the River Styx. It was dark and cold. I wasn't sure where I was going but I liked the sensation of getting there."

"With Doreen, you told me that after the reading you had a vision of a flaming banner on a stick. What about this time -- any vision other than the River Styx?"

"It's a blank."

"I wonder if you'd humor me. Would you lay out the cards the way you did that night and pretend Ivy Starr is here?"

Without looking at him, she suddenly shouted, "Ama!" When the woman reappeared a few minutes later, Mama Bee asked if she remembered how the cards had been laid out when she cleaned up. Ama nodded. "Then bring me the deck I used that night, plus a fresh one." While Ama was gone, Mama Bee looked nervous. "If the Lovers card is missing again . . . ."

"If it's missing, what?"

She shook her head. "I don't understand. I truly don't."

And, indeed, the Lovers card was missing from the deck she used at the party. So Ama silently picked up the faulty deck and laid out the same spread with a fresh deck, the Lovers upside down at the top of the cross. Ama waited, then cocked her head at her mother.

"You can go, Ama."

Dave watched the woman walk over the bridge again. "Does your daughter ever speak? I've never heard her voice."

"Ama doesn't like words, that's all. She thinks they get in the way."

In the way of what? Dave waited for Mama Bee to proceed.

"You realize that without the querant here, the reading doesn't mean much."

"Could the reading have been about Mrs. Royce rather than Miss Starr?"

Mama Bee gave him an appreciative look. "Mrs. Royce's was the last palm I read, so that might be right; she was probably still on my mind. Very insightful." Mama Bee studied the cards, touching each in turn. "The strange thing is, there's both fire and water here, leading to a secret love that explodes like massive fireworks when it's revealed."

"Is your memory coming back?"

217

"Sort of." She looked at him with genuine astonishment. "Strange, isn't it?"

"So whose face do you see?"

"A pretty face, bloated and drained of blood, distorted as if a fish was looking at her from the bottom of a pond."

"Mrs. Royce's face?"

"Not exactly. But it isn't anyone else's either. I also see another face, mouth open, screaming like in that famous picture you see everywhere, but the features rearranged like in a Picasso."

"Whose face is that?"

"I don't know."

Dave's focus returned to the idea of a secret love. "Do you think Mrs. Royce secretly loved someone who didn't love her back? Maybe someone she shouldn't love in the way she did?" Grace Venable, for example. Maybe the sexy old mermaid reacted harshly to an unexpected and unwanted advance.

"What are you thinking, Detective?"

Dave stood up. "Nothing specific." *Something so perverse I don't even want to put it into words.* "If anything more comes to you, please call me, day or night. We might be getting somewhere."

47

Taken for Granite
Monday, June 25, 2012

When Dave got back to the station Monday afternoon, Captain Schmoll was waiting for him. "I've been looking over your binders for the Barrel and Ice Pick Murders. One of the names caught my attention."

"Which one?"

"Plato Jones. I know something about him you might not."

"What's that?"

"When he was in high school, he was our primary -- and only -- suspect in a murder. Did you know that?"

"No. He's about my age, so I was probably in high school too."

"I pulled the case, colder than a witch's tit now, of course, but it's interesting. I'd forgotten a lot of stuff but it's come back." Captain Schmoll got comfortable in his chair, took another sip of coffee, and began the tale. Plato Jones, a senior with a bad reputation at South Side, was dating a girl named Bitsy Thaler, who dumped him after he slapped her around one night. Then she began seeing a guy a few years older, a high school dropout working at an auto supply store. Plato wouldn't leave the poor girl alone. He kept calling her; in just one particularly memorable day he made forty-one calls to her parents' house. He followed her. She'd be walking through Glenbrook Mall, turn around, and there he was. She'd walk out to the school bus and there he was again, sitting in his jalopy across the street. He sent her flowery cards, not Hallmark quality, cheaper stuff, but for a couple months after the breakup, she got one every day, mostly through the mail but sometimes stuck in her front door. There was always an illiterate message scrawled inside, sometimes lovesick stuff about how beautiful she was and how much he wanted her back, sometimes threatening to kill himself if they didn't get together again.

Dave interrupted. "Threatening to kill himself or her?"

"Himself."

"Were those scrawled messages just ordinary sentences or poems?"

"I don't think you could call it poetry. There weren't even any real sentences. Some of the words were hilarious." Captain Schmoll laughed. "For years my partner and I would kid each other at the end of a long day that we just weren't in the right frame of *mime* to keep going -- that's how Plato wrote it. Or, like Plato, we felt we were being taken for *granite*."

Actually, that's funny, but I'm not letting on. "Did he end up killing the girl?"

"No. One night, the dropout boyfriend was in Scuttlebutt's. Somebody told him his car had a flat tire. He walked out to the parking lot. We think he opened the trunk to get out the tools to change the tire, but he was rudely interrupted. When the joint closed up, Scut, the owner, spotted the car and had it towed. I don't know if you know Scut, but he don't mess around. A few days later at the tow yard the car started to smell like -- well, you know the smell. Rotten potatoes and dead bodies. Barny Shinmeister -- that was the boyfriend's name -- was in the trunk, shot once in the head."

"What's Plato's connection?"

"A lot of evidence pointed his way but we could never make the forensic links a prosecutor would hang his hat on, let alone that a jury would hang the defendant on." Captain Schmoll laughed heartily. "That's a good one, ain't it? Hang your hat on, hang the defendant on."

Yes, sir, Captain Moonpie, you're a regular Jay Leno, ready for prime time. "So Plato was never charged with anything."

"He even passed a lie detector test, the bastard."

"I'll take another look at him. Did you notice, by the way, the notes left at the scene of Mrs. Royce's murder and on the Wrights' pool house look like they're related?"

"I noticed that. The spider and the fly. One's about love, the other's about death."

"That suggests that whoever is stalking Mrs. Wright is the murderer of three people -- Digby, Soren-Kawzy, and Royce."

"All the more reason my money's on Plato Jones, my favorite spider. One of those women you interviewed thought the note she found at the Wrights' house was written by Plato because of all the misspellings, so I think he's your man." Captain Schmoll patted his chest. "There's no substitute for experience, you gotta give me that much. I can spot a spider web a mile away."

Interesting. Now you know our murderer isn't Lexie but won't admit you were wrong.

48

Take a Breath
Thursday, June 28, 2012

Dave got a break. A tip from one of Matilda Royce's neighbors led him to the pickup truck -- a Dodge Ram -- spotted in front of her house late Saturday afternoon. It turned out to be a rental. The neighbor noticed the truck because the sign reading "BBB Enterprises" was duct-taped to the doors, which looked odd to him. The license plate was easy to track. There was a fuzzy picture on the neighbor's cell phone of a woman sitting in the driver's seat the fifteen minutes it was parked on the street.

The rental car agency, Benny's Beaters -- Can't Beat our Beaters -- was a scuzzy operation west of Lima Road hidden behind a strip club. The cars and trucks were dented and rusted, the lot cracked, with weeds providing the only landscaping. The office, a decrepit old trailer, was occupied by a big, beefy guy who sounded like a parrot on steroids. Surprisingly, he had decent records. The pickup was sitting in the lot.

The driver's license, which had been copied, belonged to Astrid Wikfelder, the Wrights' former nanny. Dave was surprised. He knew the Wrights had sent her back to Sweden months ago. The story was she had to visit her family because of something unfortunate that happened to her father, but Dave always wondered if that was the real reason. A saucy nanny like that, bouncing around the house -- well, that could be trouble. He hadn't heard about her coming back, though, and he knew that Sadie, the Mennonite cleaning lady, was now the Wrights' nanny.

"Did the girl who signed these documents look like this picture?"

"Oh, yeah. Smashing babe, accent I couldn't place, wearing overalls that left a lot to the imagination but a bikini top that didn't, a painter's cap on her head, sexy sunglasses, but she pushed them up when she signed the papers, so you could see her eyes were really deep, as blue as the ocean. I never seen the ocean, but I know what it looks like, a little dangerous but you wanna plunge in anyway, see what happens, might be fun. I was hoping to fall into those eyes and get caught in her rip tide, you know what I mean? She coulda swept me right out to the middle of the sea and done anything she wanted."

Benny, for God's sake, take a breath, would you? I'm not here about your sexual fantasies.

"There was a sign taped to the doors," Dave said. "Did you see that? It read 'BBB Enterprises.'"

"She and the guy taped that on by themselves, wouldn't let me help, before they drove out of here. Even in overalls, the babe's ass looked mighty tasty, all bent over like that, let me tell you, set my blood on fire, couldn't walk right for an hour."

If I gave you a swift punch in the gut, would those fantasies fly out like so much dust from an old seat cushion? "The guy? What guy?"

"Didn't get a good look at him. Taller than little blue-eyes, wearing painter's overalls and t-shirt. Sunglasses the size of headlights, a painter's cap, work gloves."

"Which one drove out of here?"

"The babe. She drove the truck back too."

"Was the sign still on the pickup when it was returned?"

Benny walked to the door and pointed toward the north boundary of the lot. "We ripped off the signs and threw them in that dumpster."

Dave retrieved the crumpled signs, then arranged to have the pickup impounded and a technician to start going over it. He sent a junior detective out to find Astrid Wikfelder.

49

Blow a Casket
Thursday, June 28, 2012

Plato Jones was hiding at his aunt's house in Antwerp across the state line in Ohio.

It hadn't been that hard to locate him. Dave started at Plato's Studio, where he found Petra Kuzmin standing behind the customer service desk doing paperwork. Two men were sweating on treadmills and another was lifting weights. Otherwise it was empty and smelled like what Dave imagined an East European wrestlers' pit smelled like.

When he told Petra he had an arrest warrant for Plato, Dicky Dickson having changed his mind and filed charges, and she'd be arrested for obstruction of justice if she didn't reveal her boyfriend's whereabouts, she folded instantly.

"The shit, he give me this, so okay, I help you," she said, pointing at the left side of her face. Her eye was purple, her cheek swollen.

"He hit you?"

She nodded.

"I thought his hand was broken."

"It is." She laughed shakily, tears welling in her eyes. "Now more broken, I hope. Bleeding too."

"Why'd he do it?"

"We got in fight, me having to go to Duchess' house every

damn day, take care of his business."

"The Duchess?"

"Mrs. Wright."

"Why do you call her the Duchess?"

"Rich peoples . . ." she made a spitting gesture, " . . . keep rest of us peoples down like slave pigs." She held out her hand to show him the big amber ring she had on her finger. "I make her deal on ring, she no bite." She spat again. "Too good, Duchess think, for pigs like me. Plato and me, we make workout room," throwing out her arms to gather in the right words out of the air, "fantastical . . . fantastical, that the right word? . . . for big magazine, but she no let nothing happen. But Plato, the shit, he worship the ground damn Duchess walk on."

"So where's Plato?"

The Antwerp police found Plato hiding in a closet in his aunt's guest bedroom under a pile of dirty clothes, but other than trying to escape arrest by hiding, he didn't resist.

"For the three hours before you got to Breakpoint and smashed Dicky Dickson's face, tell me where you were," Dave asked.

Plato couldn't remember other than that he must have been at home with Petra. Recalling everything that happened so long ago *entailed* a better memory than anyone could be expected to have, he whined. He probably left the studio at the usual time, around seven. He couldn't remember what he ate, whether at home or out, or any television show he watched. He might have taken a nap but couldn't be sure. Maybe Petra could remember.

It mattered, those missing hours. The Coroner bracketed the time of Doreen's death between ten at night and one in the morning. Plato didn't get to Breakpoint until eleven-thirty. Between nine, when Doreen's friends left, and eleven-thirty, when Plato reached Breakpoint, he had time to kill Doreen. Plato had no better alibis for the time of the Digby and Royce murders.

When asked to write a poem about Mrs. Wright, he gave it his best.

Rosses are red

226

vilents is blew

I do anythin for ewe

☺ ☺ ☺

He looked up at Dave. "I'm free to go now?"

"What's that first word in the second line? Violets or violence?"

"You know, the flower. Want me to draw it?"

"No."

"You ain't gonna show this to Mrs. Wright, are you? Petra will blow a *casket*."

Dave laughed. "No, I'm not showing it to her." He held out cuffs. "Welcome to your hotel for the night. We got you a nice little cot and and a toilet. We'll even let you shower; in fact, we insist. I wouldn't drop the soap, though, not if I were you."

"Why I gotta stay here?"

"Dicky is ready to testify." *And I buy a little time on a bigger problem.*

50

Narcissus
Friday, June 29, 2012

Astrid was taking her lunch break at Ziffles Ribs next door to The Hair-Raiser, where she'd been working since Tuesday. When she saw a pretty redhead, obviously pregnant, come in and start walking through the place, alarms went off. Jean Pitt! What was she doing in Georgetown Square? And why that look on her face?

Leaving her rib basket untouched, Astrid hurried to the restroom, hoping Jean hadn't seen her. She let herself into a stall, locked the door, got up on the toilet, and balanced as best she could so her feet weren't visible. That door, of course, was the one Jean wouldn't stop pounding on.

With a sigh, Astrid finally got down and opened the door. "What?" she asked in her haughtiest tone.

"You are back!"

"Duh!"

Jean raised her hand, then dropped it again. "I should slap the shit out of you. What are you thinking, sending those pictures to Lexie?"

"I didn't send them. I didn't even know they existed until a few days ago."

"Then who sent them to her?"

"I'm not telling."

But when Jean followed her back to the salon and said she was

228

coming in and she wanted answers, she didn't care who heard what she had to say, maybe the boss needed to hear too, Astrid said okay, she'd talk if Jean would buy her another rib basket. She couldn't afford to lose her job. And she was hungry.

During lunch, Astrid ate ribs and talked while Jean drank iced tea and listened. Then, Jean firmly gripping Astrid's elbow, they made their way to Narcissus, a little gift store on the other side of the salon. "This is where you bought the Tarot cards?" Jean asked.

"Yes."

"Show me what you bought."

Astrid took her to the back of the shop. "I bought one of every deck they have on display."

"And how did you pay for them?"

Astrid got out her billfold. "This credit card."

"American Express. Royce Enterprises." Jean gave Astrid a long look. "Why do you have that card?"

"I found it."

Jean snorted. "And no one here raised any question when you signed for the purchase."

"No. But I was ready. I brought Mrs. Wright's business card with me. I also had letterhead with her signature saying I'm authorized to sign."

"Who signed it? Do you still have it with you?"

"It's in the apartment. Ivy signed it on Mrs. Wright's behalf."

"Really? Well, you won't need this any more," Jean said, putting the credit card into a zipper pocket of her own purse. "Now we're going to Benny's Beaters."

"But that's a long ways away, and it'll take too long. I'll get fired."

"I'll talk to your boss, you wait out by my car. What's his name?"

"Pat. What are you going to say?"

"Enough to get you an hour longer lunch break without risking your job."

Benny was beside himself with joy when he saw Astrid. He tried to hug her. He babbled compliments. He quivered and leered and babbled some more. He invited Astrid to reenact the duct taping of the signs to the doors of the pickup. He remembered everything about the two times she signed for the pickup, even what she was wearing.

Jean thought they'd never get out of the stuffy office, where the temperature must be over a hundred. But by the time they left she understood the odd charges that had appeared on the last three monthly statements from American Express.

Before Jean let Astrid out of the car in front of the salon, she grabbed her arm. "Listen to me, Astrid, and listen good. You say one word about this day to anyone and you'll be talking out of your ass because that's where your larynx will be."

Astrid looked puzzled. Anatomy might not be the girl's strong suit.

"You're in a lot of trouble, so keep your mouth shut. Do you understand that?"

"For what?"

"Misuse of a credit card. Harassing the woman you once worked for."

Astrid looked unconvinced.

"Obstruction of justice and accessory to murder. Now do you get it?"

Astrid shrugged.

"I'd be especially careful of talking to your roommate."

"What do you mean?"

"I don't think she likes you as much as you think she does."

"What did you tell Pat? I have to know the excuse for being gone so long."

"Your kitten got run over and we had to take her to the vet."

"I don't have a kitten."

"Well, you did. Remember that."

"What was the kitten's name?"

"Oh, for God's sake, girl," Jean exclaimed, "name it anything you want. But remember, it's dead now, so there'll be no more trips to the vet. Pat will like that."

"I don't understand you Americans," Astrid mumbled as she

got out of the car.

51

Unwanted Delivery
Tuesday, July 3, 2012

Phyllis was puzzled at first. Who in the world was ringing the bell to the auto gate? She walked out of the kitchen to see what was going on. A large delivery truck was idling on the street, blocking access to the gate. The truck driver, without removing his finger from the bell, was waving a piece of paper. Sweat was running in rivulets down his face.

"Stop ringing that bell! What's that?" she asked.

"An invoice for assorted consumer fireworks."

She'd forgotten all about it. "Who gave you this order?" she asked.

The driver pointed at a line on the invoice. "Todd Fingerhutt. Let me talk to him about where to put this stuff."

"He's in Kentucky at his mother's funeral. He told me last week he canceled the order because Fort Wayne isn't allowing any private fireworks this year. The drought, you know."

"I don't know nothin' about any cancellation. Are you the lady of this house?"

"No. I'm the housekeeper. But I speak for her."

"Where's Mr. Wright? The name on the credit card is his."

Phyllis was used to this maneuver, implying she had no authority because she was an employee and a woman to boot. There must be somebody somewhere -- preferably a man -- who could override her. No matter how many times the insulting maneuver was tried, she never got used to it. She wiped her sweaty forehead with her apron, trying to get hold of her temper, willing herself not to explode. "Mr. Wright's not here either. He's away on business. You can't unload that stuff here. Take it back."

"I'm not takin' anything back."

"Just keep it on the truck then. You and Mr. Wright can sort out later who pays for what. Or better yet, take it to the Clubhouse. That's where it was originally supposed to be delivered. Somebody there can figure out what to do with fireworks."

He turned his head and spat on the driveway. He adjusted his cap. "Not on your life. I don't have an address for the Club. My instructions are to deliver it at the credit card address, 13339 Stonehaven Lane, and by God that's what I'm doing. Now where do I unload?" He looked at his arm as if his dragon tattoo told time. "I got more stops and I'm way behind schedule, so let's get moving."

Phyllis started to walk away. "I'm not opening this gate. Get back in your truck and leave. Go to the Club if you have to unload. The address on your form is a mistake."

Now it was the driver's turn to get hold of himself, but he didn't. He exploded in a torrent of curse words. When Phyllis heard him order his assistant to start unloading in front of the gate, she swallowed her pride and buzzed the gate open.

The driver sneered in triumph. "We're backing in. You better figure out where this stuff goes in about two minutes."

The empty bay of the garage between the boat and Todd's improvised workshop was the only place she could think of. She watched as two huge crates of fireworks were unloaded onto pallets.

The driver held out a clipboard. "Sign here."

Phyllis laughed.

"I said sign here."

"I don't think so."

"I'll wait as long as it takes."

"You're late, aren't you? And I saw a load of crap in the back of your truck, so your day isn't done." She took her cell phone out of her apron pocket. "You stay here one minute longer and I'll have you arrested for trespassing."

Her little act of revenge felt hollow. Mr. Wright was bound to be furious about the unwanted delivery.

52

Lucky Gun, Lucky Coin
Tuesday, July 3, 2012

When Drago dropped Lexie off around eight Tuesday night, the house was unusually quiet. Steve was again in Hilton Head, where he was scouting property for a condo development and maybe a vacation home for the family. He promised to be back in time to host the Club's Fourth of July celebrations tomorrow evening. Sadie, who had a cold, had driven back to the family farm to recuperate. Jean and Dover were in Warsaw visiting his parents. Trent and Cricket had been invited to a pre-Fourth party. All of the office staff had had the day off.

Phyllis greeted them at the door, giving her son a kiss and Lexie an update on Lacey's day before returning to Huntertown to wait for Todd, who was driving back from Kentucky. So, except for Lacey, who was upstairs asleep, and Henry, who had greeted her effusively at the door and was following on her heels, Lexie would be alone.

It was an uncommon experience. She was not used to being alone. She ran upstairs to check on Lacey and change into a lightweight shorts set. Before Drago left, he walked around the house with her, checking doors and windows. Lexie was amused. He was once again affecting his ghetto walk, which involved a lot of shoulder swing and his severe P. Diddy look. For Drago, the walk and the look were like a nervous tic, signaling he was concerned about something and ready to do battle.

"You sure you going to be all right, Mizz Royce?"

"I'm a big girl, Drago. I think I can stand an evening by myself."

"I'm a big boy too, but I don't like being alone anymore, now that I'm used to all the racket from the boys and the dogs and Lucy talking my head off about the liquor store and Todd showing me every damn rock he ever collected. So if you need something, you just give me a call, hear?"

"Off you go."

He hesitated at the door to the garage. "You aren't worried, are you?"

"Worried?"

"About Detective Powers thinking you're somehow involved with all those murders."

"I am a little, of course. How could I not be worried?"

"It's not fair."

"Whose life doesn't have shadows in the corners? Why should my life be an exception?"

"Are you gonna hire that private investigator Mom said you interviewed?"

"I am. I not only want to clear my name, but I want to know the truth. Who's the madman lurking in the dark, writing poetry and leaving Tarot cards everywhere after he sticks some poor soul through the neck? Until he's caught, nobody's going to rest."

"Where's your gun?"

"In the library."

"Go get it before I leave. Put a clip in it and keep it with you tonight. Phone too, of course."

Lexie shivered. "Good advice. I'm going to grab a glass of wine and maybe watch a movie on the screened porch. I'll have the gun and phone within easy reach."

"Tell you what," Drago said, after Lexie returned from the library. He dug into his trouser pocket as they walked to the porch. "Keep my lucky coin with you tonight."

Lexie held out her hand to stop him. "No need for that, my

friend. I don't believe in lucky coins anyway, but if you do, then it should stay in your pocket."

"I don't believe in silly things like that either, but this one works. I'll tell you about it sometime. It's old and it's got magic in it." He smiled a tight little smile. "It's not a gift, mind you. I'll pick it up tomorrow morning. Tell you what, put your gun and your phone on that table, grab your wine, and I'll get you settled out here, Henry too, baby monitor working, make sure everything's copasetic. . . . Copasetic. Is that the right word? It's hotter than Hades, so you're gonna need the overhead fan. If you're gonna watch a movie or something out here, I'll get that set up too so all you have to do is punch a button. We'll put this lucky dollar right beside the gun. Okay? One more thing."

"What's that?"

"Lock this screen door after I leave."

Lexie giggled. "What would I do without you, Drago? You're more like a brother than Rolie was."

He smiled shyly. "I hope you never can do without me, you wanna know the truth."

After Drago left, Lexie changed her mind about a movie. Instead, she detoured to the library for an armload of books about Tuscany and then got comfortable on the porch. Tuscany was where she was taking everybody for Christmas. All she had to do was choose between a rambling old farm house on a hillside of olive groves and an ancient palazzo overlooking a cobbled village street.

But what hillside or what village? There were so many.

53

Unexpected Visitor
Tuesday, July 3, 2012

An hour later, still confused by the possibilities Tuscany offered and growing sleepy, Lexie put the books aside, turned off all the lights except a table lamp in the corner, and settled back into her chair. It was so strange, she thought, the absence of fireworks. Usually, they boomed and popped from sunset until midnight for a week before and a week after the Fourth. The ban was necessary, of course, because of the drought that had dried every cornstalk and blade of grass into a torch waiting to burst into flame. But, somehow, celebrating the country's independence without fireworks felt vaguely sacrilegious.

The last thing she heard before dozing off was the Parkview medical helicopter rattling its way north.

She was awakened by someone shaking her shoulder. "Oh, my God!" Lexie exclaimed. "You scared me."

"It's just me," Ivy said. "Don't get up."

"How did you get in?"

"The screen door was unlocked. But don't worry. I've locked it now."

Lexie glanced at the door, puzzled. "I'm sure I locked it after Drago left."

"You need to be careful, Lexie. Whoever killed all those people connected to you might have you on his list. Maybe you're the grand finale."

"What a terrible thought! What time is it?"

But Ivy had already entered the house. She returned a few minutes later with a chilled bottle of Prosecco and a flute for herself. Without asking, she refreshed Lexie's glass before pouring one for herself. In the dim light, Lexie noticed that though Ivy was wearing casual linen shorts and a simple sleeveless top, they were perfectly pressed and her hair and makeup looked professionally done, as if her motor had only one speed. "Here's to us," Ivy toasted.

"To us," Lexie said, not sure what the woman meant but not wanting to be rude. "So what brings you here this time of night?"

"Concern for you. I knew you'd be alone."

"Heavens!" Lexie exclaimed. "Why is everyone so sure I can't bear to be alone?"

"It's not that. We have some important things to talk about."

"We do?"

"So what has Steve found in Hilton Head?"

Why is Steve's business an important thing for you to talk about? "In nearby Bluffton, a sweet little town we visited one day, he found a golf course community where the lots are selling for a dollar and houses for a third of their original price. He's thinking of buying the whole development and revamping it so it becomes profitable."

"Are you going to invest in the digital book printing company you looked at today?"

"I don't think so. I'm going to sit on my cash awhile until I find out which way the country's going. If it goes down the wrong path, I'm going overseas."

"Investing there, or moving there?"

"Investing. I like this country too much to leave -- except for a vacation, of course."

"I don't blame you. This house -- it's so perfect, huge but homey, like you."

"Huge?"

Ivy giggled. "You're not huge, of course. All that dieting and exercise -- you could pose for a fitness magazine. No, I don't mean huge physically but spiritually." Ivy wiggled in her chair and put her feet up on the ottoman. "And you make everything comfortable. Take these chairs. They're so big and cushy you could live in them. My apartment's got a little screened-in balcony but nothing like this. And your kitchen is bigger than the bungalow I grew up in."

Lexie's comfortable silence induced Ivy to digress about the little town near Evansville where she grew up and where her parents still lived with her older sister. There was no opportunity for a bright girl to do anything but leave the town, where the population was less than a thousand people, mostly shopkeepers and retired farmers. Her family was dysfunctional. Her mother, who came from a prosperous family, married beneath herself and was now embittered and depressed. Her father, a handsome scoundrel who'd spent some of his teenage years in a reform school, drank and was thinking of leaving the Post Office and going on disability. Her sister, a cashier at a grocery store, did her best to save them but was losing the fight.

Ivy suddenly grew pensive. Lexie was still curious about what important thing they had to talk about but said nothing, torn between wanting to hear what was really on Ivy's mind and wanting her to leave so she could go to bed.

"My sister, Nan, and I used to be close," Ivy said. "Do you have a sister?"

"No. I had a half-brother, but he's dead."

"Nan and I shared a bedroom and traded clothes. We knew each other's secrets. Just to stay out of the path of our crazy parents, we shut the door to our room and played every game you can think of."

"Like what?" Lexie asked out of politeness.

"We started with Ouija boards and palm reading. We led séances with friends. Then we discovered Tarot cards. We were in heaven then."

"You never mentioned that before. Tarot cards were found, you know, at the murder scenes of Digby, Doreen, and Matilda."

"I know. Some people think Tarot is evil, an occult game played in darkness, like playing chess with the devil."

"That's my impression."

"Tarot is very deep. When Nan and I discovered it, we were in heaven. Mama Bee isn't bad, but I can tell you she doesn't know half what I do."

"Really? I wouldn't have guessed that about you."

"Would you like a demonstration, Lexie?"

Not really, but I don't want to denigrate something that's important to you -- and I'm curious, I have to admit. "I don't have any Tarot cards here."

"I have some in my purse."

54

Two of Cups
Tuesday, July 3, 2012

Lexie had never seen Ivy so animated. Her eyes glittered, her cheeks flushed peony pink. She turned on lamps that an hour earlier Lexie had turned off. She coaxed Lexie to sit at a round table near the screen door to the auto courtyard. Barely pausing for breath, Ivy explained everything she was doing. The deck she was using was the Aleister Crowley Thoth Tarot Deck, not for amateurs but very accurate for skilled readers. She would use the five-card spread, The Cross of Truth, the same one Mama Bee used for her readings.

Ivy laid out the first card. "You see the bottom card, The Hierophant upright."

"Weren't you supposed to shuffle the cards?" Lexie asked.

"It doesn't matter."

"What's a hierophant?" Lexie asked.

Ivy looked thrilled to be asked. "A priest, a holy person who brings others into the presence of the divine. A hierophant interprets sacred mysteries and arcane principles for lesser people. In Tarot, the hierophant is part of the Major Arcana, known as the Trumps, which indicate the important spiritual principles governing a person's life."

"Does it matter that it's the first card to turn up?"

"Yes," Ivy said. "It has many possible meanings. It's the spiritual place you are in now. It symbolizes conformity to prevailing moral principles, to traditional thinking."

"Meaning I'm a conformist who's sure she knows how other people should live?"

Ivy briefly looked off into space, then back at the Hierophant, finally resting her gaze on Lexie. "You do things the way you think you should, the way you've been taught. And you like other people who live the same way. You like tradition."

"That's true."

"You go to college, get married to a man, have a baby, go to church, make money honestly, pay your debts, save some money for a rainy day, treat people generously, do no harm. You're an entrepreneur in the American tradition. You believe in God. You vote. You give away a lot of money."

Lexie dipped her head in an attempt to understand the strange tone of Ivy's recital. "And that's good, right?"

Ivy patted her hand as if comforting a child. "Well, you think so. You want to impose your principles not just on your own life but everybody else's, as if you really were a priest. You're doing what you've been taught to do. Now we move to the card indicating your desires."

"Wait!" Lexie said. "You made a point of saying the hierophant is upright. Does that matter?"

"Of course. If it were reversed . . . well, then, your generosity would be foolish, your moral principles confused, and you'd be a vulnerable person, disorderly, prone to repeating errors."

"God knows I've made enough errors in my life," Lexie said, thinking about Ferrell Hawke, her first husband, a greedy and arrogant man; Jacintha, the troubled girl she and her husband had adopted several years ago; and a number of stupid investments she had made since selling her businesses.

Ivy laid out the second card, The Ace of Wands upright in the middle of the cross yet to be formed. "This card indicates your desires. It's part of the Minor Arcana. The Wands predict spiritual growth and change. In your case, I think this card means you want to try something new in your life, something exciting and different.

Perhaps a journey or a new business enterprise or even a new personal relationship."

Lexie made a face. "I'm confused. Are you saying I'm a conformist, cocksure I'm right, but now I want to try something new?"

Ivy smiled. "That's what the cards say so far." She laid out the third card. "Now the card on the right arm of the cross indicates what is helping you. As you can see, it's the Seven of Pentacles upright."

"What's a pentacle?"

"A five-point star inside a circle, connected with Solomon. People wear pentacles as amulets or talismans, symbolizing divine or earthly energy. Like Wands, Pentacles are part of the Minor Arcana and typically predict material gain."

"So what about the Seven of Pentacles is helping me?"

"You're used to hard work and material gain, but you know material wealth isn't everything. And right now you seem to be between projects, relaxing a bit; maybe you're ready to reevaluate your life. And the number seven suggests you're completing one cycle and about to start another."

"I have no idea what that means."

"You're 35 years old, right?"

"Soon to be 36."

"Cycles take seven years each. You've completed five. You're about to start the sixth stage of your life and it will be very different."

Suddenly, Ivy got to her feet and reentered the kitchen to refresh their drinks. "Here's to us," Ivy said after sitting back down. "Ummm, that's good. Now we move to the left arm of the cross." She laid out the fourth card. "This is the card indicating what might be holding you back, the obstacle you're facing, the spiritual forces opposing your desire for growth and change. . . . Oh, my!"

"What?"

"It's the King of Swords reversed."

"Meaning what?"

"There is someone in your life with evil intentions, a very strong-willed person who means to harm you and doesn't want you to change."

Lexie smiled grimly. "I can think of three strong-willed people who wanted to harm me -- Digby, Doreen, and Matilda -- but they're dead. And, in case you're wondering, I had nothing to do with their deaths."

"I never doubted your integrity. But let's think about other people in your life. What about Astrid?" Ivy asked.

"She's in Sweden, where I don't think she can do me much harm."

Ivy shook her head gently. "No, she's not."

Lexie watched Ivy's eyes, alert for any sign of deception. "So those pictures on my phone really were taken in this country -- and recently."

"I'm sorry to be the bearer of bad news -- it's a thing no woman wants to tell her best friend -- but your husband paid to get her here. You couldn't have known that, of course. He's keeping her in an apartment on the other side of town."

"I don't believe you."

"Your husband, of course, doesn't want you to change because he's got the best deal any man can have. A beautiful wife and child, more money than he could ever make on his own, a mansion to live in, a staff to cater to his every need, a business that gives him an excuse to take unexplained absences, the respect of the community, and a secret girlfriend on the side."

Lexie pushed herself away from the table. "That's quite a list. But that's not my husband you're describing."

Ivy reached across the table to grab Lexie's hand. "Don't get mad at me. I'm just the messenger. And don't run away before we complete this reading."

Lexie sighed. "I don't think I want to know any more but let's get it over with."

"The card at the top of the cross tells us what the outcome will be." Ivy stared at the card, then smiled at Lexie. "You're the world's luckiest woman, I tell you. It's the Two of Cups upright."

"What's lucky about it?"

"It's the love card. It promises a life of bliss between two people who love each other deeply."

"Steve and me."

"No. It's about new love, leaving the past behind. First, you have to live in the moment, not in the past. Second, you have to love yourself after discovering who you really are. Then, you have to acknowledge you love someone you thought you couldn't but who, deep down, is your soul mate."

"Ivy, my dear, I don't believe in soul mates. We're all too imperfect for that."

Ivy shook her head. "The cards say otherwise, and they don't lie. You already have a perfect friendship in your life, a very harmonious relationship with someone who has already done a lot to protect you from your enemies. And guess what?"

"What?"

"That friendship will turn to romance."

55

Bummed Out

Tuesday, July 3, 2012

Lexie was relieved when her cell phone rang. "It's Steve," she said as she rose to go into the house for privacy. She walked into her cubby and shut the door. "I'm so glad to hear from you, darling. How are you doing in Hilton Head?"

"As I told you, I've found a golf course community I'm thinking of buying. Remember Bluffton?"

"Of course. Sweet place, very leafy and quiet, lots of antique shops."

"Golf courses are in the doldrums everywhere, but this project is worth thinking about." There was a pause. "It's hot as hell here, but at least there's a little ocean breeze. How about in Fort Wayne?"

"It's still ninety and not cooling off, dry as the Gobi desert, no ocean breeze of course and unusually quiet. No fireworks at all, which makes me sad."

"I didn't wake you, did I? You sound tired."

"Of course you didn't wake me, but, yes, I'm tired. It's only . . . let's see, it's only eleven. Ivy dropped by and has just given me a Tarot card reading."

"And?"

"She thinks it's a great reading, but I'm pretty bummed out. She says I'm a conformist who wants to change my life but somebody with bad intentions is stopping me, and somebody else who is now my friend is my romantic soul mate."

"A romantic soul mate? Are we talking about the guy leaving you all those mash notes?"

"She didn't say."

"Tell her that for even suggesting such a thing I'll kill her when I see her."

Lexie lowered her voice. "She's pretty sure you paid to bring Astrid back from Sweden and are keeping her in an apartment somewhere in town. She implied you're really not in Hilton Head."

Steve made an exasperated sound. "I wish we'd never hired Astrid. And, for the last time, I assure you I never had any feelings for that girl and never will. I wouldn't lay out a dime to help her leave Sweden."

"So are you still getting back tomorrow afternoon?"

"Maybe late morning, depending on how my day goes. But don't meet me at the airport. Remember, I drove myself and my car's in the long-term lot."

56

Silent Screams
Tuesday, July 3, 2012

When Lexie returned to the porch, Ivy was once again relaxing in her armchair. "I didn't upset you, did I?"

"No. Well, maybe a little," Lexie said, taking the companion armchair. "I think Tarot's nuts, if you want the truth, but you don't, and I know Astrid doesn't, and apparently Mama Bee makes a living off of Tarot, so I can't help being a bit disturbed. Maybe everybody else is right and I'm wrong."

"Let's have a little more of this lovely Prosecco before I leave," Ivy said, getting up and going to the kitchen. She was there a long time. When she was again seated, she lifted her glass in another toast. "Here's to all the spiritually corrupt people who've tried to hurt you."

"Who are you talking about, Ivy?"

"Alastair Rutherford Digby III." Ivy laughed derisively. "What a name to carry around for sixty years! And what airs he put on, all the while hiding his wicked envy of writers behind that ridiculous *nom de plume*. He thought I couldn't find the real man behind Atticus Solon, but I did. Weren't you surprised to learn he lived here?"

"I was. And what do you mean, you found him. When? How?"

"The computer is the best investigative tool ever invented.

Once I tracked him down, I went to a couple of his lectures and made sure he noticed me. It was so easy to gain his trust. He thought I was just a little sycophant, brighter than most of his fans and more adoring too. I never told him, of course, that I had just started working for you."

"Why did you want to gain his trust?"

Ivy ignored the question as if giving a lecture herself. "His lecture on Oscar Wilde clued me in, so I pretended great interest in his thesis that gay intellectuals are much wittier than other people. He was besotted with the Emperor Hadrian and Leonardo da Vinci not because of their talent but because they were gay men who made it big. You know that old book of homoerotic drawings the cops found under his feet?"

"What book of drawings? The paper never mentioned anything like that."

"It was a rare old book, very costly, that he bought in London. Calf binding, gilt lettering, vellum pages. Once he realized where my . . . my inclinations lay, he showed me his precious book, sure that I shared his interests."

What inclinations are you talking about? What interests did you share?

"He told me all about the artists. He was thinking of having a few of the drawings framed for his bedroom." Ivy refilled Lexie's glass. "Once Digby was engrossed in a subject, he let down all his defenses."

"So Digby was a fool for real."

Ivy barked out a laugh. "The Fool card was perfect for him, especially because he thought Tarot was silly stuff, beneath the dignity of rational people. He let me give him a reading once, but all he did was make little jeering remarks the whole time. Digby was a clown who thought he was a prince. Mocking him with his own prejudices was delicious."

Comfortably tired, Lexie only half-listened. How many glasses of wine had she had? The flute beside her seemed to be refilling itself.

"My readings are spot on," Ivy continued, "but Mama Bee

. . . well, sometimes she gets lucky. After I attended the Ostara party, Mama Bee invited me to join her in saging the place where Doreen died, bragging about how intuitive she is, how she just knows people. Such hogwash! I was standing a yard from her for an hour but she never suspected anything about me."

"Why would she suspect you of anything?"

"Wrong word. I mean, she just didn't get me at all. She did better with Doreen and Matilda, I give you that."

"Better how?"

"I didn't know I was going to learn Doreen's and Matilda's weaknesses at Mama Bee's party, but I did. Doreen was sure she couldn't be deceived. Matilda was going on a fishing expedition and a sea voyage no matter what warning she received. The cards that turned up were perfect for mocking the two women who were threatening you. Anybody who loves you wouldn't let them get away with that."

"You think I can't take care of myself, Ivy? That I let people get away with things?"

"You can take care of yourself. I admire you more than any other woman in the world, Lexie. But the fact is, you're too nice and generous, you take too long to defend yourself. You don't strike like a snake. You need me to protect you."

Lexie, who had been growing more and more languorous after her phone call with Steve, suddenly was faintly alarmed, yet too relaxed, as if drugged, to respond.

"You know what I like best in the world?" Ivy asked.

"No," Lexie murmured.

"Finding a person's weakness by finding his point of pride, then using that pride to do him in."

"That's a complicated thought."

"Take Doreen. What a foolishly proud woman she was, thinking she could take over our Scrapyard!"

Our scrapyard?

"All I had to do was dress up like her sidekick Maynard and pretend I was rescuing her. The funny thing about people who want to save the world is they can't wait to be saved themselves.

They don't love anybody but they're sure they're deeply loved. They want to destroy every good thing in their path, but they can't believe anybody would want to destroy them. Oh, that was an easy one."

An easy one? The meaning of Ivy's words hit Lexie like a bolt of lightning. Ivy -- her super-competent, cool-as-a-cucumber assistant -- was the destroyer of Digby, Doreen, and Matilda. Surely not; she couldn't be a murderer -- but she must be. Ivy knew too much about the victims. She felt too triumphant to be a mere bystander.

"And then there's your uppity step-mother," Ivy continued, hardly taking a breath. "How did you live with that battle-ax all those years? She thought she could muscle her way into the top position in your life, make decisions for you, but that's my place. Killing her was like shooting fish in a barrel."

"What do you mean, the top position in my life is yours?" Lexie asked with great effort, slowly forming the words as if she were drunk, not finding it particularly hard to sound as if she understood nothing.

"Do you love Steve?" Ivy abruptly asked.

"Very personal question, but of course I do," Lexie said. Trying to bring Ivy's face into focus was like looking through the wrong end of a telescope.

"It's an important question. And maybe your answer is a little . . . maybe you're denying the truth. I denied the truth for a long time. I dated a boy in high school. Then I fell in love with a woman in college, but that didn't work out either, so I decided to give men another try, but I don't love Matt at all. Once I met you, I knew where my heart was. I don't think I can ever love a man the way I love you."

The way you love me? What way is that?

Suddenly, Ivy was at her side. Lexie felt the woman's arms around her shoulder. Her cheek was kissed, then her mouth. She tried to draw away but her body wouldn't follow any commands. More kisses, words like caresses. Lexie wiped her mouth and turned her head away, but strong hands held her face still. Then she felt something being wrapped around her torso, pinning her arms to her side.

"You look like you're about to fall asleep, sweetie. I want you to stay awake, so no more wine for awhile."

Sweetie? What kind of endearment is that from an employee?

As if from a great distance, Lexie heard Ivy telling her that she had nothing to worry about ever. She watched Ivy leave the room, Henry trotting after her, and then return with Lacey. Settled back in her chair, Ivy rocked the baby in her arms as she chattered on about the life they could create together. She loved Lacey like her own child; in fact, she said with a little laugh, "I think she has my mouth." The two of them, Alexandra Royce and Ivana Starr, would live happily ever after with Lacey and Henry. They'd be rich and travel the world and be the envy of everyone they knew.

Lexie's eyes flicked to the baby. *Put Lacey down. Get out of here.* Though she was trying to scream, the words were stuck in her throat. She wanted to take Lacey away from the woman but she couldn't move her arms or get to her feet.

Was Ivy really holding the baby in one arm and her gun in the other hand? Why?

"I'm going to untie you later, Lexie. I'm not trying to be mean or scare you, but I want you to hear me out without getting all crazy."

Who's the crazy one here?

As if listening to a bad phone connection, Lexie heard Ivy say, "If you accept my terms, both you and the baby will live. Do you understand me?"

Do anything you want to me, but put Lacey down.

Lexie heard Ivy assuring her that they didn't need anyone else. They'd live happily ever after.

57

More Silence
Tuesday, July 3, 2012

When Steve reached the Fort Wayne airport, he smiled to himself. Lexie had had no idea he was calling from the plane, not from Hilton Head. He punched in her number again as he was being driven to the long-term parking lot, but he got only her voice mail. He tried again. Nothing. She'd sounded tired; perhaps she fell asleep after he called the first time.

He hoped she was wide awake, though, eager to see him and hear about his trip. He had a surprise for her. One afternoon, while aimlessly driving around Hilton Head to get more familiar with the island, he'd found a beachfront lot that would suit them perfectly. The house was a tear-down from the Eighties, but the location was perfect, and though buying a house in foreclosure was always a headache, taking months longer than it should, the Wrights were in no hurry.

Frustrated at not reaching his wife, Steve punched in Dover's number as he reached 469. "I just got back in. Everything going okay for the celebrations at the Club?"

There was a puzzling silence. Finally, Dover said, "My wife wants to talk to you. It's about Astrid and Ivy. Jean thinks she knows what's going on."

58

Wild Imagination
Tuesday, July 3, 2012

Todd was more upset than Phyllis had ever seen him. Normally, he was the calmest of men, as solid as the rocks he collected. But tonight his chubby cheeks were aflame.

"I cancelled the fireworks order weeks ago," he scolded.

Phyllis was hurt. Todd had never taken that tone with her before. "I told the driver that."

"My original order clearly said he was to unload at the Club, not at the house."

"He claimed the contrary."

"And you let him unload even though I'd cancelled the order!"

"He wouldn't take no for an answer. He was going to block access to the auto courtyard if I didn't."

"And you let him store the stuff in the garage!"

"Where else?"

He was pacing, gesturing wildly. "Out by the pool house or the creek. At the far end of the courtyard over by the wall. Anywhere but in a place attached to the house. What if something happens? The whole house will go up. Sadie lives above the garage."

"Sadie isn't there. She drove back to the farm this afternoon."

"The baby's room on the second floor isn't far away from the garage apartment over that bay. If those fireworks explode, she's in danger."

"Stop it, Todd. I don't want anything bad to happen either, but you're getting all worked up for nothing. Unless there's a lightning strike directly on the garage, nothing's going to happen tonight. Your imagination is running away with you."

"Anything can happen. The stuff's got to be moved tonight."

"The crates are huge, Todd. You can't move them by yourself."

"Then I'm calling Drago. He can haul a pallet truck over from the Scrapyard. I'll meet him at the Wrights' house."

"At this time of night?"

"Yes, at this time of night. Does Mr. Wright know about the crates in the garage?"

"No. I forgot to tell Miss Royce when she got home."

"I can't believe this. Crates of fireworks sitting in this heat in an enclosed space! That's just an accident waiting to happen."

59

Sign Language
Tuesday, July 3, 2012

At Ama's urging, Mama Bee agreed to try one more time to recall from out of the dark void the events of her summer solstice party. The Tarot cards laid out for Ivy Starr -- what did they mean? Were they a clue to Matilda's spiritual life because Matilda's was the last palm she read, or to Ivy's because she was the querant?

Mama Bee was as surprised as anyone when Matilda was the next to die after Doreen. When she warned Matilda not to go on a fishing expedition and to expect her voyage to take longer than she planned, she recited the words as if reading from an invisible script. The words that flowed out of her mouth sounded slightly strange, too strange to predict anything real. The words came from another brain. Who had written the script?

Not knowing what else or who else could be responsible for her new-found wisdom, Mama Bee credited the feathered serpent, who was now visiting her in dreams almost every night. Sometimes he looked like a giant pagan god with dark wings that brushed the ground and a glowing face haloed in otherworldly light. At other times, he was a fire-breathing reptilian monster with a scaly tail and a stony look that stopped her heart. And, once, he was just a hairy man in a mask with goat horns and hooves and an enormous leathery penis waving about. But he could not fool her. Whatever form he took, she recognized him as the feathered serpent, the speaker of proud words, the ruler of the air and the underworld, a mighty hunter of the past, bringing her the gift of forbidden knowledge -- knowledge of the future -- from the great void.

It wasn't yet midnight. With the help of fans, the gazebo had cooled off a little. Mama Bee and Ama sat across from each other at the very table where she laid out the cards for Ivy Starr, a tea light their only illumination. Mama Bee laid out the Tarot spread exactly as Ama remembered. Then she moved in order through the five cards as if Matilda Royce were the querant. When she got to the Lovers reversed at the top of the Cross of Truth, she hesitated. "Mrs. Royce loved the wrong thing."

Ama shook her head.

"She loved the wrong person."

Again, Ama, still fixated on the cards, shook her head.

"Speak to me, Ama. You are so beautiful, why won't you speak?"

Ama closed her eyes.

"Why did you shake your head?"

Ama did not speak but she opened her eyes, stood up briefly, then sat back down on her chair. She tapped the Lovers card, then the table in front of her.

"You're sitting where Ivy sat."

Ama nodded.

"So it's not about Mrs. Royce. It's about Ivy."

Ama, almost smiling, looked at her mother and nodded again.

"Ivy loves the wrong person."

Ama nodded a little more vigorously.

"Who does she love?"

Ama pointed toward the roof of the gazebo.

"What . . . who . . . God?"

Ama shook her head vigorously.

"She loves somebody above her? Somebody greater than her."

Ama nodded.

"Her boss. Mrs. Wright."

Ama shuddered.

"Why did you shudder?"

Ama didn't move but simply stared at her mother with pained eyes that begged to be understood.

"And Mrs. Wright doesn't love her back -- not in that way. She'll even be offended."

Adjusting the stack of bracelets on her arm, Ama nodded affirmatively.

"So there's going to be trouble."

Sighing deeply, Ama rose from her chair, first wet her finger and stuck it in the flame of the tea light, then tipped her head back at the sky and mimed an explosion. She stood there a few more seconds to see if her mother understood. Satisfied, she folded her hands together in a namaste and glided back across the bridge to the house.

60

I-V
Tuesday, July 3, 2012

Astrid had enough life in her to dial 9-1-1. Dave arrived as she was being strapped onto a stretcher. One of the investigators pointed to a gun lying on the floor on Astrid's left side. "We learned from a neighbor that this girl has been living here for a few months. The lessee is Ivy Starr. He heard what he thought was a car backfiring a few hours ago, so the girl's been like this a long time. She's lost a lot of blood."

The girl was in very bad shape. Dave knelt on the carpet anyway. "Can you tell me what happened?"

Astrid's eyes were open but unfocused. Her long blond hair was matted with blood and her pale skin was blood-spattered and spectral. The lower half of her face was a mass of tissue and blood.

"She can't talk," one of the EMTs said. "She was shot in the jaw."

"Did you do this to yourself?" Dave asked. "Blink once for no, twice for yes."

She blinked once.

"Did your boyfriend do it?"

She blinked once.

"Did your roommate do it?"

She blinked twice.

"Ivy Starr?"

When the girl's eyes closed and stayed closed, Dave feared the girl had lost consciousness, but after a few seconds, she held up her index finger for a second, then raised her third finger, forming a V. He touched the red string bracelet on her wrist, then gently folded her hand in his.

"Thank you, Astrid. First an I, then a V. Ivy, your roommate. I get it."

As Astrid was being taken down to the ambulance, Dave's phone buzzed. He glanced at the screen impatiently, but the moment he saw the name on the screen, he took the call.

"Detective? This is Mama Bee."

"I recognize your voice."

"I just had a breakthrough. Ama and I reenacted the night I fell off the gazebo into the pond."

"And?"

"I think something bad is going to happen and I know who the players are."

"Tell me fast, because I'm standing in the middle of a pretty bad scene as it is."

"The crossed lover wasn't Matilda. It's Ivy Starr. I had a vision about her."

"What vision?" Dave was practically dancing with impatience.

"She thinks she was protecting Mrs. Wright by murdering her enemies, but Mrs. Wright is now in danger. I see Mrs. Wright tied up. And I see flames."

"Oh, God. Sorry to be so rude, and thanks for the tip, but I've got to call somebody else. I'll catch you later." Dave punched in Lexie's cell number but only got voice mail. Then he was about to call Steve when Steve called him. "Steve, my friend, where are you?"

"A few miles from home. I just got back from Hilton Head."

"I just tried reaching Lexie but I didn't get an answer."

"I just tried too, pretending I was still in Hilton Head so I can surprise her. But why are *you* calling her, Dave?"

"Astrid just got shot, and I think -- this is not to be repeated -- her roommate, Ivy Starr, did it. I wanted to warn Lexie not to let Ivy into the house."

"What a coincidence! I just heard from Jean that they're roommates. My wife got some photos sent by e-mail suggesting Astrid came back from Sweden, but we weren't sure what to believe. That's why I was calling you -- to see if you'd send somebody out to check on my wife because Jean thinks Ivy may not be the law-abiding citizen we all thought she was."

Dave took a deep breath. "That's for damn sure. I think Ivy may be on the way to your house."

"She's already there -- or was an hour ago," Steve said.

Dave almost dropped the phone. "Are you sure Ivy's at your house?"

"Not this moment, but she was an hour ago. When I called, Ivy had just given Lexie a Tarot card reading promising a new romance. She even tried to make my wife believe I'd paid to bring Astrid back from Sweden as my mistress. But when I called again a few minutes ago, Lexie didn't answer."

Shit, shit, shit. "I have reason to believe from one of my sources that this may not be the first time Ivy Starr has killed someone, so she's really dangerous. Do you have a gun with you?" Dave asked.

"No. I didn't want to leave it in a car parked at the airport."

"The gun used on Astrid is still in the apartment, so I don't think Ivy Starr is armed unless she's got a secret arsenal, but be careful. I'm sending squad cars out and I'll get there myself as soon as I can."

61

To Be Free
Tuesday, July 3, 2012

Lexie shook herself, struggling weakly against the ropes. She couldn't pass out again. Suddenly, Ivy was standing in the middle of the porch, reciting a poem as if from the well of an amphitheater.

How do I love you?
Let me count the ways.
When I'm with you
My nights are bright as days.

How do I love you?
Look at me and see
that to you I will be true.
The two of us are meant to be.

And how do you love me?
I see it in your eyes
The pleading to be free
of all your other ties.

Not my other ties, Lexie thought. *These ties. If you had that poem ready all along, then you planned all this. Were there signs I should have seen?* She struggled again against the rope binding her arms to her side and her ankles to each other. *I have to get free.* "You left all those notes, didn't you?" she mumbled. "Why?"

"Because I love you, Lexie. I was just too shy to say so at first. But now I'm not."

Now that you've tied me up and I'm alone with you, you're a very brave woman!

And then, just as Lacey began to cry, Ivy vanished with the baby. Lexie was alone again. Where had Ivy gone? Why was Lacey crying? Where was Ivy taking the baby?

She turned her head, hoping her gun was back on the table beside Drago's lucky coin. The coin was there but not the gun. Where was it?

Once again, she passed out.

62

Tire Iron
Tuesday, July 3, 2012

When Steve reached the Stonehaven *cul de sac*, he spotted Ivy Starr's Buick on the street. His heart pounding, he pulled into the auto courtyard, punched the electronic garage door opener, but didn't waste time pulling into the garage. He leapt out of the car and looked around. The only light he could see was on the screened porch. Did that mean the women were there? Or in some darkened part of the house?

It was hard to think straight. Ivy had shot Astrid. Would she do the same to Lexie? If Ivy didn't have a second gun, did she have some other weapon? Had she already done something to Lexie that prevented his wife from taking a phone call?

His gun was in the library. To get it, he'd have to sneak into the house and then, gun in hand, start looking for the women. Or should he simply get out his tire iron and storm the porch, where the light beckoned?

Tire iron in hand, he crouched and made his noiseless way to the porch. At first glance it looked empty but as he inched toward the porch door on the courtyard, he spotted Lexie slumped in a chair, bound with rope, eyes closed. Was she alive or dead? He whispered her name. She was silent so long he feared she really was dead. Then with relief, he heard her whisper something. "Baby." Over and over she whispered "Baby." He looked around. Where was Lacey? And how about Henry?

Throwing caution to the winds, he stood up, ran to the door, and tried to jerk it open, but it was locked. He tried punching through the screen. "Lexie! Lexie!" he screamed. "What's going on?" He began smashing the door handle with his tire iron.

And then, in the midst of his efforts, his eye caught movement in the doorway to the kitchen. In a split second, a shadow resolved itself into a human figure. Was it Ivy? Was that a gun she was pointing at him?

When two shots whizzed by his head, he knew she had a gun. He crouched again and scrambled back toward the garage, all the while counting the rounds. If Ivy was using Lexie's gun, then eight rounds meant an empty gun -- unless somehow she'd found more clips.

Steve was so frantic, he didn't notice that on the other side of his boat were two crates that shouldn't be in the last bay. All he wanted was a weapon better than a tire iron.

63

Sniper

Wednesday, July 4, 2012

Ivy cautiously scuttled to the table lamp to shut it off so the porch was completely dark, then made her way to the screen door, her eyes straining to see if Steve had been hit. No bleeding body that she could see, no sound of pain that she could hear. She debated whether to follow him to the courtyard or stay put, like a sniper in her nest.

She walked over to Lexie and checked her pulse. She was warm to the touch and breathing. Ivy leaned down to kiss the love of her life. She wished none of this turmoil had to happen. Love ought to be simple.

But it wasn't.

What she had started she now had to finish. She unlocked the battered screen door and crept out to the courtyard. Yes. It was worth risking everything for the love of her life.

The first thing she noticed was Steve's Expedition parked at an angle. The second thing she noticed was the open garage doors. All the bays were full except the one Steve should have parked in, two cars on the left of the empty space, a boat and then some crates on the right. The coward was probably hiding in there.

"Steve Wright. Come out wherever you are," she called out in a singsong voice. She felt brave. There had been no return fire, so Steve must be unarmed.

Then she heard something metallic hit the cement floor on her left. She turned that direction and fired two shots. She heard glass shattering. Then the metallic sound came from her right. She fired another two shots into the darkness but heard no screams, nothing more satisfying than bullets slamming into brick.

She was suddenly sweating with fear. Killing hadn't been so hard before. It should be easier than this.

She whirled when she heard a truck grinding toward the auto courtyard. Crouching at the side of the garage, she watched the truck pull in, stop without the ignition being turned off, and the door open. In the overhead light of the cab, she recognized the profile of Drago Bott. She had never liked the man. He spent far too much time with Lexie. Impulsively, she took a shot at him but it went wide, pinging off the truck.

Given Drago's reputation for violence, Ivy suddenly realized he might try to get his revenge by coming after her. Frantic, she looked for a place to hide. The wooden crates in the last bay were the only safe place she could see.

64

Fireworks

Wednesday, July 4, 2012

"Drago," Steve yelled. "Watch out! Ivy's got a gun."

Drago was startled. Steve's voice seem to come from his left, somewhere in the dark depths of the garage. What the hell was going on? "So do I. Where is she?"

"Never mind Ivy. I'll find her. Lexie's tied up on the porch and she's moaning about the baby. I don't know where Lacey is."

Drago scrambled out of the truck on the passenger side and ran to the porch. He jerked open the battered door, freed Lexie from the ropes with a pocket knife, and, spying his lucky coin, pocketed it before carrying his boss to the kitchen, where Todd had just come downstairs with the baby, Henry at his heels, barking with excitement.

"You've already been upstairs?" Drago asked. "How'd you get in?"

"Went up the back way to get the baby. First things first. I'll find a safe place for her. Then we've got to get the fireworks out of the garage."

"Where in the garage are they?"

"In those crates next to my workshop. You didn't see them?"

"It was a little dark and I was being shot at, Todd. By Ivy. I think she took Mizz Royce's gun because it's not where I left it. I take it you didn't hear the gunshots."

"Is that what I heard?"

"It wasn't backfire from cars, that's for damn sure. I think Ivy ran into the garage and is probably holed up somewhere near Steve."

"Why are you holding Miss Royce like that? What's wrong with her?"

"Don't know. She was tied up. Maybe she's been drugged."

"Then she needs fresh air." Todd cocked his head. "I don't hear guns."

"It was the OK corral out there a few minutes ago, so don't count on it staying quiet."

"Then we've gotta get out of here. Let's get her in a fireman's carry on your back. Then follow me," Todd said.

They raced through the kitchen and down some corridors to the lap pool area and out the French doors. They didn't stop running until they reached the creek.

65

Law-Breaker
Wednesday, July 4, 2012

Meanwhile, Steve was still crouched in the garage. When he heard the shot pinging off of Drago's truck, he was ninety-nine percent sure that Ivy's clip had only one round left.

He didn't want to kill Ivy but he wanted to flush her out without getting killed himself. The garage was practically an armory of makeshift weapons -- hedge trimmers, nail guns, drills, hammers. But, really, what were they worth against a gun? Besides, he thought he heard the woman enter the far end of the garage, where Todd's workshop was. He couldn't get at those weapons without somehow getting past her.

He dug into his trouser pocket for coins. From behind Lexie's Mini Cooper, he threw the coins out to the courtyard, hoping Ivy would take a shot in that direction. But she didn't.

Mentally scrambling for a way out of the impasse, his eye fell on his boat. The gun he normally carried in it was also stored in Todd's workshop in a special locked cabinet, but the boat flares should be where he left them on the boat. He crawled toward it, wincing at the possibility of being shot in the process.

After retrieving two flares from the boat and keeping the boat between him and where he thought Ivy was, he crab-walked out of the garage into the courtyard, his eyes on the space between the crates and the workshop, straining to see whether Ivy was hiding behind them, cautiously trying for a better angle without getting shot, his ears tuned like an owl's to the slightest furtive sound.

And then it came, a shuffle from somewhere behind the crates. But no gunshot.

He wished he knew how to throw his voice like a ventriloquist. "Ivy," he called, crouching and creeping to his right as he uttered the lie. "I know your gun's empty. Come out. I don't want to hurt you."

And then came the shot that emptied her clip. He reflexively fired the boat flares.

Steve leapt back in shock when the front crate caught fire and the fireworks began igniting, one after another, then in clusters. The deafening noise, the blinding light, the fireballs shooting every which way -- it was as if a mad gunner had been let loose in a war zone. Then a Roman candle struck him in the shoulder, burning a hole in his shirt. Time to run.

Steve heard a scream from the back of the garage. He knew there was no way out for the woman. Fire had engulfed the bay.

More rapid-fire explosions followed -- not just Roman candles, but rockets, Chinese lanterns, mortars, dragons, wheels, and fountains, quickly blowing a hole in the ceiling and through the apartments above, then spraying the sky with ear-splitting bursts of fire and smoke. A fireworks display that was meant to last an hour was going up in minutes.

Steve ran for his life. Drago met him before he reached the screened porch. "Mizz Royce and the baby are safe. Follow me!"

Twenty minutes' later, Dave found everyone he was looking for out by the creek. "You're all surviving?"

Drago answered. "So far, so good. We're all hot as hell, of course, but the creek's right here if we need to dive in. Mizz Royce is waking up, I think. Todd's got the baby. Look at her. She's wide awake, watching the sky, enjoying the spectacle like it was meant for her. Unlike Henry, who's cowering behind my back."

Dave, looking back at the house, said the fire was pretty well confined to the garage and the porch but men had been sent into the house to look for survivors.

"You're not going to find much," Steve said. "I'm pretty sure Ivy was behind the crates. Once the fire started, she couldn't get out."

"I hate to say this," Drago said, "but I'll say it anyway. I always thought that woman was cold as a frozen mastodon turd."

"Well, she's hot as a firecracker now," Dave said. He looked at Steve. "By the way, why were you storing fireworks in the garage?"

"I can explain that," Todd said, and he did, diverting all blame from Phyllis and himself and heaping it on the asshole truck driver with the dragon tattoo.

Dave shot Steve a stern look. "You realize you've broken the law." He ducked as a dozen Atomic Tornados suddenly exploded overhead, ripping fiery fissures in the inky sky -- and splitting eardrums below.

Steve tried to read his friend's face, flickering from light to shadow in the glow from the garage fire and the random bursts of Atomic Tornados. He could barely be heard over the noise. "It was an accident . . . self-defense . . . no gun . . . only a boat flare . . . I didn't mean . . . ."

"Oh, stop. You know I'm not talking about whatever might have happened to Ivy."

"Then what?"

Dave smiled grimly, waiting for the noise to die down. "I'm talking about violating the ban on fireworks. We have a drought, you know. Every part of the landscape is tinder."

Todd started to protest, saying that's why he and Drago had driven over -- to move the fireworks to safety. They never meant -- .

Drago punched his arm. "The man is messing with your head, Todd. Relax."

"So sorry about that," Steve said, collapsing on the grass. "I didn't realize what was in the crates or I'd never have fired the flares. I just thought Lexie had ordered more furniture. But at least we celebrated independence with lots of light and noise. You gotta give us that much. I don't know if the flag on the side of the garage is still waving, but by God there are bombs bursting in air and we

273

can see the rockets' red glare." He wiped the sweat off his face with his shirt. "In case you're wondering, guys, don't go thinking you're going to see this kind of spectacle next year. I don't plan to put on a show like this ever again."

Epilogue
Life Goes On
Summer 2012

★★★ Doogy Starr, Ivy's father, was angry with the lawyer he consulted. When Doogy heard his beloved daughter Ivy had been blown up in a Fourth of July accident, he saw dollar signs. Surely, he could sue her employer, the rich-bitch Alexandra Wright, for millions. There must be some whacky theory that would work. Rich people didn't deserve what they had. He did. He'd never have to work again.

Well, actually, he wasn't working now, and when asked for particulars about his beloved daughter, couldn't remember the exact date of her birth or whether she had a middle name. No, he hadn't seen her in months and they never talked on the phone. But all that was beside the point. A father should get something out of the disaster.

Wasn't that what the law was for?

And he needed the millions. His wife was more depressed than ever and his sullen daughter Nan no longer spoke to him. If he couldn't squeeze a few million out of the Wrights, how about a few thousand so he could escape somewhere his wife and creditors couldn't find him? Somewhere like the Alaskan frontier. Maybe he'd become an ice road trucker. He'd never driven a big truck, let alone over ice roads, but he was sure he could do it.

Oh, hell, there were lots of lawyers in the world. The dumb ass in the fancy suit probably had a diploma from an on-line school handing out diplomas to whoever could pay for them. Years ago,

Doogy himself got one certifying that he was a minister of the Lord, even though he'd never read the Bible in his life.

Once again, Doogy got out the phone book and turned to the Attorneys page. He'd keep looking. He had nothing else to do.

★★★ When Mama Bee got the call from Detective Powers about Ivy's death, she mumbled the appropriate words of sorrow through her smiles. She knew it wasn't right to smile, but it was only human. She was proud. After all, she'd predicted that Ivy would rise to heights no one could imagine, and she'd seen the woman's face rearranged the way Picasso did it in those paintings that sold for millions. Like a good citizen, she warned the Detective about what was going to happen -- not in time to prevent the tragedy, but still she tried.

Now she had some deep thinking to do about how to advertise her part in identifying the most unusual serial murderer ever to commit her crimes in Fort Wayne and her skill in predicting the future -- all without coming across as indelicate.

She called Ama to the gazebo to share the exciting news.

At first, Ama was silent, as she always was. And then, miracle of miracles, she responded with words. Mama Bee could barely hear them, but Ama was undeniably talking again.

Once started, Ama couldn't quit talking. She talked and talked, all through that day and then long into the night. Mama Bee wondered how she would ever shut her up.

★★★ Astrid returned to Sweden with help from the Wrights. There, she underwent surgery after surgery to repair her jaw, plus speech therapy and psychological counseling. Unfortunately, she would never again look like the beautiful blond bombshell she had once been.

Astrid was not a praying woman, but she prayed that Ivy Starr's soul was in Hell. Ivy had used her as bait to separate Mrs. Wright from her husband. Then, when Astrid confided that Jean was nosing around about the Dodge Ram, the Tarot cards, and the misused American Express card, Ivy shot her.

Once upon a time, she had loved America. Now she hated it. She was tempted to join an anti-globalization, anti-capitalist demonstration that the media said would take place in Malmö on the weekend, but she was still reluctant to be seen in public. Besides, her hatred of America was much less than her fear of being assaulted by radical protestors eager for violence.

★★★   Plato Jones spent thirty days in jail for misdemeanor battery. Petra never visited him. When he got out, he found out why. She had sold all the equipment out of Plato's Studio and absconded with what was left of the ten thousand advance he'd gotten from the Duchess.

★★★   Dave Powers eventually closed his file on the Digby, Soren-Kawzy, and Royce murders. Captain Moonpie was not pleased. Detective Powers hadn't solved the case in time to prevent the murderer's death. And neither of Moonpie's theories -- that either Alexandra Royce Wright or Plato Jones was the murderer -- had worked out. He didn't like being wrong.

★★★   Two days after the explosion, Steve Wright got his construction crew back on the job. By the Labor Day weekend, the kitchen was once again usable, and of course the main courtyard on the opposite side of the house hadn't been touched. So the Wrights had a courtyard party.

Steve grilled a beautiful prime rib. Phyllis laid out a feast of side dishes, including Todd's special recipe for baked beans made from scratch. Lucy brought a case of the best Bordeaux she could find, plus a few bottles of Skinny Girl cocktails so popular with women. Dover presided over the bar. Henry stayed close to the grill.

Before dessert was served, Lexie proposed a toast to Jean. Her baby, a boy she planned to name Jonathan, was due in a matter of days. Then Lexie announced that she and Steve were taking everyone to Tuscany for Christmas.

After a short, shocked silence, Cricket asked in disbelief, "All of us?" She looked around. "You'll have to rent an awfully big house." She started counting the couples. Herself and Trent, Jean and Dover, Phyllis and Todd, Drago and Lucy, Sheila and Dave, Jessica and Ed.

"Seven, counting our hosts," Trent said before Cricket was done.

"And an eighth room for Sadie and Lacey," Steve said.

"I have goody bags for everyone," Lexie said, holding up one of them. "In here you'll find some euros, Rick Steve's guide to Florence and Tuscany, a pocket dictionary for those who don't speak Italian --" hoots of laughter " -- and some truffle oil so you know what delicacy to avoid when you order pasta."

Cricket got up and did a little dance. "Are we all going to be there at the same time?"

Lexie giggled. "Probably not, since Steve and I are planning on the entire month of December. The rest of you will have to figure how much time you can take off, so I expect people to be checking in and out for two-week stays. But if you're all there the last week to celebrate Christmas -- which is Lacey's birthday, don't forget -- that would be perfect. So start checking your passports and schedules."

Author's Note

Margarite St. John is the pen name of Margaret Yoder and Johnine Brown, two sisters who were born in Iowa, live in Fort Wayne, Indiana, and vacation in Florida.

Margaret, the Storyteller, is a fan of true-crime stories. Formerly a school teacher with a B.A. in Education from Indiana Purdue at Fort Wayne (IPFW), she now leads a Bible study group. Married to a surgeon, Margaret has three children.

Johnine, the Scribe, is a retired attorney and college professor with a Ph.D. in English Literature and a J.D. from the University of Chicago. She has two children and five grandchildren.

We both love beautiful shoes and dogs -- even dogs who eat shoes. People seem to be surprised by our dark, irreverent sense of humor about everything. Our favorite fan comment is, "I couldn't put the book down."

Visit us on our web site at www.margaritestjohn.com or on our blog at www.margaritestjohn.blogspot.com. Our books are available for Kindle and other electronic devices and in paperback.